Ellis Peters has gained universal acclaim for her crime novels, and in particular for *The Chronicles of Brother Cadfael*, now into their eighteenth volume.

'Ellis Peters writes as well as ever and her many fans are in for another treat'   *Today*

'Thought-provoking, intriguing, stylishly written and superbly told'   *Woman and Home*

'Versatile as well as prolific'   *Daily Mail*

Never Pick Up Hitch-hikers!

Ellis Peters

HEADLINE

Copyright © 1976 Ellis Peters

The right of Ellis Peters to be identified as the Author of
the Work has been asserted by her in accordance with the
Copyright, Designs and Patents Act 1988.

First published in 1976
by Macmillan London Ltd

First published in paperback in 1992
by HEADLINE BOOK PUBLISHING

10 9 8 7 6 5 4 3

ISBN 0 7472 3840 5

Printed and bound in Great Britain by
Cox & Wyman Ltd, Reading, Berkshire

HEADLINE BOOK PUBLISHING
A division of Hodder Headline PLC
338 Euston Road
London NW1 3BH

Never Pick Up Hitch-hikers!

CHAPTER ONE

'Well, for Petesakes,' protested Alf afterwards in indignant self-justification, 'how was I supposed to know? There was I, more than an hour behind time already, and no sign of that cagey bastard Boycott, and with what I had on board, I wasn't aiming to hang around much longer, even if I'd still believed he intended showing up, and by then I was damned certain he didn't. Gawd knows what put him off, I reckon his thumbs had started pricking. I *had* to move off, didn't I? And then there was this kid, standing on the edge of the run-on, pointing his thumb down the motorway, solemn as an owl, with his suitcase in his other hand, and his feet at ten to two, so clean and green I'd swear he'd never even hitched a lift before. In a grey suit and collar and tie, short back and sides, the lot! I tell you, if there'd been two of him I should have taken him for a Mormon on his missionary year, nobody else goes around looking like a tailor's dummy these days – come to think of it, tailor's dummies don't look like that any more, either – only Mormons. But those boys hunt in pairs, and anyhow, they don't hitch lifts. So I thought well, if you need me, boy, maybe you're what I need, too. And I slid the old van up alongside, and I said: "How far you going, kid?" and he said: "As far as Braybourne, with luck, sir!" That did it! Anybody as polite and simple as he looked and sounded was my luck. I said hop in, so am I. And he hopped.

'Well, damn it, he looked like the answer to prayer, the spot I was in, and he came out with his life-story so pat on the way down, you wouldn't believe. He was a gift from heaven!

'How was I to know he had a nose like Sexton Blake's bloodhound, and a squad of guardian angels tougher'n a Rugby scrum?'

William Anthony Patrick Banks was twenty years old, the only son of his mother, and she was a widow.

She was, admittedly, a very active and well-heeled widow, full of good works and a prop of many committees, but she still had time to keep a close eye and a loving hand on Willie, whose life from infancy, through school and into his late father's partner's business, had been planned for him without overmuch consultation of his wishes. His trouble was that he was of a sunny, guileless and contented disposition, not at all given to raising objections, and by the time he realised that he was in danger of being stuck in that office for life, and ending up a solicitor and a partner in his turn, it was almost too late to break out of the shell. Moreover, he was so well-brought-up, so amiable and so genuinely fond of his mother that almost all the courses open to more ruthless young men were impossible to him. He couldn't just say that he'd discovered he didn't want to be a solicitor – she would have taken it as a wounding insult to his father's profession. He couldn't state tersely that he had to get away from her shadow and stand on his own feet – she would then have made it impossible for him to do any such thing by being heart-broken and forgiving. Forgiving, that is, with the implied suggestion that she was about to smile and wave him away bravely and with her blessing, and go into a mortal decline as soon as he was out of her sight, of course without a word of complaint. Nor could he simply vanish without trace – she would have had the entire police force of the county out looking for him.

So he went about it in his own fashion. Anything his father had done was admirable and worthy in his mother's

2

eyes, and to quit his father's profession in order to pursue his father's hobby would not be an offence. She had several of William Moncrieff Banks's execrable watercolours and one very odd oil framed about the house, and rated them as the offspring of a great lost talent. Willie took to oils, and began to produce canvases certainly no more alarming than his father's, but a good deal more highly coloured, and in an abstract style which allowed remarkable rapidity of execution, and sometimes achieved, as a result, fresh and clean colour effects. Occasionally he even liked the results, to his own astonishment, and that made it all the more convincing when he suddenly confided to her that painting was what he wanted, and must have if he was to be happy, and that with her permission he proposed to start learning his business properly, and wanted to enrol in a good School of Art.

He had London in mind, but she, once she had digested the idea of parting with him at all, quickly cut down on the distance. There was a palatial new art school in the next county, where one thriving market town and four or five outlying villages were halfway through the painful process of being transformed into a new town. Willie closed with the suggestion thankfully. Forty miles was a start. You can always add another forty to the first instalment, after a cautious interval.

He wrote off, early in the year, for a prospectus of the courses offered by the New Braybourne School of Art, and his mother accepted this as evidence that he had actually enrolled. He hadn't. But he let her have a hand in finding him respectable lodgings in a house approved by the school itself, and that satisfied her. After Easter she saw him off by the bus, he having declined further fuss or a taxi, and for all her reluctance to let go of him at all, was able to reassure herself that she had merely let him out on a long leash, which could be wound in at any time she pleased. She thought, of course, that he had boarded the evening train south, and would go straight to his landlady's house and his chosen class.

Willie, on the other hand, foresaw that for a time he was going to need all his savings, and with railway fares as high as they were, and the service station on the motorway only a few hundred yards from the bus route, saw no reason to spend good money on a more formal method of travel.

Which is how he came to be standing on the edge of the run-on, pointing his thumb down the motorway, clean and green in his grey suit, with his feet at ten to two, when Alf Jarrett gave up waiting for his defecting passenger, and came driving along past the service buildings and the petrol pumps and the coach park, did a double-take at this improbable bourgeois apparition, and pulled up beside him.

'How far are you going, kid?' he said, leaning out.

He was not a big man, but compact and broad, with a weathered, froggy face under a peaked cap, and a bent nose that gave him a droll and slightly surprised look. He could have been an experienced groom, or a fairly prosperous scrap-dealer, or a small farmer. At any rate, he appeared friendly and well-disposed, which was the main thing. And since he was obviously Willie's elder by at least fifteen years, Willie addressed him according to custom: 'As far as Braybourne, with luck, sir!'

'Hop in,' said Alf, 'so am I.'

Willie hopped.

By the time they were halfway down the forty-mile run, cruising along steadily but fast in the centre lane, Willie had confided a good part of his life-story. He was not generally given to this exercise, but pick-ups like this, in common with train journeys, lend themselves to confidences which need never produce any echoes, since the parties are unlikely ever to meet again. And the large, misshapen brown ear cocked towards him seemed to attract conversation.

'So your Ma thinks you're going to this art school,' said Alf, shaking his head over the deception, but grinning without noticeable disapproval, 'and you ain't intending any such thing. Well, I won't say but what mothers can be a bit of a problem when they've only got one. And you won't be that far away. If you're going to stay in Braybourne?'

'Oh, yes,' said Willie. 'I couldn't just ditch her and go off into the blue. I'll be close by if she gets desperate. But art was just one way out. It isn't my forte.'

'What *do* you fancy, then?'

'Oh, I'll just get a job, practically any job, I haven't thought yet. Not in an office, if I can help it.'

'You've got nothing fixed up yet, then? Got to have a look round first, I suppose.'

'That's it exactly,' said Willie.

'You got somewhere to stay in town? It'll be past eleven, time we get in. But maybe you got friends there?'

Alf had round, earnest eyes that showed a gleam of white all round the iris when passing lights spilled into the van.

'No, I don't know the place at all, but I've got a room waiting for me. With a Mrs Dutton who takes in art school students. I thought I'd better let my mother in on that part of it. You know how they are about who's going to cook and manage for you, and what sort of household are you going into! Booking with an approved house seemed to be an insurance.'

'Yeah, keep her happy, eh? Where is this place? I'm on the late side, myself, and my missus will be waiting and worrying, but maybe we can see you right.'

'Do you know New Braybourne well?'

'Nobody knows *New* Braybourne well,' said Alf feelingly. 'Used to be a nice market town with a real centre and good shops, and a clutch of villages round it, not the best farm-

5

land ever, but not bad, either. Now it's halfway from somewhere to nowhere, with a whacking great new road system that uses up half the available ground, and umpteen schools, about as pricey as Buckingham Palace, only gimcrack, and two estates of rabbit-hutches and a couple of tower blocks, and a few oddball private blocks of flats in among the rest. But mostly traffic islands. At traffic islands those boys are real good! What's this address of yours? I might know it if it's an old 'un.'

'Dutton, 35, Rainbow Road, Norden Common,' said Willie obligingly.

Alf whistled. 'Norden, that's one of the old villages they've taken in. It's a good way out. I doubt the buses will be running, time we get in. She expecting you tonight?'

'It's sort of left open. She knows I'm coming down tonight, but I don't suppose she's going to sit up all night for me, or worry if I don't show up till morning,' said Willie easily. 'If I have to book into some hotel, I can always telephone her.'

'Oh, you've got a number for her?'

Willie had, and cheerfully shared it. Alf's rubbery lips moved, memorising. He had a very good memory.

'You won't make it tonight, that's sure. I know the buses, they pack it in after eleven. But I got an idea, and it does me a favour, as well as you, if you're on. My missus has been waiting an hour for me right now, and I don't aim to lose any more time than I need. I was supposed to run into the town, I mean the real old Braybourne, and drop off a parcel of stuff at my sister's place, in a block of flats there. I've got their spare key, and they're back from an Easter trip tomorrow. I can give you the key, and the address, and the parcel, and you can save me twenty minutes going out of my way, and sleep in the flat overnight. Why pay for a hotel, laddie, if you're starting out on your own with no job in hand? All you need to do is post the

6

spare key back through the letter-box when you leave in the morning. How about it?'

'That's terribly kind,' said Willie, touched and impressed, 'but I couldn't possibly take advantage of your relatives, when they don't even know about it. I mean, they might not like it at all, if they knew.'

'Sure they would! You don't know my sister Jess. She'd say go ahead, and bless you! And it would save me going along there.'

'Well, of course, I'll be glad to take the parcel for you and leave the key, in any case.'

'Then you might just as well make yourself at home for the night,' pointed out Alf reasonably. 'You won't find it easy to get a room, anyhow, this time o' night. I'm surprised you left it so late starting.'

'It had to fit in with a train time,' Willie explained almost apologetically, 'and there aren't many on our line, it's about due for the axe. It was either this morning or tonight. You see, my mother thinks I've taken the train. She wouldn't approve of hitch-hiking.'

'Afraid you might get picked up and done for your wallet by some crook,' said Alf, and shook with bronchial laughter, shifting his crumpled, home-rolled fag to the other side of his mouth. 'They're like that, ain't they? My mum used to be just as bad, when I first started shifting around on my own and thumbing the occasional ride. Then I started driving heavies up to Scotland, and she switched to: Never pick up them no-good hitch-hikers, Alfie, you don't know when you'll get knocked on the head and chucked out the cab. Ah, well, they can't help it, can they? Born to worry!'

Willie forbore from remarking that Alf's mother's advice seemed to have fallen on deaf ears, in view of his own very similar case. He pondered the advantages of a free night's lodgings, and was tempted.

'Well, if you're sure it would be all right . . . Naturally

I'd take care of the place as if it were my own home. It's very kind of you.'

'Think nothing of it! And you could switch on the heating and warm the place up for Jess and Tom to come home to, tomorrow,' said Alf, and went off into another paroxysm of wheezy laughter.

The fitful terrestrial stars that hover at intervals about motorways drew together ahead, and congealed into an intricate constellation. New Braybourne unfolded its attenuated garlands of street lights, blue of mercury and orange of sodium, over its vast, invisible site, a map of Alf's whacking great road system pinned together with traffic islands. 'Here we go!' said Alf thankfully, and slid into the left-hand lane ready for the run-off. 'I'll take you into the square, and show you how to find the block. It's one of the new three-storey lot, back of the church – Cromwell Court, number 24, top floor. Name of Smith. I've got a couple of miles to go in the opposite direction, or I'd take you all the way. But you'll find it, all right.'

New Braybourne by night was a strange vision, composed of long avenues of lavish city lighting, in places devoid of traffic, houses or apparent life, punctuated by sudden narrower stretches comfortably built-up with old dwellings, glimpses of former village greens, groups of shops, chapels, precincts and halls abruptly loud and cheerful with people, and dark and almost rural places where the changed order had not yet either healed old scars or left new ones. And everywhere Alf's islands, lit by soaring, modern lamps, where a few lonely cars swirled in elaborate round-dances and shot off in all directions like sparks from a Catherine-wheel.

'Here's where the old Braybourne starts,' said Alf, as the monstrous dual-track highway on which they ran, solitary under the tall lights, shrank gradually into a normal road, and began to be fringed with modest semi-detached houses perhaps forty years old. Petrol stations marked the rim of the market town, suburban shops rose on either side. 'Not much changed here, not yet, just two new estates outside, and those flats down towards the river. More like a real place, this is.'

The buildings on either side drew further apart and grew taller and nobler, and they were in a short street of well-proportioned shop-fronts and pleasant Georgian houses. They came into a spacious square, with an unidentifiable monument in the centre, a garden of shrubs round it, and half an acre of cobbled parking space. Against the night sky a square tower showed over the roofs, and a lighted clock-face. A few people, headed homeward from various evening entertainments, strolled unhurriedly along the pavements. Alf pulled into the parking-ground.

'This is it. Don't forget, Cromwell Court, number 24, top floor. Now look, you take that little road down towards the river from the corner of the square, and that'll bring you into Marley Street. Turn left into that, and keep on till you come to Prince's Garage, on the right, then down the little alley just beyond it, and you'll see the three blocks ahead of you. Cromwell's the first block. Right?'

'Right!' said Willie. 'And many thanks! I say, I'd like you to have my card, in case you ever want to get in touch.' He presented it matter-of-factly, not noticing Alf's passive amusement and wonder. 'That's my home address, of course, but I've written in Mrs Dutton's as well. Could I telephone her from your brother-in-law's flat? I'd leave the money, of course.'

'No 'phone there,' said Alf promptly. 'I wouldn't worry about it, I'll call her when I get home, and tell her you'll be in in the morning. Here you are, then, here's Tom's key, and here's the parcel.'

It was about the size of a large shoe-box, and heavy, wrapped in thick brown paper. Willie tucked it under his arm, and slid out of the van, gravely offering his hand. 'You've been awfully kind. I hope you'll let me know if there's ever anything I can do for you. We'll both be around in the town, I take it.'

'All around!' said Alf, and choked on his latest home-rolled fag, quaking with benevolence and mirth. 'Don't you worry, kid, you're doing me a favour right now. A big favour!'

'Goodnight, and thanks again! I won't forget the key.'

Alf Jarrett turned the van in a tight and rapid circle on the cobbles of the square, and drove away by the same street by which he had entered. And Willie Banks tucked the box under his arm, took up his suitcase, and marched jauntily into the dark and narrow street his guide had pointed out.

If Alf's knowledge of the progress of the new town had not been in one particular out of date, Willie Banks's story would have been different and shorter. Very much shorter! As it was, he found Marley Street according to instructions, and began to walk along it, looking for Prince's Garage. There were broken places in the façade of shops, sites cleared for development. But no garage, and garages are easily recognisable phenomena, even by night. It must be further along. The shops gave place to homes, semis with little front gardens, here and there a larger house, with-drawn more austerely behind its shrubs and trees. It was a long street, well before its end more residential road than street. And still no garage. And finally it stopped at a T crossing, and the last of the old town finally faded into the dark.

Willie stopped and considered, wondering if he was capable of missing so obvious a landmark. He retraced his steps slowly, all the way back to where he had begun. Prince's Garage was gone without trace. One of those stripped sites must be where it had stood, arguably the newest and rawest, since at least one native was not yet aware of its demolition. There should be a narrow alley beside it. He could easily have asked for directions on his first transit, having met two or three late pedestrians. Now there was no one in sight to ask, and he hesitated to open one of the little garden gates and knock at a door.

He was standing beside one of the empty sites, assuring himself that no alley penetrated the darkness beyond it, when someone turned the corner he had turned, coming from the square, and came walking briskly towards him. A girl in a long skirt and a light, belted raincoat, with a springy step, and a cloud of curvy, light hair that bounced in time with her gait and just touched her shoulders.

Willie waited until she drew near, and then took one discreet and peaceable step forward – not that she showed any sign whatever of being wary of a solitary male at past eleven o'clock – and not having a hat to raise, made her what can only be described as a respectful bow.

'Excuse me,' he said, 'can you direct me to Cromwell Court? I seem to have mislaid a garage where I should have turned off.'

CHAPTER TWO

New Braybourne's largest surviving cinema had ceased to show films, like so many others of its kind, but had been rescued from becoming a Bingo hall by the Development Corporation, because it was still a sound and handsome building, suitable with a fairly modest conversion for concerts, municipal balls, charity performances, political meetings and produce and flower shows, not to mention the annual meeting and presentation of awards of the local fishing club. It also ran a Tuesday night disco for the young, and its solid walls and isolation from dwellings preserved the ears of the older inhabitants. All they boys and girls who counted for anything in the town attended these discos regularly, and among them, as usual, on this particular evening, was Miss Calli Francis, aged twenty, who did the office work and helped with sales at Forbes and Wrighton, 21, Market Street, Stationery and Artists' Materials.

It was just before eleven o'clock that Calli, coming back into the main hall from taking a breather on the front steps, was suddenly hit by the warmth, the noise, and the sight of the deadpan, jiggling mutes, her contemporaries, all at the same time, with a bombshell effect for which she herself could not account. After all, she had seen it all and heard it all before, many times. Too many times! All at once it occurred to her that though the record now turned up full-throttle must be ten minutes separated from the one on which she had turned her back a while ago, it sounded exactly the same, and on the whole there was too much of it. Also that as she looked from dancer to dancer, with sudden acute attention, it was hard to tell one from another. All the girls were wearing the draggled granny-prints they would have giggled at a year ago, and all the boys pulp-cartoon tee-shirts, and hair like Medusa. Both were doing clog-dance routines five inches off the floor, on soles the weight of which should have nailed them down, but didn't. There was nothing the matter with their energy. It was just that they all sounded alike, and they all looked alike, and they all thought they were gloriously nonconformist, when they were conforming desperately with every breath they drew. People always have, of course, but they haven't always called it doing their own thing!

Her escort came weaving across to her from the bar with a Cola. It had never dawned on her before that she didn't like the stuff, but now in this dazzling enlightenment the fact was made plain, and she had no intention whatever of touching it, ever again.

'You have that, Bill,' she said kindly. 'I'm not thirsty. You know what, all of a sudden I don't know what I'm doing here. Do you?'

'Sure!' he said, shaking his snaky locks to the thumping beat of the record. 'Living it up! Come on and stomp the boards!'

'I left a pretty good thriller turned down at page fifty-three, with the second murder coming up any minute,' said Calli, marvelling. 'I must be out of my tiny mind!'

'Aw, c'mon!' urged Bill. 'What's bitin' you, girl? You'll be a long time old! Don't go square on me yet!'

'Square!' said Calli, taking fire. 'You lot are all so square you could be used for building blocks at the nursery! *Square!* You daren't any one of you go out on a limb and look, or sound, or act, different from the rest. You haven't got an idea or a taste or a principle to call your own, you're prints off a print off a print! I've had it! I quit!'

She didn't wait to see what he did about it. He had plenty

of second strings and third strings hanging around, he wasn't going to suffer, and he certainly wasn't going to stop and think about it, or follow her into any rash void outside the norm. He'd be all right! Calli got her coat, and walked out of the door and down the steps, in no hurry because she had plenty to think about, and was on the eve of some sort of discovery connected with growing up. It was a nice night, cool but not cold, clear and still and suggestive of spring. Quiet, too, out there on the square. Square! Marvellous word, dozens of meanings, precise, factual, figurative and moral. Like back to square one. And a square guy. And squaring the circle.

Calli walked down the square and into the lane that led to Marley Street with a curious feeling of being slightly drunk, though she had no idea whether this conception was accurate, never having been anywhere near intoxication in her life. She turned along Marley Street in a state of wonder and exhilaration, striding like an Amazon in her long, black skirt – not a granny print, that must mean something! – and lifting her eyes from the surface of the roadway, worn by clearance traffic, beheld a young man standing under a street light by the bare gravel where Kidd's bakery had once been. A rather tall, rather slender, rather rigid young man in a grey suit, with a parcel under his arm and a suitcase in his hand, his large feet in classic, low-soled black shoes turned out at ten to two. He had hair that looked fair under the street lamp, and was cut short but not too short, curling agreeably about his ears. He had an oval, solemn, wide-eyed face, so clean and innocent you could wash your hands in it. He was so square, or so original, that he might have dropped out of nowhere as a symbol of what she was missing.

It was a matter of regret to her that she could not, in the circumstances, make the first approach. She marched steadily ahead, though acutely aware of him, and would have passed, if he had not taken a step towards her as she drew level, and said, in a soft, considerate voice, ready for maiden alarms: 'Excuse me, can you direct me to Cromwell Court? I seem to have mislaid a garage where I should have turned off.'

The girl halted willingly, confronting him with large, bright, candidly curious eyes. He still couldn't tell what colour the cloud of light, lively hair would be in daylight, but under this lighting it looked a kind of translucent golden-green. She had a round face, slightly tapered to a neat but challenging chin, and wide across brow and eyes, like a bold and intelligent cat. She didn't smile, but her look was friendly.

'Prince's,' she said matter-of-factly. 'They knocked it down just over a week ago, they're going to build more flats. It's a bit further on – *was*, I mean! I'll show you. I'm going that way myself.'

'That's very kind of you,' said Willie, relieved, and fell in beside her, as she clearly intended he should. Though he topped her by at least three inches, he hardly had to curb his stride to match it with hers. Even in a long skirt she walked like an athletic boy. He wasn't sure it might not give a wrong impression if he made conversation, at least on any topic more personal than the weather, and the mild spring night hardly called for much comment. But she, it seemed, had no such qualms, and was willing to make the going.

'It does get a bit confusing,' she said cheerfully, 'when they keep demolishing landmarks. Nothing's quite the same for two weeks running in this town nowadays. When I'm expecting visitors I have to draw maps for them, or they never find me at all. It must be hell for delivery men.'

'In a way,' said Willie, 'I'm a delivery man. I promised to leave this parcel at one of the Cromwell Court flats, for a

16

chap who gave me a lift down. Do you happen to live in the same block?'

She shook her head, and the cloud of fair hair danced on her neck. 'I've got a little bachelor flat in Nelson – that's the third block, lower down towards the river. But it's the same way. Look, here we are, this is where Prince's used to be.'

It was a big, blank site now, even the rubble cleared away but for a few irregularities in the scarred and hard-packed soil. Beyond it the narrow lane opened on the right with a deceptive bend between walls left standing round rear properties.

'No wonder I couldn't find it,' he said, as they entered the deep shadow, side by side. It was curious how the quite modest houses above and the natural slope of the land beyond had completely concealed even the roof and tower of the church, now visible again on their left as they descended, let alone the three three-storey blocks that gradually loomed below, terraced down the slope. Between the masses of masonry lights glimmered lower still, along the embankment of the river.

'Are you visiting relations here in Braybourne?' Calli asked, eyeing his suitcase.

'No, I don't know anyone here. I thought I might look round for a job in the town. There ought to be something going, with all this redevelopment going on.'

'Oh, I see,' she said thoughtfully. 'You've left it a bit late to find a room tonight, haven't you? I mean, the *Lamb* and the *Eagle and Serpent* keep open into the night, but they're awfully pricey.'

Willie found himself telling her the whole story, starting with the delicate deception practised on his mother, and ending with the provision made for his night's lodging, and his eventual destination at Mrs Dutton's boarding house in Norden. Calli appeared to receive the situation with consider-ably more doubt than he had shown.

'Open-hearted lot, this chap's family, wouldn't you say? Oh, well, I suppose there are people like that. And anyhow, of course, he was getting rid of his own errand, and making free with his sister's place, no skin off his nose. I suppose it's all right,' she said, and studied Willie sidewise in the fleeting patches of light under the street lamps, with profound and dubious attention. 'Yes,' she said finally, making up her mind, 'he got you sized up easily enough, he knew he could trust you. Some people do bet on their own judgment, like that.'

'Well, I wouldn't abuse his confidence, naturally,' said Willie, aghast, 'after he'd been so kind.'

Calli sighed, as much with astonished pleasure as with resignation. He might as well have been Candide setting out into the best of all possible worlds, where to be trustworthy was to be trusted, and people offered one another their front-door keys on sight. It was the other fellow's end of it that still worried her, even though she could see no obvious snags.

Calli had read *Candide*, and many other equally surprising works of classic literature, being the sole offspring of a happy misalliance between an optimistic but incompetent classics scholar and a hard-working down-to-earth shopgirl, who had kept her husband by her own efforts during their brief married life, while he dreamed fondly of academic glory, and provided sturdily for herself and her daughter when he died absurdly of absentmindedness in a busy street, stepping off the kerb to cross to his tobacconist's as though traffic did not exist, and even the wheel had not yet been invented. To him Calli owed her name and her intellectual curiosity, to her mother her good sense. Together they made a formidable equipment.

The wall on their left-hand ended in a wide car entrance into an open court edged with lawns, and before them loomed the long block of Cromwell Court, each upper floor drawn back in a terraced shape, and faced with small balconies. There was a row of garages built into the ground floor, and an open staircase climbed squarely round a roofed well in the centre.

'Cromwell, Marlborough and Nelson,' said Calli, leading the way to the staircase. 'They got ambitious when they named them. Well, here we are.'

Willie halted, prepared to be abandoned on the doorstep. 'Thank you very much, you've been very kind.'

'I'm coming up with you,' said Calli. Not asking, telling. She herself didn't know why she should still be suspicious of such rash benevolence. What could this boy possibly have to lose? He had the key, he had, presumably, the flat to himself for the night. He could – in theory, not, of course, in practice, being the person he was – but in theory he *could* make off with everything of value there was in the place, and vanish. There was nothing comparable that could be done to him. And yet . . . 'I'm coming up,' she said again, and set off determinedly up the stone stairs.

Their edges were already chipped here and there, the paint of the balustrade soiled and daubed, and one floor up, an unexpected and chilly wind cut through the open well, out of what had seemed everywhere else a windless night. A covered corridor spanned each floor on the side away from the balconies, where narrow, white front-doors peered out through squares of reinforced glass at a bare brick wall and dusty windows. These were not luxury flats, but rehousing for slum clearances and provision for working-class families coming into the new town.

'Not bad, though,' Calli assured him, in a whisper because many of those workers were undoubtedly asleep behind these none too solid walls. 'Quite well equipped inside, only no storage space to speak of.'

She knew how the numbers lay. 24 was the end flat on the left-hand half of the top-floor corridor. They went

19

quietly along the chill stone passage, and there was the numbered door, silent and dark within, and through the end window of the corridor a view of the lower ground, terraced and built-up, one layer of roofs below another, a few lights glimmering, and a heaving of tree-branches in between causing them to blink like stars.

Willie put down his suitcase on the mat, and fished out Alf's key from his pocket. I suppose that's it, Calli thought, with a sense of disappointment, and even made a move to draw back from him towards the stairs. An abortive movement. She couldn't go. There was something that still worried her about the whole business. She watched him fit the key into the lock and turn it. In getting his other hand to the latch he almost let the brown-paper parcel slip from under his arm, and Calli quickly put out her own hand to steady it. The door swung inwards silently on a chill darkness.

It looked better when he felt inside and found the light-switch. A small hallway with cream-coloured walls and orange carpeting on the floor, a mirror with a console table under it, and a row of pegs, some with coats and scarves hanging from them.

Willie turned and looked at Calli somewhat uncertainly, much as she was looking at him. 'Well . . .' he said with a hesitant smile, and made to hold out his hand to her.

'Don't!' said Calli abruptly.

'I beg your pardon!' he said blankly.

'Don't!' She put her hand on his arm, pulling him back a little from the bland interior. Afterwards he remembered the inevitable china ducks soaring up the cream-coloured wall opposite, and a pair of men's shoes, elderly but once trendy and probably expensive, tucked under the table. 'Don't stay here! I wouldn't! Personally I wouldn't touch it. Look, you can do all you promised to do, you won't be owing him anything if you just put that parcel on the hall table, and lock this door again, and slip the key through the letter-box, and get right out of here. If it's all on the level, he won't even know you turned his hospitality down, will he? That's what you were going to do tomorrow morning, in any case, push off and post him the key. Mr Smith will have his parcel, and your Alf can keep his illusions. Just *don't stay overnight here!*'

'But why?' he said helplessly, his eyes round as saucers. 'What on earth could be wrong?'

'I don't know. I just don't like it. It smells wrong, somehow. Put the thing in there and come away, and that'll be that, and nobody any the worse even if I am being needlessly cagey.' She reached out and took the parcel from under his arm, and he let her take it, whether out of politeness or conviction there was no knowing. She carried it to the hall table, and placed it neatly in the very centre, under the mirror.

'You really mean it, don't you?' said Willie, marvelling, and studied her respectfully as she came back to him, switched off the light, and drew the door to. They eyed each other in silence for a moment. 'All right!' he said, and locked the door and dropped the key through the letter-box. 'You may very well be right,' he said. 'But now I *had* better push off and get myself a bed somewhere, hadn't I?'

She had made a comprehensive inventory of his appearance, his clothes and his manner long before that point, and concluded that he was accustomed to living easily enough, and without worrying about where his next meal was coming from. It didn't follow that he was in funds at this moment. It might well be his family that had the money, and if he was here in the town to look for a job, then what money he had might have to tide him over some days. No need to waste any of it. And she had certainly persuaded him out of a free lodging. And it was rather late, and he had that suitcase to carry . . .

'Look,' she said, 'down there below is the block where I

live, you needn't go back into town and start on the hotels. I've got a studio couch in my living-room, I often put people up, family, and friends of mine. You're welcome to sleep there tonight, if you'd like to. It's quite comfortable.' He was listening to her with his mouth slightly open, and a thoughtful look on his face, but they were thoughts she couldn't read, and she nearly added bluntly: 'And don't get any ideas, either! You'll be a guest, and that's the lot.' And then, after all, she didn't say another word. She was half waiting for him to grin a meaning grin and accept with nudging alacrity, or else back away in embarrassment and blushes, and talk his way out of it, but he didn't do either. He brightened like a lamp switched on, and heaved a perceptible sigh of relief and gratitude.

'If you really mean that,' he said heartily, 'and I shan't be a damned nuisance, then all I can say is, thanks a lot, and it's immensely kind of you. Yes, I would like to.'

That, she thought, was the way invitations should be accepted, or as briskly and simply declined if the answer was no. She was glad she hadn't laid down conditions, and not particularly concerned about whether they might yet turn out to be necessary. It might be interesting to find out, and she was not at all worried about her ability to cope with whatever transpired. Calli was a virgin because up to now that was exactly how she wanted it, and she was in no mind to throw away something of value on any twit who happened along. She was something essentially modern and marvellous, a virgin without illusions, grudges or timidities. There was a lot of her exuberant, fearless and generous mother in Calli.

'Come on!' she said. 'What are we hanging around for? Let's get out of this place, I still don't like it. And you must be hungry as well as tired.'

There was a strong sense of gaiety and thankfulness in their exit from Cromwell Court, in contrast to the tension of their entry. Willie had one arm free now, having disposed of his parcel, and he used it to help her down the angular staircase, her warmth and his matching between their sides. Outside, astonishingly, again they felt no wind, the bulk of the block shielding them.

'We needn't go back to the lane,' said Calli, aloud now that they had left the sleepers behind. 'There are steps along here. They go down all the terraces to the embankment. Ours is the second level.'

Marlborough Court heaved out of the night on their right-hand at the first level, blinking at them with an uneven sprinkling of lighted windows, and vanished again behind the roofs of older houses as they went on down the second flight of concrete steps. With every step they took away from 24, Cromwell Court, their spirits lightened. Each of them felt it, but neither of them questioned it. They were used to being light of spirit. Neither of them believed too seriously in any genuine threat or oppression left behind, it was simply that now they had no more commitment to that uncertain and slightly distasteful recollection. It was over, and they could get on with their (almost!) uncomplicated lives.

Nelson Court occupied a jutting level that overlooked a stretch of the embankment and the curve of the River Shelma. It had a different design from the two family blocks above, being intended for single workers or newly-weds, in need of easily manageable and economically viable dwellings. The balcony on each floor here was the roofed but not walled corridor from which the flats opened, and the southern aspect was given to the broad windows of the living-rooms. Calli had a middle flat on the first floor, a tiny lobby with bathroom opening from it on one side and bedroom on the other, and over the river a fairly generous living-room-cum-dining-alcove, and a minuscule kitchen off.

'It's nothing special,' said Calli, not apologetically but with critical appreciation, as she closed the outer door and snapped the lock against the world, 'but it's warm and easy to run, and enough for me.'

She crossed to the windows that filled most of the far wall, and drew the deep blue curtains upon the true stars above and the terrestrial and reflected stars below. When she turned, Willie was gazing with rapt and speculative approval upon the full-length studio couch that filled most of another wall, and was by far the most impressive piece among the modest furnishings.

'No miniature would have been much good,' she said, 'my mum married again, a six-foot-three lorry-driver, and my sixteen-year-old brother's only two inches short of him already, and there's two more not far behind. You won't have any trouble. I'll dig out some sheets and a quilt for you.'

Only when she was hauling out the necessary linen from the bathroom cupboard did it occur to her that this mention of a giant step-father and three matching brothers, however juvenile, might well be taken as a timely warning to a male guest not to get any wrong ideas. She smothered a giggle in the towel on top of the pile in her arms, and shot a glance back at her visitor before she rejoined him. But Willie was looking about him with wide eyes and a delighted smile, quite oblivious of any real or imaginary aspersions on his intentions.

'I could easily run a flat like this myself. Just the job for a working bachelor. I supposed there aren't any going begging?'

'This is just the place where there soon may be,' she said seriously, 'if they keep building like this. The thing is to get your name down now, *before* they build. You don't want to stay in lodgings, then? Some men like to know the cooking and washing's going to be done for them.'

'I wouldn't mind that at all. It's having a place of your own that matters.'

'Would you like a hot drink now? And something to eat? Tea? Cocoa? Or there's a can of beer left from when Dad was here last.'

He chose tea, and followed her into the tiny kitchen while she made it, all curiosity about this compact and desirable way of life here revealed to him in detail for the first time. She produced biscuits, and butter, and a hunk of Cheddar, and they ate and drank there in the kitchen, one on either side of the diminutive fold-away table.

'I'm sorry,' said Willie suddenly, 'I haven't even told you my name, have I? This seemed to happen so naturally, I hadn't realised. I'm Willie Banks.' It was, in fact, the one thing he had omitted to tell her when he had explained his situation.

'My name's Calli Francis. I work at the art shop in Market Street.'

'Calli,' he said, pondering. 'What would that be short for?'

'Calliope, as a matter of fact. And don't say: I thought that was a fair organ,' she added promptly, seeing his mouth open to utter the inevitable. 'It is! But she also happened to be the muse of eloquence and heroic poetry. Dad – my own Dad – was a classics man, and had great aspirations, but I'm his only surviving achievement.'

Willie looked at her gravely, and did not protest that he had, in fact, been about to remark that Calliope was one of the Nine, and that Calli had been paid a graceful compliment in her baptism. She might, he thought, be considered quite a satisfactory achievement for one life-time, too, but he didn't say that, either. He had just been reminded that she was a working girl, and tomorrow a working day, and that he must not keep her from her proper rest.

'What time do you have to leave in the morning?'

'About half past eight is all right. I usually open the shop, so I have to be there about a quarter to nine. So if you don't mind, I'll have the bathroom first, and then you can take your time.'

Willie sat on the studio couch with his suitcase open on the floor beside him, and listened in sleepy wonder to the brisk sounds of her beyond the closed door, tapping in heeled mules from bedroom to bathroom and back again, and reflected in astonishment how far he seemed to have travelled in one evening. Too modest to assume that there was anything in himself to attract happenings on this scale, he could only suppose that life, once one struck out on one's own, habitually followed this sort of pattern. He thought it remarkably interesting and highly promising.

Calli put her head into the living-room to say: 'Goodnight!' before she disappeared into the bedroom and closed the door. It had a spring catch inside, but she did not set it. If, after all, he surprised her by pushing his luck, she was quite ready to deal with him with good-humour, and quite certain of her ability to do so effectively. She did have one moment of astonishment and doubt, when he hesitated in the lobby, and then softly approached her door. But all that happened was a gentle tap, and his voice enquiring softly: 'Do you like tea or coffee in the morning?'

'Coffee,' said Calli matter-of-factly, and added: 'But you won't know where to find it.'

'I'll find it,' said Willie serenely, and went cheerfully off to his studio couch, and slept with the aplomb of a tired pup.

It was very quiet, there in the southern face of Nelson Court, overhanging the river and open country. Sounds from the town came in only distantly, and from the network of new town highways not at all. The long corridor and the outer screen wall being between them and the slope, neither of them heard the sirens in the night; and their windows being darkly curtained and facing mainly south, neither of them was disturbed by the red, glowing light that came untimely in the small hours, and was gone before dawn.

CHAPTER THREE

Willie arose early, having tapped himself on the forehead seven times before falling asleep, performing his private magic, to indicate the hour at which he wanted to awake. It almost always worked. He opened his eyes to a room unfamiliar without feeling in the least strange, and instantly remembered exactly where he was and what had happened. There was no sound from bedroom or bathroom, presumably Calli was still asleep. Willie got up, drew back the curtains from a morning view of the embankment and river and scattered dwellings and fields beyond, all faintly hazy and shot with slanting light. He dressed, washed and shaved, folded up his sheets and blankets and restored the studio couch to its daytime shape, cushions and all. Then he went into the kitchen to hunt for the coffee.

Breakfast seemed the sort of meal that would normally be taken in the kitchen, at that fold-away table. He found a percolator, and had it plopping contentedly, and bread sliced for toasting, by the time Calli came in fully dressed and freshly polished from the bathroom.

'I hope you don't mind,' he said quickly, instinct warning him that kitchen rights are fundamental. 'I thought I might as well try to make myself useful. I've put everything back where I got it from.'

'Don't spoil it by apologising,' said Calli, eyeing his arrangements with appreciation. 'None of my brothers ever knows where to find a cup, let alone anything else, and they've been here several times. There's marmalade in the little cupboard on the wall. I've got bacon, too, if you'd like a proper breakfast. There's time. It isn't eight yet.'

He declined bacon, and surrendered the toast to her care. They were sitting facing each other across the table, sipping coffee, when the little clock on the cupboard hiccuped and began to strike in a thin, tinkly voice. 'Might as well hear the news,' said Calli, and stretched out an arm to switch on the transistor radio beside her on the window-sill. The usual headlines, half disaster, half routine, but both distant, flowed past them and were not heard. They were several minutes past the hour, and down to the scattered items that just make the national news, and are elaborated in later regional bulletins, when Calli suddenly stopped crunching toast and sat very upright, eyes round and ears pricked.

'*What* did he say? About New Braybourne? Something about a fire . . . Listen!'

'. . . families from three other top-floor flats were evacuated,' said the radio drily, 'and some damage is reported, but no other casualties. The body which has been recovered from the burned-out apartment, in a recently built block of flats known as Cromwell Court, has not been identified, and the police say positive identification may be difficult owing to the intensity of the fire, which is a puzzling factor. But it is assumed that it is that of the tenant of the flat, Thomas Smith. The cause of the fire is so far a mystery, but it appears to have started in the entrance hall of the flat, and to have spread with great rapidity.'

That was the end of the item. Before the reader could get out ten words about an impending industrial dispute in another Midland car factory, Calli reached a hand to turn it off. They sat staring at each other mutely, digesting, or at least taking in, what they had heard.

'Cromwell Court,' said Calli, recapitulating points in a stunned voice but calmly. 'Top floor . . .'

'He didn't say the number,' said Willie, clutching at a straw he found he didn't much like when he had it.

30

'He didn't need to say the number. Thomas Smith, he said . . . the tenant. There couldn't be two Thomas Smiths in one block of flats. In the entrance hall . . . it started in the entrance hall . . .' Calli opened eyes and mouth into stricken circles and clutched the edge of the table. 'Willie! My God, when we were opening the door . . . You nearly dropped it! Don't you remember? And then I put it inside, on the table . . .'

'Oh, *no*!' said Willie on a whistling breath. 'It couldn't have been . . . could it?' And he recalled the moment when the parcel under his arm had started slipping, and his toes curled up inside his shoes with horror.

'I told you! I said it smelled wrong. I knew there was something fishy about it, just handing over the place to you like that. People *don't* take in strangers so readily.'

'Why?' said Willie, momentarily side-tracked. '*You* did.'

'That's different. I didn't hand you my keys and go rushing off in the opposite direction. Willie, don't you understand? That body they can't identify . . . *that was meant to be you.*'

'Oh, no!' protested Willie again, but with no conviction at all. His mind laboured, recalling details that had meant nothing to him at the time, and meant nothing at all pleasant now, but couldn't be evaded.

'Oh, yes! If I hadn't smelled a rat, it *would* have been you! And that's what you were carrying in that parcel – the incendiary bomb, or whatever it was, that set off the fire. That lovely acquaintance of yours, who gave you a lift down the motorway, was looking for a stooge, not just to install the bomb, but to get blown up by it, too. How else can you account for it?'

'Oh, no, this is silly,' said Willie, holding on to the everyday while his mind pursued minutiae he knew would refute all his efforts at sanity. 'Why should he want to knock me off? He'd never seen me before. He didn't know

31

me from Adam, why should he have anything against me?'

'Idiot, he *didn't* have anything against you. It just happened to be you wanting a lift. Anyone would have done – well, anyone male and young, maybe. Anybody within pretty wide limits, if the body wasn't going to be recognisable. He just wanted somebody to be found in that flat and taken for Thomas Smith. What is it?' she asked, seeing that Willie was boiling up gradually into speech, and that whatever he said was going to be evidence for him, not against.

'This Alf . . . I'm just remembering things. He seemed to think it was killingly funny when I said my mother wouldn't approve of my hitching a lift. And then when I agreed to take the key he said I could switch on the heating and warm up the place for Jess and Tom to come home to . . . And then he laughed like a drain.'

'What did I tell you? It *was* a plant!'

'But I can't make any sense of it,' he protested. 'There *wasn't* anybody there when we opened the door. Not only because it was dark, it was cold, too, there hadn't been any heating on. And it felt empty, absolutely empty. So where did this chap they've found there spring from, in the middle of the night? It can't be the real Thomas Smith. It was his key Alf gave me; whatever's going on, they must be in it together. So why should he go back there and get killed?'

'He didn't,' she said with conviction. 'Somebody else, somebody who *didn't* know what was going on, must have got in there afterwards. And he was the unlucky one!'

'But what was the big idea? What purpose would all this serve?'

'Well, it would give "Thomas Smith" an out, wouldn't it? Supposing he badly needed to disappear? Supposing he was in a spot he had to "die" to get out of? People leave you alone if you're dead. Your enemies. The police. You stop being interesting. Maybe "Thomas Smith" badly needed to make everybody lose interest in him. Now, safely dead, he can move on without anybody watching him, and get himself another identity, and live in peace.'

'You realise, don't you,' said Willie, 'what follows if it really is like that? We won't be the only ones who've listened with interest to that news bulletin. Alf from the van will have been listening with all his ears to find out how it went, and now he'll know, won't he? It went fine, all according to plan. I delivered the bomb, or whatever it was – well, I must have done, mustn't I? It went off! – and a badly burned body was found in the flat. So who could it be but me? He can't have known somebody else was going to show up, and he can't know now that somebody else actually did. There's no telephone there. So he thinks – no, he's certain! – that everything went like clockwork, and I *am* dead. The neighbours, the fire brigade, the police, the whole town is sure T. Smith got killed last night. And Alf-with-the-van and whoever was in with him in setting me up for the chop are just as certain that's *me* they've got in the mortuary. *And they're all wrong!* It gets more interesting, doesn't it?'

'And more dangerous,' said Calli very seriously, and stood staring at him in deep thought for a moment, until the clock hiccuped the half-hour, and made her gasp and look round. 'Oh, lord, I shall have to go! Look, Willie . . . do something for me! I must go to work, but please, don't go out of here, not even out of the flat, today. Don't let anyone see you. Stay here today, until we get the story in the papers and find out more about it.'

'But I must,' he said, slow to assimilate the implications, 'I must let Mrs Dutton know I've come, she'll be wondering and worrying about her rent if I don't show up.'

'*Will she?* I'm not so sure. We were saying, T. Smith is free to jump off into another identity now. What's the matter with *your* identity? You told this man the address and the telephone number, and he knows she's never seen you.

You gave him your card, you said. What's to stop T. Smith from showing up with a suitcase at Mrs Dutton's, complete with your card? I wouldn't mind betting she's got her new lodger by this time, or very soon will have. And look, if he does play it that way, that's the only means of locating him now, and we're the only people who know it. And I want to find out. And I know a way of finding out!'

'But if he takes on my identity,' said Willie, 'he takes on my mother, too. Alf must have got a pretty good idea what my mother's like. If she doesn't hear from me within three or four days, she's going to be telephoning Mrs Dutton's house, and if she doesn't find Willie Banks in and get to talk to him on the second or third try, she's going to be driving down here to pay me a visit. He *can't* be taking a risk like that!'

'He can,' said Calli positively, 'if three or four days is all he needs before he vanishes again.' She flew into the hall, and came back with her coat bundled in her arms, and from well-mannered habit he rose and took it from her to help her into it. 'Even if your mother reported you missing,' said Calli, wriggling her sleeves down, 'there'd be nothing to connect her report with T. Smith and this fire, you being dead. Would there? All he's got to do is move out in another name, and a few days would give him time for that. And that's why you've got to stay here and stay dead, at least for today. Because if once they realise you've survived, knowing what you know, and able to identify Alf, as you are, they'll pull out all the stops to dispose of you for good.' She picked up her bag, and shot towards the door. 'So stay put,' she said over her shoulder, 'until I come home. *Please!*'

'We ought,' said Willie sternly, gazing after her, and raising his voice as she receded from view, 'to go to the police with this whole story.'

'Sure we ought,' said Calli from the hall. 'And will!

34

Tonight! With any luck it'll be a longer story then.'

He heard the outer door open and close. She was gone. And he didn't even know what she had in mind. He might, in fact, have rebelled against being given orders. He couldn't resist the: Please!

Slowly and thoughtfully he went back into the kitchen, washed up after breakfast, did a little tidying, and a lot of thinking. But he didn't open the door of the flat, and he didn't even play the radio above a whisper. She had urged him to stay, and remain incommunicado. He stayed.

All the morning Calli, between ringing up charges and selling Wattman paper, colours and envelopes, went over and over the ground in her mind, arguing against herself to test her own certainty, and it remained, if not unshakeable, singularly clearly defined. Because she could be wrong about the fire having been laid, about the plot having been worked out to take the heat – no grim joke intended! – off a man possibly wanted by the police, or ducking out from burdensome responsibilities. But always the fact remained that there was a way of finding out, and only she and Willie Banks had the knowledge to test it.

'I may be a bit late getting in this afternoon,' she said to her colleague Marian, when one o'clock came round. 'Hold the fort for me, will you? I'll try to make it on time, but I've got to go out and do some shopping.'

'You'll be safe as houses,' said Marian cheerfully. 'Old Forbes has gone out to lunch with a rep., he won't be back before half past two, you can bet on that. I should push off now, if you want to catch some of the shops that close midday.'

Calli took her at her word, and beat the clock by eight minutes. Not that she really wanted the shops, but where buses were none too frequent those stolen minutes might save her a twenty-minute wait for the next one. She left by way of the office and the rear door, picking up on the way a complete set of Forbes and Wrighton's folders and brochures of paints, pastels, brushes, papers, boards, and a sample case full of materials. On the bus for Norden Common she went over her role carefully. There were things she couldn't use. She couldn't say she got the names of new students from the School of Art, because Willie had confided that he had not actually registered there. But she could appear hopefully, making the rounds of the approved lodgings, and work round to names without herself naming them. Luckily she knew her subject when it came to artists' materials, she could talk paints and brushes till the cows came home. Why should anyone find it suspicious that Forbes and Wrighton should send a saleswoman to push their goods as the new term began?

Norden Common was a fifteen-minute run by the bus, owing to a complex route designed to make the most of those portions of the new town already populated. The village itself lay at the very fringe of the designated area, on the same side of town as the school itself, and so far remained a village, only loosely attached to the urban regions. Rainbow Road made a long curve behind the church, and was lined with solid Victorian houses, withdrawn in well-treed gardens. Number 35 had a dark, overgrown shrubbery, a little Gothic turret, and a flight of seven steps to its front door. Calli rang the bell, and put on her bright, hopeful, saleswoman's face as footsteps approached from within, and the door was opened.

'Mrs Dutton?'

'Yes?' She waited with a vague, polite smile, but her eyes were shrewd and observant, and were taking in Calli as though she were a one-minute memory test. She was not the kind of comfortable landlady the house might have been expected to produce, but a spry, thin, angular woman of about forty, very trim and genteel in a nylon overall, with sallow skin and a greying fringe. Calli decided to participate in her own share of the sizing-up that was going on here; owns the house, and prefers maintaining it this way to selling up and taking a job. Could dabble in art herself, she looks the part, and I'm sure she made that chunky ring she's wearing.

'I work for Forbes and Wrighton, artists' materials. Now that the Easter term's beginning, I'm making a round of the approved lodgings for students. We can offer very reasonable terms, and a full range of brushes and colours. I believe you do have students staying with you?'

Mrs Dutton saw no reason to deny it. She'd taken them ever since the school opened. 'I have three gentlemen at the moment. But I should imagine they're quite well equipped already. Your shop is well known, of course, they probably do shop there regularly.' And she added, which was helpful and encouraging: 'I believe I've seen you at the counter sometimes.'

'Oh, yes, certainly, I've been with them nearly three years now.' How useful a thing is truth, when you can afford to stick to it! 'I'm sure all the established students do use our goods, but at the beginning of term I thought there might be some newcomers to whom I could introduce them. I wouldn't want to trouble those who already know us, but if you have anyone new . . .?' She let the delicate question hang in the air.

'Well,' said Mrs Dutton, on the whole kindly disposed, 'there is one young man only just arrived. He's hardly had time to unpack yet, he came very late last night, but you can try him, if you like.' She drew back and held the door wide on a hall that was floored with coloured tiles and smelled of polish. 'It's the first door at the head of the stairs. You'll see the name on a card at the side . . . Banks, William Banks.'

Calli walked into the hall and towards the stairs as

jauntily and eagerly as if the world had not just trembled under her feet. She hadn't known there was so much doubt left in her certainty until it was suddenly withdrawn. She was not crazy, she was not imagining vain things. Somebody had stolen Willie's identity, and believed himself to have eliminated Willie. He was there. Now she wanted to look at him.

'Thank you so much! I do appreciate this,' she said, on the first step of the stairs. Privately she thought, don't overdo it! She'll think I'm getting a commission on what I sell, I wouldn't blame her if she asked for a cut.

'You won't mind letting yourself out?' said Mrs Dutton mildly. 'I have things cooking I must see to.'

'Of course! I mustn't take up your time.'

So much the better. Mrs Dutton vanished through the old-fashioned green baize door at the back of the hall, and Calli was left to make her way up to the door at the head of the stairs. A neat, printed card thumb-tacked to the doorjamb said: WILLIAM A. P. BANKS. No doubt about it, no getting round it. No other explanation for it. Whoever was behind this door was responsible for a fire, a death, and an impersonation, and he thought he was in the clear. His mistake!

She knocked, the insinuating knock of a practised saleswoman. She put on the tentative smile and eager charm. If you play the part, you have to look the part.

There had been a stirring behind the door, now there was abrupt and absolute silence, then the gradual sense of movement again. He was not quite proof against too much wariness, he had to reassure himself he'd become another person, and only his ally knew where to find him. No doubt brother-in-law Alf, if he really was a brother-in-law, worked rational hours, and wouldn't be expected at this time, and it took a minute or two to shrug off the lingering fear that someone else of significance would turn up. Then he had reasoned himself out of suspicions. She heard rapid steps, and the door opened. Not very wide, but it opened. There was a body and a face in the interstice.

'Yes, what is it?'

The voice was muted and low. The face, which was well above the level of her own, and attached to a lean, well-made body in grey slacks and a darker grey roll-neck sweater, was long and brown, and draped with an intricate network of dark russet hair, a thick bush of it on his head and curling down on to his neck, the rest deployed in artful lines about his face, twin curving moustaches on his upper lip, drawn finely and not at all concealing his mouth, though they might well alter his appearance just as much as if they had, and twin curves of trimmed bandit beard on his chin, running from the corners of his lips to meet in a short imperial. He could pass for an artist any time he liked, maybe he'd made himself over – from a full beard? and with a dye job? – to fit the image. But what she noticed above all was the colour and form of his eyes, long ovals of tawny, greenish gold, with a lot of iris, and pinpoint pupils. The sun through the front door's glass panels was directly on him, she had an excellent view. Tiger's eye is a beautiful stone. She saw how true the name was.

'Mr Banks? Forgive me for intruding so soon, but I represent Forbes and Wrighton, artists' materials. I understand you're beginning a course at the art school, and I would like to introduce you to our range of oil and water colours, brushes, canvases, everything you may need. We also carry . . .'

'Oh, you're selling, are you? Not now! I haven't time.' He was weighing her up, all the same, and he didn't altogether dislike what he saw. What he wasn't keen on was being seen. Not until he was sure of whatever changes he'd made. 'Some other time,' he said, and the long lips inside the etched frame of russet hair started to smile almost against his will. She thought he might lick them if he wasn't careful. But he was careful, and the moment passed. The door started to close inexorably, veiling one eye. 'I'm barely in here yet,' he said reasonably. 'Come in a week or so.' The door continued its advance, obliterating his long, straight nose.

'We do carry everything you will need,' she said rapidly, 'and we give special prices for our own students . . .' Safe enough, lie though it was. This student was never going to buy any materials of any kind, or draw a line, or apply a wash. 'I'll call in a week or so,' she said, brave to the last. Saleswomen have to be.

'Good on you!' he said, the other eye narrowing by the second. 'Do that!' The door closed, softly and firmly.

Calli went down the stairs with her unopened sample case and her unperused price lists, light as air, floating on a cloud of achievement.

She bought a newspaper on the way back, the first edition of the evening *Journal*. It hit the streets around noon, too early, probably, to have more than the bones of the story. Her interview with Thomas Smith had been so brief that she was back in the rear office by two o'clock, in good time to restore the sample case and lists to their places. They had served their purpose. It was no surprise to find the paper simply recapitulating what had already been said in the morning bulletin. There were just two additional points. The tenant (tacitly assumed to be also the deceased) had been in residence for three weeks only, and passed for a single man. And point two, the police had made a cagey statement to the effect that Thomas Smith was in all probability a pseudonym. That was one way of putting it. The implication was that it covered a wanted man, or one whose record was suspect, to say the least. Which was no more than Calli had already decided.

As soon as she left the shop that evening she bought

another paper, the last edition. She had intended to do so in any case, but the banner headline caught her eye from across the street:

FIRE VICTIM THOUGHT TO BE BASTABLE! FATALITY RECALLS BRAYBOURNE'S GREAT BANK ROBBERY

She walked home with her nose buried in the columns, and her spine tingling with sharp excitement. When she let herself into the flat at Nelson Court the quietness within gave her one moment of doubt as to whether Willie had obeyed orders and stayed. But he was there, sitting peacefully on the studio couch with a book in his hand, and tea was already made and waiting for her. She put the paper into his hands without a word.

'I know,' said Willie disappointingly. 'I caught a news flash on Radio Two a little while ago. They think this fellow who took the flat was using an assumed name, and he's some sort of criminal.'

'There's more than that. You read it! This is harking back to something that happened right here in Braybourne, three years ago. I remember the fuss at the time. Read it! You'll see!'

She sat down beside him while he read through the article. The front page had the police release, made early in the afternoon. The tenant 'Smith', the body in the case, was believed to be Stanley Bastable, Braybourne born and bred, the youngest and undoubtedly the mastermind of a trio which had pulled off a big robbery at the Regional Assurance bank in High Street, three years previously. Bastable had got clear away, and had been on the run from the police ever since. The first trace of him had been discovered some eight months ago in Australia, but he had again vanished from there before he could be picked up or investigated, and eventually, after many false alarms, had been traced back to England, with reasonable confidence to this district, and, more dubiously, this town. Now with the aid of hindsight and the belongings in the burned-out flat, identification of the tenant was quite definite. That was all the police had guaranteed, the identification of the body with the tenant being left to the public imagination. Stanley Bastable, successful bank robber, was dead, in a fire apparently accidental.

'Turn to page eighteen,' read Willie hungrily, and did so. The paper had hurriedly set up a feature story recalling the robbery, and the persons concerned. Three men had been involved, and they had broken into the bank through the cellars of an adjoining shop which happened to be vacant at the time, done an expert job on the vaults, and got away with something like a quarter of a million pounds. None of them had ever been caught. It was known that they had split up after the coup. Thumbnail sketches of the three were appended, with photographs obviously old, and by no means good. Bastable, a vague, expressionless oval of cleanshaven face, with neat, short hair: then twenty-five years old, and without a police record. George Collins, described as the wheel man, brilliant with cars, whether stealing them, driving them, finding his way with them or faking them for resale, also quite a bright boy on the chemical side, five years older than his chief. And Denis Sievwright, twenty years older again, the technical expert on everything to do with safes and strong-rooms. His photograph showed a long, sad, almost apologetic face, like a deprecating mule. He had a record, and had been inside twice for short spells, but on such minor charges that he was practically unnoticeable. He was known to be a man who disliked violence, never carried or possessed firearms, and relied on his wits to keep him safe.

There was also mention of Bastable's wife, carefully

42

worded to convey, without fear of libel actions, that she came from a minor criminal family, owning several members who had form, but almost respectable by modern standards, playing the game by the rules, owning a fair cop when there was no way out, and never resorting to violence. Née Jessamine Jarrett, Mrs Bastable was some years older than her husband, and the age of their first and so far only child was discreetly given, along with the date of the marriage, thus avoiding the necessity of stating in so many words that she had become his wife only in a shot-gun wedding, her upright menfolk being prepared to make an exception on this occasion in their objection to violence.

'Alfred!' cried Willie, still deep in the details of the Jarrett family. 'She has a brother Alf! And Alf-with-the-van said his sister was T. Smith's wife, and called her Jess. Would you believe it, he was telling the truth!'

'Why not? It's always easier to use the truth where it does no harm, you don't make silly slips that way. And *you* didn't matter, *you* weren't going to be there to compare notes with anybody when the enquiries began, were you? Not in Alf's book.'

'Good lord!' said Willie, momentarily shaken. 'I keep forgetting that. No, he could say what he liked to me, couldn't he? So Mrs Bastable's family is playing on her husband's team. If Alf is helping him to plan his disappearance now, then it's long odds the wife is in it, too. It says here she's been living quietly in Birmingham all this time, with her little girl, and has never admitted to knowing anything about the robbery. But if Alf's helping him, then she can't have been left destitute – just waiting here for the affair to blow over and the next thing to happen. And comfortably off while she waited. It says here the police are bringing her to try and make a positive identification of the body. By his belongings. I suppose, if . . . well, it sounded as if there isn't much identifiable about *him*.'

'She'll identify him,' said Calli positively. 'I bet she's been sitting ready and waiting to be asked. She knows all about it, she must do. Obviously her brother's in it up to the neck, he was prepared to go to the length of murder for Bastable, wasn't he? They want this body nicely docketed and buried in that name, so that the real Bastable can start life somewhere else without the police forever snuffing the wind for a scent of him. And you can bet his wife aims to be with him this time, wherever it is. She'd identify that body if it was seven feet high, ninety years old, and female.'

'You don't think,' asked Willie thoughtfully, going back over the possibilities, 'that there's the slightest chance – somehow, by accident – that it *could* be Smith-Bastable, after all? I mean, obviously the police think so, they wouldn't simply jump to conclusions.'

'No, I don't. Not a chance in a million. And for good reason,' said Calli triumphantly. 'I *know* Smith-Bastable's alive, and I know where he is – or was at twenty-five minutes past one – because I've seen him and talked to him. He's at 35, Rainbow Road, pretending to be a new art student called William Banks, and to prove it he's got *your card* on his door saying just that.'

She told him all about it, in a rapid flood of short sentences, gratified by his open-mouthed consternation.

'You shouldn't have,' he protested indignantly, genuinely disturbed about her. 'A man as dangerous as that! Whatever possessed you?'

'We had to find out, didn't we? And better me than you – supposing Alf had been there, and recognized you? Well, he wouldn't have been able to help it, would he? Come to think of it,' she said, producing an unexpected giggle, 'you'd probably have frightened him to death if you had turned up. But nobody knows anything about *me*. And it wasn't dangerous at all, why should it be? Just to pretend I

44

was hawking artists' materials round the student hostels? Now we know, don't we? Nobody else could be using your name, and sticking your card on his door.'

Willie thought about it for a few minutes in silence. 'Two things I still don't get, though there are possibilities. Who – since it isn't Stanley Bastable and it *certainly* isn't *me* – who *is* the man in the flat?'

'I don't know. But someone connected with Bastable. He came there to see Bastable, he settled in to wait for him.'

'Somebody keeping tabs on him,' said Willie. 'And he was a man who had no trouble breaking in when he found nobody at home. Someone closely connected with Bastable, but somebody who didn't trust him and wasn't in the plot, or he certainly wouldn't have stayed to get killed. Calli, what happened to all that money they stole?'

'None of it was ever recovered, and none of the three seems to have been throwing it around in a style to draw attention to himself, wherever he's been. It says in Australia this chap was living in a suburban semi, and working in an office. And there was a girl who passed as his wife. Maybe he did intend to ditch his proper wife, after all.'

'Uh-huh!' Willie shook his head decidedly. 'Or her family wouldn't be standing by him. No, he just wasn't letting her cramp his style during the wait for the heat to go off. And all this time they never made any arrangements for her to join him. When he felt safe he was coming back here. Not to stay, but for a good reason.'

'The money,' said Calli.

'There'd hardly be another reason good enough, would there? According to that account, they split up the same night they did the job. I think they took just what money they needed for current living, and planted the rest until it was safe to collect it, and the hunt was over and forgotten. They must have had an agreement to meet and split it

45

fairly, if that's so. And Stanley was planning to beat the pistol and get away with the lot. Otherwise the inner circle would have known about what was going on, and they didn't, or one of them wouldn't have walked right into the trap and got himself incinerated.'

'If that *is* one of the other two,' said Calli, 'which one?'

'Collins, the wheel man,' said Willie without hesitation.

'Why him?'

'Because he was only five years older than Bastable, and the other one, Sievwright, was over fifty. Even a badly burned body must retain some trace of its age. Pathologists can tell.'

'And you think he came in the night to call on Bastable because he got wind he was there living as this Thomas Smith, and was planning to do his pals down and skip out with all the money? It wouldn't exactly endear him to his mates, would it?' agreed Calli thoughtfully. 'Tell me, if Collins had managed to get hold of it first, would *he* have shared it up fairly?'

'You never can tell. Some crooks do keep their word to their mates. But probably not.'

'In that case, seeing Collins is thought to have been lying low under another name in England all the time Stanley was doing the same in Australia, why didn't Collins lift the money long ago, and say nothing to anybody?'

'Easy!' said Willie, And indeed, in the light of this inspired conversation it did seem to him that they had been proceeding along a chain of reasoning that was quite inevitable. '*He didn't know where it was!* That was why he was so desperate to keep a close eye on Bastable, as soon as he found out he was back here. Only one person knows where that money was hidden, and that's Bastable. Because he hid it, and he made sure there weren't any witnesses. And he's *still* the only one who knows where it is. *And we're the only ones who know where he is!*'

46

They stared at each other, a long, considering stare. Then Calli rose briskly and grasped the forgotten teapot.

'Get your tea. You might as well. Once we get to the police with this lot, we'll probably be there some time.'

CHAPTER FOUR

Somewhat before this point in the proceedings a number of other actors had arrived upon the Braybourne scene, all drawn by the same news story, though for differing motives and by differing means.

Mrs Jessamine Bastable, thirty-three years old in February, had been waiting all morning in her best frock, a demure navy number with white trimmings, in a modest semi-detached house in a Birmingham suburb. Before the police arrived she had a lot to think about. She had her orders, but was not yet sure whether she was disposed to obey them or kick the hell out of them and please herself. Self-interest argued, disconcertingly, both ways. Fear had nothing to say to Jess. There was very little around that she was afraid of.

She did not look at all like a Jessamine. She was not very tall, and actually not fat in any sense of the word, but she was one of those ebullient women who give the impression of being as broad as they are long, and pushing whatever clothes they wear outwards in all directions, even when they fit immaculately. She had a vast erection of dark-red hair, part attached to her head – quite enough, if she had not had delusions of grandeur – and part added in a hair-piece that almost matched, so that when fully decked and draped with a chiffon head-scarf she was four inches taller than her actual height, and looked very much indeed like a Cretan goddess with one of those tower head-dresses that occur in the ceramic figures. Her arms and shoulders might have been sculpted by Epstein in his more lush moments, and her legs, well-shaped but twice as large as life, were as solid as the pillars of the temple, and aggressive under short skirts. She had a waist, astonishingly small, and breasts like gun-emplacements, and about as safe to challenge. As for her face, it was large in feature, but not at all displeasing, and her eyes were as notable in their blue self-assurance as her chin was in its belligerence.

'They're here,' said Mrs Jarrett, putting her head round the parlour door about three o'clock in the afternoon. She was half her daughter's size, dehydrated and stringy but made to last for ever, and had the leathery skin and straight, tightly wound hair that went with her build. She had looked fifty when she was thirty, looked fifty now she was fifty-nine, and would probably still look fifty when she was seventy-five. The look she gave Jess was disapproving, and her sniff was critical, but both were perpetual with her, and neither affected her total purpose in life, which was to stand by her family, right or wrong, in anything they undertook. They told her everything, because they knew from long experience that she would find everything out in any case, and also that she could keep her mouth shut. 'Two of 'em,' she said, peering from behind the lace curtains at the big police car drawing up outside. 'Brought a she to hold your hand, they have. I told you you should have had a bit o' black ready. Don't forget you're supposed to be too cut-up to face it, and leave it to Alf.'

'I'm forgetting nothing,' said Jess grimly. 'I know why they want me to stick around here and keep out of their hair. Give Stan one good chance at that money, and me sitting here like a fool, and he'll be off again to the South Seas, or somewhere, and this time there won't be any allowance, either, I'm telling you.'

'I don't believe it,' said Mrs Jarrett stoutly, folding her arms over her skinny breasts. 'Alf wouldn't let him get away with anything like that.'

'Alf'll do his best, but Alf's best will make a fat lot of impression on Stan, won't it? Alf couldn't even run his end of the set-up properly. He was going to have Snuffy Boycott safely hooked, and then Snuffy smelled a rat, and left him waiting like a dummy at the motorway, and he had to pick up this kid and plant him instead. Besides,' she said, coming to the real grievance with a spurt of flame in voice and eye, 'don't pretend you don't know about the gaudy bit Stan's got hanging around in Braybourne. If you think I'm going to sit here pretending to be in mourning for him while he's shacked up cosily with another girl, you can think again, and so can he.' She rose on her monumental legs and stood braced as the door-bell rang. 'Go and let 'em in,' she said.

Mrs Jarrett shrugged and went. Hers not to reason why. She was there to stay out of trouble herself and provide discreet aid to all the rest of the family when required, to look after Jess's five-year-old daughter, and to keep a home going on the money that always came in from somewhere, and the origin of which she never queried. During Stan's absence abroad, once the initial interrogations were over and nothing admitted but total injured innocence, they had lived very cosily, if not in luxury. If there was any prospect of Stan Bastable trying to make off with the rest and leave Jess high and dry, Mrs Jarrett was all in favour of taking any necessary steps to put a spoke in his wheel. Times were liable to be hard if he got away with it, what with her old man inside for a string of larcenies, and Alf's younger brother Joe tucked away on remand. She wondered if there was anything in it about this girl Stan was supposed to be keeping on ice in Braybourne. It was something Alf had let fall that had planted the suspicion in Jess's mind.

Mrs Jarrett was still shrugging, and still dubious, when she opened the front door and let into the parlour Detective Sergeant Wells and Policewoman Millward, a solid matron who might have been specially selected to be able to bear Jess's bulk if the widow collapsed on her shoulder. Mrs Jarrett closed the door upon them and left them with Jess, and went to see what her granddaughter was up to in the kitchen. As often happens when two tough characters skip a generation and meet on intimate terms, those two got on like a house afire.

The police were very correct, very considerate. So, in her own fashion, was Jess. She went so far as to keep a handkerchief in play, as if it might be needed at any moment, without ever actually making any use of it except to find her fingers something to ply and twist.

'Yes,' she agreed, with the lofty calm of resigned widowhood, 'I heard the news. No, I didn't know he was back in England, I never had any idea where he was. He never took me into his confidence while he was alive, and I'm completely in the dark about his death. If he really *is* dead? But I suppose you're in no doubt about that.'

'In circumstances like these,' said Sergeant Wells weightily and woodenly, 'there's always an element of doubt. Even the forensic evidence can't always make it a hundred per cent certain. No use trying to make it sound prettier than it is, Mrs Bastable, you'll have heard and read that this was a very sudden and very intense fire, and there's not much left to identify as a person. But there are things that may settle the matter. Cuff-links, and the remains of a watch by the bed. Things like that. I'm sorry it's impossible not to distress you. It must have been a bad shock when you heard.'

Jess considered applying the handkerchief, and then rejected the idea. That wasn't her line. She was a woman of stone, long-suffering, loving but sorely tried, abandoned by an unworthy but cherished husband, and now confronted with his unexpected reappearance in death, when for three years she had lived blamelessly without a word from him, and learned to live without him. Who was going to believe in tears or hysteria from her? Certainly not that hawk-eyed female hiding beneath the peaked cap that looked good only on leggy twenty-year-olds. I'll give her something better than that, thought Jessie.

'I went through enough shocks from him while he was alive,' she said robustly, 'and in a way he's been dead now three years, as far as I'm concerned. Never a word where he was, or whether he was living or dead, in all that time. I suppose you could call it a shock to hear suddenly that he was so near, and still never a message from him, and now he really is gone. But I've done without him long enough to know how to manage. And I'm not pretending to more than I feel. I'm sorry he's gone, and sorry he had to go that awful way. But I shall get by without him.'

'Very sensible of you,' said Sergeant Wells, 'and I admire your pluck. Well, it's possible you can help us to clear up any doubts that remain, if you don't feel too overcome . . .?'

Leading up to it sneaky, thought Jess. Getting me to put on this rock act, and then ask me to come along and identify the cinders, thinking I'll try to chicken out and leave it to Alf. Same as Alf thinks I'm going to do, according to Mastermind's plan. Their mistake! Whatever's going on, I want to be on the spot and know what it is. And above all, I'm going to sort out this fancy bird Stan's found himself. So, I'm putting him at risk, butting in? So who started it?

'You want me to come back with you and identify the body,' she said stonily.

'The belongings, perhaps, might mean something to you,' he prevaricated soothingly.

'Whatever you want,' said Jess. 'I'm quite prepared. Give me ten minutes to get a few things together, I can stay at my brother Alf's place overnight. And don't worry about me folding up on you. I need to know if that really is Stan you've found, just as much as you do. Till I'm sure about that I shan't know what I'm to do with the rest of my life, shall I?'

She strode across the room and went out, closing the door on them. They gave each other a long, thoughtful and eloquent glance as soon as she was gone, but neither stirred nor said a word until they heard the unmistakable energetic ascent of her feet upon the stairs.

'Could be true,' said Sergeant Wells then, pondering. 'Shot-gun wedding in the first place, but from her point of view she didn't pick much of a winner. She may have written him off.'

'With a little help from her friends,' said Millward in a lipless, sidelong and poker-faced utterance, just calculated to reach his ear, 'she may even have *knocked* him off?'

'I hope you know what you're doing,' said Mrs Jarrett, tight-lipped, when she saw the small suitcase descending the stairs, and Jess in her best navy coat looking like a call to battle.

'That's just it, I don't, and I mean to find out. I'm fed up waiting for Mastermind to pull off the coup of the century, I'm going to look out for myself this time. And I'm going to sort him out, him and this model of his. You look after Susie, and leave the rest to me.'

'You'll be sorry,' said Mrs Jarrett, but not with complete conviction.

'I shan't. He may,' said Jess, and marched back into the parlour to announce that she was ready to leave.

The mortuary was no test of Jess's nerves. She had been in such places before, and in any case was acquainted with death, as a younger member of a large and prolific clan. Nor were dead people any threat. Whatever menace there had ever been in them was over.

But it was a shock, though she rode it majestically, to find that the body of a burned man may be contorted and fixed into a sitting posture with arms half-extended, like an old-fashioned doll before the flesh-like plastics got into the act. Or like a roasting-fowl, badly over-cooked, springing into quite a changed shape in the oven, joints bristling in all directions. Not that she was confronted with the phenomenon unveiled. A sheet was draped over it, and remained so, but the figure under it sat almost upright, all its flexible members and tendons carbonised into a jaunty paralysis. Aware that Policewoman Millward was close and attentive at her shoulder, waiting for her to screech or collapse, Jess did neither. She stood close, and looked the relic virtually in the eyes, through the protecting sheet.

'Is that him?'

They had shown her the things salvaged from the bedroom of the flat, and she had confirmed that all the recognisable clothes and personal properties were her husband's, judiciously excluding some, which she said must have been acquired since, if they were his. But she had declined to know the watch, and been doubtful about the cuff-links. If they wanted to confront her with the body itself, she was determined not to do anything premature to make the confrontation unnecessary. The truth was that she was curious. She needed to know everything she could about a business in which she trusted nobody, least of all her husband.

'What would you say his height was,' she asked, 'when he was alive?' That was by way of a back-heel into Policewoman Millward's stomach, in the teeth of a horror which even Jess recognised.

'Five feet eleven, according to the pathologist,' said Sergeant Wells without a quiver.

'That would fit. Stan was about that. Well, you going to let me see him?'

That could pass for hysterical defiance, or marble hardness, they could take their pick, either way it ought to find them something to think about.

'This,' said Sergeant Wells, 'is what we thought you might know. His left hand, by a complete freak, is almost unmarked.'

He was very delicate in uncovering the hand without showing more than the edge of blackened corruption. And it really was a hand, projected at the end of an invisible wrist and arm, open and empty and curved like a doll's, again, the fingers brown, short-nailed and blunt, but quite long, suitable for a tall, lean man. Just a hand that seemed to be waiting to receive something. Maybe the pay-off?

'The ring . . .' prompted Sergeant Wells, perhaps not expecting hysteria, but prepared for it and ready to side-track it.

It was on the little finger of the mendicant hand. The silver was tarnished by fumes, but the heavy bezel still showed its tracery of curlicues, rather clumsily and errati-cally cut, and the square black stone was slightly askew in its setting, and bore a crude intaglio pattern that looked, if you had sharp eyes, like a lion's head from a heraldic crest.

Jess's eyes settled upon it, and flew so wide open that her towering hair-piece tilted back and threatened to topple. Her jaw dropped, and her massive knees shook under her. No doubt about the shock effect this time. She croaked: 'My God, he still had that . . .' Then she really sagged for a moment. Sergeant Wells whipped a chair round to insert behind her knees, and Policewoman Millward took her by the arm and turned her so that she ended sitting with her back to the body. The sheet covered it decently again, hand and all.

'Get your breath a minute,' said Policewoman Millward sensibly, 'and then we'll get you out of here and I'll find you a nice strong cup of tea.' And she added sympatheti-cally: 'He didn't burn to death, you know. The smoke got him first.'

Jess sat breathing hard, and thinking even harder. When her voice came back she said, to herself rather than to them: 'He said he bought that off a barrow, some street market in London. I'd know it anywhere. Come to think of it, I never saw him without it. Nor I never saw another like it.'

'It is distinctive,' agreed Sergeant Wells, carefully watching her, for the ring had undoubtedly shaken her, and clearly she took a lot of shaking. 'You're sure of it?'

'I'm sure!' She had got to the stage of requiring the cover, if not the comfort, of that hoarded handkerchief.

'And you can confidently state who the wearer must be?'

'Couldn't be anybody else,' said Jess. 'He never took the thing off. Yes, that's Stanley Bastable. I'll swear to it. Now, if that's all, let's get out of here.'

They took her somewhere more congenial, themselves relieved, and gave her a cup of strong tea as promised. She was still somewhat stunned, though that could have been an amalgam of shock on the one hand and furious thought on the other. She still shook a little, and clutched the handkerchief to her mouth.

'Well, that's the worst over,' said Policewoman Millward consolingly. 'It's lucky, really, that you haven't seen anything of him for the last few years, it'll be easier for you. And he can't have woken up at all, you know, or he wouldn't have been still on the bed. Went straight from sleep into unconsciousness, before the fire ever got to him. That's often the way it is.'

'But I still can't understand how it could happen,' mourned the widow, shaking her head. 'I mean, he was no daft kid to fall asleep smoking in bed, or anything like that. Have they found out how it did start?'

They made soothing sounds, and told her nothing, certainly not that the fire had started, not in the bedroom, but in the hall, and with unexampled suddenness and violence. If she knew nothing about it, as seemed likely – for that double-take had been genuine – then all the better for her, she wasn't going to get herself into the same sort of trouble. And if she did know, then let her fishing go for nothing.

'I should take it easy for a day or two,' said Policewoman Millward, still emollient. 'No need to cope with buses, where can we take you?'

So it was in a police car that Jess set off from the main police station near the square to Alf Jarrett's semi-detached house two miles out, in the district known, after an engulfed village, to which it now bore no resemblance whatever, as Little Felling. A great deal of felling had actually been required to reduce it to its present state, the wholesale demolition of stone-built cottages which would have stood for five hundred years more and still been weatherproof, in favour of panel-boxes in which anxious mothers felt obliged to request their hefty teen-age sons not to lean against the walls, or stand too long in one spot, for fear of buckling the construction. Their exteriors were elaborated with certain areas of wood-strip, apparently having no other purpose than decoration, but affording endless challenges to the young of the estate, who delighted in ripping them off. As they had warped considerably in their two years of occupation, even the five-year-olds could join in this game and score.

'Slum in ten years,' prophesied the police driver morosely, winding his way between the cars parked along Elmwood Drive.

'You're not kidding,' said Jess. 'Alf talks about moving out a few miles, but he's got his business to consider.' She did not state what Alf's business was, and the driver, who knew her background and the reason for her presence in the town, did not ask. 'Here we are,' she said, '56, this is it. Drop me off just past, will you?'

'I wouldn't worry,' said the driver, good-naturedly complying, 'they're used to seeing us along here. If we drop somebody off and say so-long in a civilised manner, they think it's the lady mayoress visiting. It's when we collect the rumours start flying.'

'Thanks all the same,' said Jess, 'but this will do me.' She swung her splendid legs out of the car, hoisted her suitcase out after her, and marched back the twenty yards or so to the front gate of number 56. The driver, speculatively watching her progress as he turned the car and drove slowly back out of the cul-de-sac, reflected that she had made a remarkable recovery in those two miles. Not a trace of the bereaved widow now. After all, she hadn't seen him for three years, it wasn't surprising that she'd got used to being without him. But according to Madge Millward, who was no fool, the sight of the ring that identified him had really shaken her, that was no put-up job. Anyhow, she'd got over it fast. See her go, solid as a tank, and about as broad!

He cruised by and took his ruminations away with him, just as she turned in at the gate.

Neither he nor Jess paid any particular attention to the shabby little car that had just parked on the other side of the road, nor the man who was sitting in it. And neither of them realised that the same black Mini had followed them all the way from Central.

The man inside it was just as anonymous and insignificant as his car. He was of middle height but slender, a little bowed, a little shrivelled inside his dark and unremarkable clothes, with a long, lugubrious, patient face. Short, thinning hair under an old trilby hat went with his age and kept him totally unmemorable. He wasn't shabby enough to cause comment in the town, or smart enough to be noticed here. He could have gone almost anywhere among people, and been invisible. When he had watched Jess try the front door, find it unlocked and march straight in, he got out of his car, briskly but quietly, tucked his little briefcase under his arm, and followed her.

There were shrubs along the path that gave casual cover

from anyone looking out of the front window on the ground floor, and one dishevelled cupressus that screened the door. He walked up with no concealment or haste at all, but also with no sound, being rubber-shod. The kids coming home from school took him for the insurance man, or the bloke who collected the instalments for the stuff the Jarretts had bought on the never-never.

They didn't watch to see him gently try the door, hold it a thread open while he listened, and silently vanish within. They wouldn't have been particularly surprised if they had. Insurance men and instalment collectors, like goods recoverers, regularly vanished into houses in Elmwood Drive, though not always without resistance.

In fact the man had driven from Cheshire since the morning news bulletin, studied the local paper, and waited some time outside the headquarters of Central Division for Jess to appear with her escort. He was not well acquainted with her brother, and hadn't known where he was to be found, so Jess was his only lead, and the matter was urgent. He had an investment that was threatened.

His name was Denis Sievwright.

The other arrivals during the day passed without being remarked by anyone concerned with the case. Two large and imposing cars, a Bentley and a Jaguar, drove into the car park of the *Eagle and Serpent*, which was the town's four-star hotel, and decanted five snappily dressed but widely differing individuals, laden with baggage of such superlative quality that the porters actually ran to get possession of it.

In the foyer a large, fair-haired, bluff and handsome personage detached himself from the group and approached the reception desk. He looked about twenty-eight, and was built like a Rugby player, and with a candid and mindless grin that went with the image. An image frequently deceptive, even on the field.

'Mr Match telephoned from town. Two doubles and a single will be adequate. All with bathrooms, of course. And unless you have a suite with sitting-room for Mr Match, we'd also like a small conference room. I believe he told you we've come away to hold a business confab in peace. London's impossible.'

The clerk was even more impressed than he had been by the telephone call, and hastened to provide all that they required. He was so busy reckoning up what the conference might be worth at this time of year, and organising the procession to the lift, that he had only vague impressions of the individuals in the party. But there was no mistaking which was Mr Match. He sat back and let things be done for him, which is an art. When all was prepared and everyone else waiting, then he moved, and not until then.

He was not very tall, and he was broad, so that he appeared perfectly square, with wide-set legs and thick shoulders, but with very little surplus flesh. Everything he had was bone and muscle, and when he did get up from the chair he had turned into a temporary throne, and amble across to the lift, his progress was silent and his gait as light as a feather.

As for the face, it was round and benevolent, shaven clean, and he sported a beautiful hair-cut that allowed the thick brown hair to coil attractively into his neck and shape itself away in glossy curves at the optimum point for elegance. That seemed to add inches to his height, for some reason. He had round, mild brown eyes with thick brows, and a short, fleshy nose, and a ready and beaming smile. If those grouped round him were his regional managers, or chief salesmen, the clerk reckoned they were lucky in their boss.

The Rugby type appeared to be his second-in-command. Then there was an older man, maybe fifty, in a severe black suit, and with a severe black glance and matching side-burns, who looked rather like an ultra-respectable and highly priced undertaker. The fourth was a relatively dim-looking man of about thirty, who stood aloof and looked bored, as though he'd done his part. He had certainly been driving Mr Match's car, and probably he was merely chauffeur and maybe also valet. And the fifth was a lightly built, wiry man of quick, exact movements and sharp, sidelong glances, lean-cheeked and lipless. This one looked round at the expensive accoutrements of the *Eagle and Serpent*, and so far from being impressed, appeared to be pricing them one by one, and detaching his mind meantime to some imponderable consideration of his own. He was the only one who didn't look amiable, if you allowed the grave one to show goodwill in his own austere fashion. All of them radiated confidence and money.

The lift engulfed them, and they were whisked away, separated from their luggage, of course, which travelled by another lift and was expertly delivered just ahead of them. The rooms stood open to be approved. Mr Match's suite had a spacious sitting-room quite capable of accommodating his select business conference.

'Very nice!' he said, looking about him with a round, benevolent eye, and handing out a lavish tip almost absent-mindedly, his right hand oblivious of what his left hand did. 'Very nice indeed! Yes, we shall be able to concentrate here!' He had a deep, slightly abrasive voice, but warm and smooth, too, honey with a granular content.

The conference began as soon as all the help had departed, gratified, to the lower regions, and left Mr Match ensconced in a well-padded chair, his short, thick legs spread broadly before him. From the two double rooms with bath the four henchmen returned to attend him, waiting for him to open business. Wherever Mr Match went he was in the chair..

'It ought to be a push-over,' he said, relaxing. 'Nearly a quarter of a million, if they told the truth, and Stan safely packed away in a box.'

The big blond with the handsome, brutish face stood straddling the carpet in front of the radiator, watching his chief earnestly. 'You believe the report, then? That *is* Stan Bastable?'

Alec Match spread his hands comfortably across his broad, flat stomach. 'At least, so far I believe the fuzz think so, and they're not, believe me, any dummkopfs. There were two others, weren't there, partners in that set-up? And he has a wife, and she has a family of smalltime slobs not above cutting in. I think Stan's gone. I *think*! Who sent him, that I'm not guessing, not yet. What I want is this brother-in-law of his, this Alf Jarrett. He lives here. He's on the voting register. He may even be in the 'phone book.'

'He is in the 'phone book,' said Preacher Tweddle, blackly present in the background, and omniscient as usual. He had a nose for continuities that prompted him always to look up the next information before it was requested.

'Good! He's the nearest link, and if he wasn't in on this I'm a Dutchman. I want him. Bring him.'

'Who?' asked the blond succinctly.

'You. And take Slitter. Not that a small-timer's likely to give you any trouble. But better make sure.'

The big, fair man and the little, wiry man with the unpleasant expression wheeled and went out. The little man was honing the finger-ends of his right hand with his left palm, and smiling. He had a very peculiar and unreassuring smile.

'A quarter of a million,' said Alec Match, stroking his front and also smiling, though thoughtfully and without any premature self-congratulation. 'And that I *do* believe.'

CHAPTER FIVE

Alf was sitting alone in the corner of a settee, his feet up comfortably among the cushions, when Jess walked in on him. Close by the telephone, she noticed, and for all his nonchalant attitude, not really relaxed. He had a dark suit on, and a collar and tie, very correct. Waiting for them to come and get him to do my job for me, she thought grimly. A good thing it was me, and not him. He might not even have tumbled to it, he's so damned sure he had the whole thing sewn up.

He didn't hear her come until she closed the parlour door behind her with a crisp slam. Then he jumped like a startled frog, whirling round on her with open mouth. 'What the hell,' he demanded, spluttering, 'do you think you're doing here? You're supposed to be lying low and being a poor, heartbroken widow.'

'I know,' said Jess, dumping her suitcase with a thump on the floor. 'And you all prettied up here, waiting to be a mourning brother-in-law and go and identify Stan for the nice fuzz. Well, you can forget it! I've already done it.'

'You haven't!' he gulped, already dead sure she had.

'They just drove me over here. First-class passage.'

'What the hell got into you?' he said furiously. 'You'd got your orders, hadn't you? Stan knows what he's about, doesn't he? You'll wreck the whole thing, interfering like this.'

'That's what you think! Ask me, you're going to need me to pull the chestnuts out of the fire for you. No pun intended,' she assured him acidly. 'Where's Lou?'

'Out shopping.' He had considered that perhaps she had better be. His wife had inherited his mother's role, to see no evil, hear no evil, speak no evil, and never complain provided the money came in successfully. She was good at knowing when to disappear, and how long to stay away. 'I reckon she'll be an hour or so yet. What are you beefing about, anyhow? We'd got it all under control.'

'You thought! Even if you had, you should have kept Stan off the birds if you wanted me to stay on the sidelines. Why should he get his bread buttered both sides? Get me a drink, and I'll tell you why it's a bloody good thing I did kick the script out of the window, or we'd never have known what I know. Go on, I need more than police tea.'

He got up submissively and ambled off into the kitchen. Whatever the damage or the gain, it was done now, and they'd have to make the best of it. He was jingling glasses at the sink when Jess heard, or thought she heard, the faint creak of the front door. Lou coming home? No, she'd have banged it wide open to hoist in her basket. Jess stood braced on massive legs, and listened, but now there was nothing to hear, and the first sound had been so elusive that she was not sure whether to believe in it. She went softly to the door, opened it with care, and peered through the crack. Nothing stirred, everything was as it should be.

It was an old country habit to leave the catch on the outer door fastened back, and Lou had never got out of the way of it, even in an estate where you couldn't leave a worn tablecloth hanging out on the line without risking its loss. Jess took two sharp steps along the hall to snap the catch and shut out the world, but the world was already pushing the door smoothly open and walking in. She opened her mouth to blast whoever it was back into outer air, and then after all made not a sound.

She did not know the two men who came walking coolly in, but in a sense she knew what they were, and that was

66

enough. The first was big, fair and self-assured, with his hands in the pockets of a light poplin raincoat, and a cigarette in the corner of a smiling mouth. The smile was tight, significant and conceited, calculated to knock the ladies over, and used on females from habit even when he had no such designs on them. His eyes were blue and cold. What he had in the right hand that remained in his pocket she could only guess, and she might be wrong, because even people like this didn't treat guns as casually as in the spy thrillers. But she might not be wrong, and she wasn't risking any mistakes.

'You usually walk into other people's houses without knocking?' she said, standing solidly where she was, and filling the narrow hall.

'What?' called Alf from the kitchen, and wandered into the empty living-room with her whisky in his hand. 'You talking to yourself out there?'

Without turning her head she said crisply: 'No. We've got visitors. Come and say hullo! Maybe you'll know 'em. I don't.'

His bewildered face appeared at her shoulder, and shrivelled into instant apprehension. 'What's this, then? What d'you think you're doing? What do you want?'

'Mr Alf Jarrett?' said the blond sweetly. 'Introduce us to the lady! Your wife, is she?' He took three more steps towards Jess, and without too much haste Jess gave back three. 'That's right, you're a sensible girl. We didn't expect you, but don't be alarmed, we don't mean you any harm. Or Alf, either, if you're both well-behaved, and take things calmly.'

'What am I doing, then?' said Jess. 'Screaming the place down?'

They were both inside the house now, and the second one was gently closing the door against the world, as she had meant to do. She didn't like the look of this one, either.

Very presentable in a way, well-dressed, well-groomed, well-shaven, but somehow his gait and manner and face didn't match, he wore all this correctness like fancy dress. Mean eyes, light-coloured and sidelong, and a mouth like a razor-slash. He kept one hand in his pocket, too, but she didn't think it was a gun he carried. A knife was much more his line.

'Why don't we go inside, and all have a drink?' grinned the blond, 'before we go for a little ride to a nice hotel? And if your bloke's struck dumb, lady, you can do the honours for him.' He continued his advance, like a slow battering-ram, bearing them back before him into the living-room, and the other one followed him closely, with a grin she liked even less than his friend's. Like bending double a rubber knife.

'You can't just barge in here like this . . .' Alf began feebly. But by then they were all inside the room, and the door closed.

'We have, laddie, we have. Now don't be alarmed, there's no need. We're doing you an honour, really. Our boss wants a little word in Alf Jarrett's ear. That's you?'

'It's me,' said Alf sullenly, 'and this is my house. An Englishman's home is his castle!'

'Still can be, Alf, still can be. Me, I wouldn't want to rob you of it. And this . . . No,' he said, eyeing Jess appraisingly, 'you wouldn't be his wife, not unless you were just thinking of leaving him, or why the suitcase? Wrong initials, too. J. B.! That wouldn't be for Bastable, would it?'

'It would,' said Jess. 'I'm Mrs Stanley Bastable, if you want to know. And who the hell are you?'

'Don't be like that, Mrs B.! We're nice chaps, really. My name's Sam Copper, though I don't suppose it'll mean anything to you. And this is Slitter McGoy. And we're here to invite you both to come with us for a little ride in a beautiful new Jaguar, to see a nice, philanthropic gentleman at the

68

Eagle and Serpent. That's all! Safe as houses. The original invitation was only for Alf, but then, we didn't know we were going to have the pleasure of meeting you. Mr Match will be particularly pleased to see *you*.'

The name meant nothing to Jess, but by Alf's uneasy silence, when she had expected bluster, she rather thought that it struck a chord for him. Distant but formidable, someone heard of but never encountered.

'And what makes you think we're going anywhere with you?' she said exploratively.

'Your good sense, lady. And maybe Slitter's little persuasive tricks. I wouldn't try anything, he's short on nervous restraint and very fast on reaction. And he didn't get his name for nothing. And after all, why not come with us? It's a nice hotel, and you may get a drink out of it, with luck, and a nice ride back home again – if you're good.'

'I don't understand,' she said slowly, 'what this Mr Match wants with us. I never heard of him. What's the game?'

'Put your coat on, love, and come and find out. You can sit by me in the front seat, and talk to me. And don't forget Slitter'll be taking good care of Alf in the back. Come on, get moving. Mr Match doesn't like waiting.'

'All right,' said Jess abruptly, 'why not? Come on, Alf!' There was no help for it, and on consideration she could think of no reason why these people should bear them any illwill, certainly not enough to justify the risk of harming them. Somebody wanted something from them, and apart from the wisdom of compliance with a request phrased in these terms, it might be as well to find out exactly what was in the wind. So she led the procession boldly out of the front door, and down the garden path to the Jaguar waiting a discreet fifty yards away.

Slitter McGoy leaned lovingly against Alf's side until he had got him into the back seat of the car, where Alf put as much distance between them as he could. Jess sat up straight and aggressive in the front passenger seat.

'Talk to me, love!' said Sam Copper coaxingly, as they swung out of Elmwood Drive. 'You know what, I could like you if you weren't a married woman. I'm a very moral chap, you know.'

She didn't like his tone, and she didn't like him, and she was just beginning to reason accurately and realise that she had weapons. His job was to deliver her intact, and conceited though he was, he wouldn't dare do anything else. She didn't have to worry about him.

'I'll talk to the boss,' said Jess superbly, 'not the hired help.'

'Well, well!' said Alec Match, in the charming sitting-room of his suite in the *Eagle and Serpent*. 'This is an unexpected pleasure, Mrs Bastable. I'm sorry if we've inconvenienced you, but only halfway sorry, since it's been the means of meeting you, however informally. Sit down, dear lady, sit down here, this chair is quite comfortable. And what would you care to drink?'

'Whisky,' said Jess. 'Neat. Or just a little water, if you intend the session to go on long.' And she sat down in the chair he had indicated, crossed her quite alluring ankles, and leaned her splendid erection of hair gratefully back against the high wing of the chair.

There were five of them, presumably the whole circus. Very expensive, very smooth, and potentially very dangerous indeed, but not at this moment. The hotel was full of clients sufficiently well-heeled to bring the staff running, and therefore of watchful staff ready and waiting to run at the drop of a hat. The whisky, a generous one with very little water, also helped her to concentrate. Alf was sitting opposite in a similar chair, very nervous and defensive. He wasn't much of an asset, she thought critically, and he would mess things up if she didn't watch him closely.

'I won't waste your time,' said Alec Match cheerfully. 'We're here because, of course, we've read and heard on the radio about the terrible fire that happened here in these flats at Cromwell Court last night. Forgive me if I cut corners. The Thomas Smith who lived in that flat and died there is claimed by the police statements to be Stanley Bastable, your husband, dear lady – and your brother-in-law, Mr Jarrett. So I need hardly tell you that Stanley Bastable has been a legend for some years, and anything to do with his life or death is of great interest to – certain of his fellow-practitioners, shall we say? He had a great coup to his credit, he deserves to be remembered. Now I'm interested, Alf, to know just what you know about this fire, and about Thomas Smith, and how the whole thing happened. I'm sure you won't mind telling me.'

'I'd tell you anything I knew,' said Alf bitterly, 'if I knew anything at all!' He was fumbling after the right line almost visibly. Jess thought with impatience that he must have been a dead loss to Stan, he'd have done better to rely on her. 'I never even knew he was back in this country,' urged Alf, labouring. 'All this came as a complete shock to me, and as far as I know it's all on the level – he's had it, trying to be clever. He never did take me into his confidence. All I was for him was a bloody errand-boy, and then only with the simple errands.'

'You didn't know he was contemplating coming back here?' asked Match, in a voice all too smooth for belief.

'No, I didn't. The last I heard from him was from Sydney. He told me to lay off even writing to him, and sit back and know nothing. That's the last word I had, I swear it!'

'Oh, come, come, come, Alf!' sighed Mr Match mellifluously. 'That won't do! We know you had a letter with an Australian stamp not long before that flat was rented. Just

71

long enough for a flight to bring him in. Don't take us for gulls, dear boy, we have been watching the signals. You picked him up at Heathrow and drove him up here. After all, we've been interested in him for a long while, you know. There was a lot of money involved, and it never was spent, was it? Now think, do think! Did he tell you, driving up to Braybourne, where his loot was hidden? You can't have forgotten. It wasn't so long ago.'

Sparkling with sweat, and glossy as a stored apple, Alf vibrated and agonised. He wasn't used to thinking at this speed.

'He never told me a thing.' His defensive instinct, which was always to deny, came in useful here. 'He made use of me, sure! Seems you know he told me to wait for him at the airport, and get an application in for a flat for him before he arrived. But that's all! There was nobody but him knew where the stuff was planted, and now there's nobody knows at all. Oh, all right, I knew about him being here, working like a labourer at Mostyn's. After he'd been there ten days, he told me to lay off going near, and not try to get in touch. Just stay away and know nothing. I think he thought the police had got a whiff, just a whiff, of who he really was, but that I don't even know. I did what I was told. And the next thing I know, there he is, dead!'

'Are you telling me,' asked Match, with ominous sweetness, 'that just when the hounds were getting the scent, and it was all in Stan's interest to clear out and leave them a nice, unrecognisable body, that's exactly what happened . . . *and it was Stan's body?* What, no jiggery-pokery about this convenient fire at all?'

Alf shrank and hedged and sweated still more profusely. 'Not to my knowledge. I told you, he never told me a thing. Straight, it's just like I've told you.'

'No plot to get him off the hook at some poor dolt's expense?'

72

'No! I swear there wasn't!'

He wasn't believed, of course, and Jess didn't wonder at it. He couldn't have convinced the cat that what came out of the bottle the dairyman delivered was milk. And somebody had better take over this affair quickly and get it on to a more credible footing, and wasn't it lucky she was there to be the one?

'Bunk!' said Jess, loudly and firmly. And when she had all eyes on her, which was with the minimum of movement and in the flicker of an eyelash, and a dead silence into which to project her bombshell, she went on forcefully: 'Quit hamming, Alf, and grow up. There isn't a soul here who doesn't know you're telling a pack of lies. The way things are now, what's the use? Not that the truth's going to do you a hell of a lot of good,' she added, staring Match in the eye. 'But for what it's worth, you're welcome to it. Of course Stan wanted off the hook, and wasn't going to hang around waiting to be picked up. Yes, he did cook up a plan to have somebody else sleep in that flat overnight, and go up in smoke in his place. And yes, Alf here had the job of setting up the patsy, and getting him to take the fire-bomb in with him without knowing it. And he did it, too. Except, of course,' she added grimly, before Alf could open his mouth and put his foot in it, 'that the whole damn' thing went wrong, and you might as well know it.'

'Now,' said Alec Match heartily, 'now we're getting to the real stuff. This is more like it. Now, who was this plant of Stan's, and how were you going to get him there?'

Jess gave Alf a warning glare, and said with emphasis: 'Go on, tell him about Snuffy – you might as well.' Volunteer enough information to satisfy the examiner, but no need to do more. If Alf hadn't sense enough to follow her lead she could always interrupt again. But he was licking his dry lips, and his eyes had narrowed from fright into calculation.

'All right!' he said. 'Here it is, then. I was to put it up to a chap called Snuffy Boycott that we had a nice little job fixed on a jeweller's down here, and we wanted him for the safe work. I went up with the van to fetch him, and picked up the bomb from – well, never mind, from our supplier, in a parcel, and dropped him off in the square with that and the key to this flat of Stan's, and told him to make himself comfortable there overnight, and we'd go over the job next day. And that's it! The thing went up in the night as planned . . . only . . .'

'Only not as planned,' said Jess grimly.

'No?' Match turned his beautifully barbered head and waxenly benevolent face slowly towards her, and searched her set countenance, which never quivered.

'No!'

'Go ahead! Tell! Where was Stan all this time?'

'Gone to earth at Alf's place, where your boys just fetched us from. *Supposed to be*, that is! Because when Alf got back that night Stan wasn't there, hadn't been there, and neither one of us has had a word from him since. And now you know nearly as much as we do. Nearly, not quite! One more thing I know. Not even Alf knows it yet. I never had time to tell him before these two broke in on us.'

One silent glance questioned Sam Copper. 'That's right,' said Sam. 'We saw a police car drop her off, and parked in the next street till he came back out of the cul-de-sac and drove away. Five minutes, maybe. She'd barely got her coat off.'

'Then you can guess where they'd brought me from,' said Jess. 'I don't often get police cars driving me round like taxis. They fetched me from Birmingham early this afternoon to identify the body. Yes, I've seen it – what's left of it. Don't ask me where Snuffy Boycott is now, but I can tell you where he isn't. He isn't there in the morgue! And nor is any other patsy in his place. There may not have been much left of the body to recognise, but there were his belongings, and a hand – with a ring on the finger. Oh, yes, I knew him, all right! What they've got there is Stanley Bastable! Nobody else! Don't ask me how, or why, but that's who it is. And whatever secrets he had he's taken with him, so don't look at us, work it out for yourselves.'

They were all peering at her closely and earnestly, and for a full minute there was silence. 'By heck, she means it!' said Match then, and blew out a great breath of astonishment and frustration. 'You're really telling us he's gone?'

'Nobody ever was goner,' said Jess with bitterness.

'What do you think happened, then? How on earth did the whole thing get overturned like that?'

'Your guess is as good as mine or Alf's. The only thing I can think of is that somebody got to him well before, and left him dead before he could get away to Alf's place. There's more than one,' she said with meaning, 'would have liked to get out of him what he'd done with that loot. And no stooge is going to stick around when he finds a body in the bed. But what's the use of guessing? I don't know, and you don't know, and Alf didn't even know till now what I've just told you. You're stuck with it, so am I.'

'And he never let anything out to you? You're his wife . . .'

'Huh! *Wife!*' snorted Jess, producing an inimitable sound that took scorn to its limit. 'Stan never trusted man or woman, wife or bird, with anything. You think I'd have been sitting around in a Birmingham semi all this time, if I'd known where the money was? You think those two who were in the job with him would have left it lying this long, if they'd known? No, he was a great secret-keeper, was Stan. And much good it did him in the end.'

Alex Match got up slowly and walked all round her, with deep concentration. She never turned a hair. 'You don't seem to be exactly stricken with grief,' he remarked mildly, quite without disapproval.

'Only over the money I don't suppose I'm ever going to touch,' she agreed grimly. 'What did I owe him? Three years sweating it out here and looking after his kid on next to nothing, while he lay around in the sun with his fancy girls. Don't expect me to go into mourning.'

'Well, well!' sighed Match resignedly, eyeing her almost with admiration. 'It looks as if we shall have to do some hunting on our own account, doesn't it? If Stan's gone, then his cache is still where he left it. If nobody knows where that is, then we all start fair, don't we?'

'And may the keenest nose win!' said Jess sourly. 'But I don't suppose it will be mine.'

'You never know, Mrs Bastable, you never know. Should any little piece of information ever come into your notice . . . and should you require help in putting it to use . . . you might even consider a little partnership.'

'I might, at that,' she said thoughtfully. 'Seems to me you've got the resources, as you might say. They'll have to turn over his things to me in the end, won't they? What's left of 'em! You never know, there might be something there. Nothing written down, that I'll bet on. Not Stan! But something that could set off an idea. You'll be here?'

'We'll be here. For a while, yes, we'll be here. And you'll be staying with Brother Alf, where we found you? Just in case we need to get in touch,' he said smoothly.

'I'm not giving up till I've tried everything,' said Jess, and downed the rest of her whisky. 'Now, if you've done for this time, how about a car home? Your young man knows the way, now, and I reckon you owe us that.'

Back in Elmwood Drive, with the front door securely fastened this time, and Lou indifferently ironing in the kitchen, they found time to compare notes at last.

'Lucky for you,' Jess said with a great sigh, kicking off her town shoes, 'that I was here to take the load off you.

Where would you have been on your own?'

'Where am I now?' retorted Alf, aggrieved. 'Damn me if I know now what the devil *is* going on! You've got me as mixed up as them. Oh, sure you got us out of there without any damage, but what do we do now? *They* won't let up. That's a London mob, you know that? Big stuff! If I'd known the Match Boys were going to get into this act I'd never have had anything to do with it.'

'You're in it now,' said Jess flatly. 'I've got us a few days' grace, haven't I? The police won't release Stan's things to me in a hurry, these people know that. They'll wait. *We're* the ones who can't afford to, because those few days are *all* we've got. Now come on, tell me exactly what did happen with this plant of yours. What became of that kid you picked up and brought down the motorway, that's what I want to know.'

'What d'you mean, what became of him! He got burned up, didn't he? For God's sake,' said Alf, staring at his sister with the beginnings of a broad and disdainful grin, 'you weren't *really* kidded into thinking that was Stan, surely? Oh, you did a lovely job of putting it over on them, but you can't *believe* it? I *know* where Stan is, he couldn't be more alive. You *know* that!'

'Of course I know it. I've seen all they dared show of that body. So listen to this! Not only is it not Stan, and not Snuffy Boycott, but it isn't any innocent picked up on the motorway, either. I wasn't kidding when I said I could identify it positively by a ring. So I could. The ring George Collins always used to wear. And that's George Collins in the mortuary, still wearing it.'

Alf sat with wide-open eyes and dropped jaw, staring at her for a long moment. The tip of a grey tongue moved along his lips slowly. He said feebly: 'It can't be! How could it? You're raving! He knew nothing about it, why should he turn up?'

'Word gets around. You should know that. Don't ask me how or why; all I know is, that's him. But that I *do* know. Somehow he got wind of Stan being here, and exactly where to find him, and he came to keep an eye on him. Can you blame him? He'd got an investment to look after, too. He wasn't going to let go of his share if he could help it. He must have come in the night, not to be seen, and when he found nobody there he let himself in and made himself comfortable in Stan's pyjamas to wait for him and have it out. Locks on doors wouldn't bother Collins. Too bad for him he picked the wrong night!'

'But are you sure?' insisted Alf in a dry whisper.

'Of course I'm sure. How many times do I have to say it?'

'Then what,' said Alf, his eyes rolling, 'became of this kid Banks? There wasn't any second body. Where is he?'

'Exactly what I was asking you.'

'But look at it, Jess, just look at it! He *was* there, wasn't he? He must have been there, he delivered the bomb. But if he didn't stay there, he didn't go to the lodgings where he was booked in, either. So where the hell is he, and why did he run for cover? I don't like it!'

'Maybe he wasn't as green as he let on,' said Jess.

'You're right, he is lying suspiciously low. You don't do that unless you know something fishy's going on. What can he have found in that flat to tip him off, and send him quietly scuttling away without a word to anybody? Sure he was there, he was inside, he left the parcel. And then skipped. Stan wouldn't be such a fool as to leave anything lying around that would give the show away, would he?'

'Not on your life! He had to leave nearly all his things behind, of course, to make it look right, but he'd be careful.'

'He still may have left just that one little thing too much. Because *something* certainly told that boy he'd better get out of there quick, and maybe – just maybe! – he didn't go empty-handed. And whether he did or not,' went on Jess with abrupt resolution, 'we'd better set about finding him, because he knows too much, and seeing he's kept it to himself and vanished like this – no running to the police, or anything – it looks as if he *knows* he knows it, and aims to make his own use of it. And whatever that may be, it isn't going to do any of us any good, that's for sure.'

'Find him?' repeated Alf faintly, beginning to sweat again.

'You heard me, you know what I mean. Find him and shut him up. We can't afford to leave him around.'

Alf swallowed a great gulp of air and looked sick.

'All right,' she said impatiently. 'You find him, and then it'll be Stan's job, you needn't take it on yourself. You wouldn't be any good at it, anyhow. What we've got to do is go on behaving exactly as if that body really is Stan. And what *he's* got to do is go on being the person he's being now, whoever that is, until he gets the chance to get his hands on that money. And he's got to make the chance in the next few days, because that's about all we've got.'

'But that's just the trouble,' moaned Alf, 'he's being this kid who's vanished. Well, we reckoned it was safe as houses for the short term he'd need. This Banks kid's got a managing mother. Oh, he'd fixed up this leaving home lark all right, she wouldn't be getting worried for some days, but if she didn't get a letter or a call soon she'd be wanting to know why. It can't last all that long, but we reckoned it would be long enough. But it won't last at all if this kid turns up and blows the cover sky-high.'

'That settles it,' said Jess firmly. 'We've got to get that money and get out of here fast, right out, somewhere more remote than Australia this time. And I'm going to be right there with him, and I'm going to be holding the money. But to make it work out, we've got to get rid of this young man, he really is dynamite. So where do we look for him?'

'He'd told his mother he was starting at the art school,' said Alf helplessly, 'but he wasn't really, he was going to look round for a job. But he'd got these lodgings booked, and he was going to stick to that, to keep his mother happy. Mrs Dutton, 35, Rainbow Road, Norden Common, the house is. He even gave me a visiting card of his, would you believe it? Visiting cards, yet! I gave it to Stan, he couldn't have had better credit. I was that sure . . .'

'Too sure,' said Jess flatly.

'Yeah, maybe! But it looked a treat, all sewn up and set-tled. And now I don't know where the hell he can have got to, seeing Stan's there in his lodgings, busy being William Banks. How do you look for somebody who's gone clean down the drain like that?'

'All right,' said Jess, 'you couldn't know. I should think the first thing we'd better do is make contact with Stan, and let him in on what's happening. Maybe he'll have some ideas, I've run dry. I want to talk to him, anyhow, any-where that's safe. You fix it. I suppose this dump where he's holed out has got a telephone?'

Mrs Dutton answered the telephone at the house in Rainbow Road, and hearing a male voice, and one that claimed to belong to a brother-in-law, had no qualms about answering it as frankly as possible.

'Mr Banks? I'm so sorry, you've missed him by about ten minutes. He's gone out to dinner. Who is it? Oh, his sis-ter's husband . . . I see! What a pity, it's only ten minutes or so ago his young lady called for him . . .'

The telephone made a quite inexplicable sound in her ear, no doubt a crossed line shattering the connection for an instant. Jess, leaning over her brother's shoulder, had caught the words, and uttered a snarling, strangled shriek.

'I beg your pardon? This is a very bad line . . . There, it's better now. Yes, actually I did hear where they intended going. I'm sure Mr Banks would like me to tell you, if you and his sister are in town so briefly. They were going to have a meal at the *Goat and Compasses*. Do you know the town at all? It's quite a nice, modest public house at the corner of King Street, with a restaurant. Our students often use it, it's in town, but on this side. Not at all! I hope you'll find them. Goodbye!'

She hung up. So did Alf, reeling from the contained pressure of Jess's rage, about to burst behind his shrinking neck.

'His young lady!' breathed Jess, as soon as the hand-set was replaced. '*His young lady!*' she howled to the ceiling, letting all her pent fury go in one ferocious gust. 'Let me get my hands on that so-and-so, that's all! I'll give him "young lady"! I'll murder the bastard, and her, too. I knew it! He'll never change. Not until I've got hold of the purse! You just wait until I get him where I want him, there'll be a cat among the birds, all right!'

'Now, Jess, for Gawd's sake,' begged Alf, cowering, 'remember we're all in the muck if you go shouting your mouth off. I'm not coming to the *Goat and Compasses* nor nowhere else with you unless you calm down. Christ! What with the fuzz on one elbow, and the Match boys on the other, you'll be the death of us if you go shouting the odds in public. Think of the money! Think of all that lovely lolly! Gawd, you don't even need him, if we can get our hands on that first.'

Jess had frozen as abruptly as she had blown up, though her ice was liable to fracture in all directions at any moment she pleased. She eyed her brother long and dourly, and said in the calmest of tones: 'I'm having the money and him, too, make no mistake. Whether I want or need him, whether I throw him back or hang on to him. *I'm* going to be the one who decides. He doesn't know that, yet. He will!'

Lou, small and spry and hair bleached the colour of straw, Ma Jarrett in the making, passed through the living-room from the kitchen with a pile of ironed clothes and linen in her arms, gave them both an indifferent but observant survey, and said in passing:

'You want to keep your voices down, you could shove your fist through these walls, and never need no Elastoplast. Give my love to Stan, won't you?'

'And his young lady?' said Jess, quite calmly.

'I don't suppose she amounts to anything,' said Lou. 'Just tell her to hop it. It's long odds you won't see her for dust.' She proceeded out at the further door, and up the stairs, totally unshaken.

'All right,' said Jess, dangerously placid. 'Posh yourself up a bit, and let's get going. It's a fairish bus ride to King Street.' And she went to powder her nose and repair her lipstick at the mirror in the bathroom.

Denis Sievwright had had ample time to vanish again into the cupboard under the stairs before Lou emerged from the living-room with her pile of freshly ironed laundry. He had very good ears, and quick reflexes. But he was certainly sick of that cupboard. It was a pleasure when Jess and Alf stormed through the hall and out of the house in pursuit of Stan Bastable and his latest bit of skirt. Lou was still opening and shutting drawers and wardrobes upstairs, without haste. He could let himself gingerly out of his confinement and out of the house, and slip away down the garden path to the Mini parked under the street lights. He didn't even have to hurry. He knew where they were going. He knew Stan would be there before them.

CHAPTER SIX

Central Division headquarters of the Braybourne police was housed in a handsome new building in a quiet street north-east of the square. Calli and Willie climbed the impressive front steps, and reported their names and business to an elderly desk-sergeant, who contemplated them with a benign and impenetrable blue stare, and appeared to spend some seconds in a private struggle to relate these sedate and youthful beings with circumstances of mayhem, arson and crime generally. It wasn't easy. After prolonged consideration he enquired:

'Did you by any chance hear the six o'clock news?'

'No,' said Calli, mystified but compliant. 'We were on our way here by then.'

'Ah, well!' said the desk-sergeant cryptically. 'I had a feeling that would turn out to be a red herring.' In his long experience most of the leads volunteered by the public, though not all, turned out to be not only fishy, but fish so violent a vermilion that it was difficult to see how they took in even those who proffered them. He rose to go and confide his new acquisition to Chief Inspector Cope, who was in charge of what was now certainly a case of arson, and very probably also of murder. In a few minutes they were ushered into the Chief Inspector's room, and seated facing him across a large, leather-topped desk. Sergeant Wells settled himself unobtrusively behind them with his notebook.

'I hear you have information to offer about the fire at Cromwell Court,' said Cope, looking them over with the same speculative caution as his sergeant had produced, and apparently coming to much the same conclusion. Willie was studying him just as attentively. He was quite young, really, surely not forty yet, a burly, square, sporty-looking person in tweeds and a bright, broad tie, with hair cut just long enough to be fashionable, and just short enough to curl in the nape of his neck. Willie was impressed. It seemed you could get to be a chief inspector before you began going downhill towards retirement. Promotion must be reasonably fluid and encouraging in the police force.

'You wouldn't, by any chance, be the couple who were seen leaving the block shortly before midnight?' Cope offered them a slightly sour smile at sight of their blank bewilderment. 'I see you haven't heard the item we put out with the news. A ground-floor tenant saw a young couple leaving at around a quarter to twelve, and going down the steps towards the lower blocks. The young man was carrying a suitcase. We were asking the couple to come forward and be eliminated from our enquiries. Would that be you?'

'I rather think,' said Willie, 'it must have been. The time's right, and I certainly was carrying a suitcase.'

'But it wasn't the appeal that actually brought you. So you came to the conclusion yourselves that you had something relevant to tell us!' He hadn't expected much of the alleged young couple, either, and now that they were here his expectations remained very modest. 'I shan't necessarily suspect you of setting the place on fire,' he assured them tolerantly.

'Actually,' said Willie, with aplomb, 'we probably did. Without in the least realising it at the time, of course.'

Chief Inspector Cope's aggressively large, round brown eyes popped open a little wider. After a momentary blank silence he said in a carefully neutral voice: 'I think you'd better tell your story your own way. Right end round, preferably.'

They told it, not at all badly in Sergeant Wells's opinion. For one thing, they kept it short and didn't interrupt or correct each other. He told his side of it, she told hers, recounting her reasons for visiting 35, Rainbow Road, and exactly what she had found there. Sergeant Wells couldn't see their faces, but he was alive to their reactions to the shades of expression that crossed his chief's speaking countenance. They didn't think he was taking them very seriously. In which they were greatly mistaken, even if he didn't necessarily accept their interpretation of everything that had happened. Probably they were hoping for a *quid pro quo*, but they wouldn't get one from Cope, that was for sure.

'It might, of course,' said Cope, 'have been better if you'd brought me this information earlier and left me to deal with it.'

'That was my fault,' said Calli readily. 'I wanted to find out first if I was crazy. I mean, things like that don't happen, not to most of us, it wasn't easy to believe in it. I thought if I could check that somebody really is using Willie's lodgings and identity, that would settle it. And I did check, and somebody is. I don't think you'd have had any better way of finding out, without alarming this man. And I thought it was absolutely essential, until we knew, for Willie to stay out of sight, or he might really end up dead, as well as tipping off whoever these people are to their danger. As long as they go on thinking he's dead, they'll go on thinking they're safe, won't they?'

'And you consider you've proved,' said Cope, 'the identity of this William Banks, art student, as well as his existence? You've certainly done that.'

The pair of them conferred in a long, considering glance, debated the answer, and agreed who should make it. In some ways they were as transparent as in others they were opaque and unpredictable. It was Willie who replied matter-of-factly: 'I honestly don't see how he can be anybody else, do you? Why stage the whole thing, except to get one man off the hook? The chap who picked me up is his brother-in-law. The entire operation seems to be for his benefit. We think . . .' That was significant, that 'we'! '. . . it's Stanley Bastable. Isn't that what you think, too?'

'And the hell of it is,' said Cope, after he had dismissed them with his cautious blessing and a recommendation not to be seen too obviously in public places, and to keep in touch if anything further occurred to them, 'the hell of it is, that certainly would be what I think, if only we didn't have that awkward little fact that they haven't got. It all hangs together, given that Jarrett somehow got landed without the stooge he'd expected to have, and had to rustle up a substitute. The lad's right, the whole operation has the logic of being designed purely to get us off Bastable's back, and leave him free to move around invisibly, like any other ghost. In this kid's version, of course, it leaves him and us with no answer to the question: Then who *is* the chap in the morgue? Our version, on the other hand, though it answers that all right, leaves us with an equally knotty problem: Who is this pseudo-William Banks? How did this extra character get into the act? You know what, I'd prefer it if we *didn't* know it was Stan who got himself incinerated.' He frowned at the signed statement lying on the desk before him, and looked up suddenly at Sergeant Wells. 'I suppose we *do* know?'

The sergeant mulled that over for no more than twenty seconds. 'Not exactly *know*,' he said then. 'We're only ninety-nine per cent certain. It isn't that I'd willingly take Jess Bastable's word for whether it was raining, let alone what her man was up to, and from all I could see she was all set to identify that hulk as Stanley Bastable from the moment we collected her in Brum. I'd say the set-up those two outlined was fact. Only something came unstuck. If she'd gone through with it as she expected to, and as I expected her to, I'd have been certain she was lying, all according to the scenario.'

'But she didn't,' said Cope heavily.

'She got halfway through, word-perfect. Then I showed her the ring. She knew it, all right! It hit her slam in the solar plexus. The whole thing collapsed under her, like her knees. The end of that scene definitely was *not* according to rehearsals.'

'It doesn't necessarily prove,' said Cope thoughtfully, but without great conviction, 'that it really is her husband, after all.'

'No. But that was genuine shock. She knew him, and it knocked the wind out of her. About the biggest shock she could have had would be knowing him for Stan.'

'You had her driven round to Jarrett's place? You didn't put a tail on her?'

'No, there didn't seem any point. If he was a goner, she wasn't going to be flying off to contact him. A pity, as it turns out,' he admitted. 'It might have proved it, one way or the other. Shall I get someone out there now?'

'I think we're justified in hauling Jarrett in at this stage, he's got some answering to do. I'll send Lamb to fetch him, and if his sister's there in the house we'll put Pearce on the job, and make sure she goes nowhere without a shadow.'

'And this place out at Norden Common? You want me to go?'

Cope pondered dubiously how to handle it. 'It's a tangle! Somebody's using that boy's identity, and kidding himself he's absolutely safe in doing so. And it was Jarrett who set up the retreat for him, so presumably both he and Jarrett really believe our burned body is Banks, and everything went off according to plan.'

'Or they did believe it,' said Sergeant Wells unhappily, 'until Jess drove round from the morgue in a police car, and disillusioned at least one of 'em. And their next concern will certainly be to put the other one wise. I wish I *had* thought to put a tail on her!'

'What bugs me,' fretted Cope, 'is who the hell he can be,

87

if we accept that he isn't Bastable? Jarrett planted him, Jarrett's in with him. It could be they've got another job brewing up, and this is some expert they've imported under wraps for the occasion. But then where was Bastable supposed to hole up, if everything had gone according to plan?'

'Once officially dead,' said the sergeant, 'he wouldn't be limited, provided he looked different enough. This could very well be some pro they need for a special job.'

'Go get a look at him,' said Cope, making up his mind. 'But play it very cool. Up to now, unless Mrs B. has made contact already, he's happy in his hide-out; I'm happy to have him stay where I can find him. I don't want him frightened away, and I don't want a household of art students alerted, either. I'd rather pick him up quietly outside, if possible. It only needs one alarm, and the whole colony will go to ground and stay there. Go get a close look at him, and use your judgement whether you bring him in on the spot. But if you can't land him at once, don't scare him away! We might never find him again.'

Chief Inspector Cope's plans were due for total frustration, by a margin of something less than half an hour. At Elmwood Drive Lou Jarrett, up to the elbows in darning, an occupation surely outmoded in these days of nylon and polyester, gave Inspector Lamb a bleak but civil welcome, but was about as helpful as a migraine. Obviously alone in the house, she indifferently made him free of the whole place, and expert in knowing nothing, which was her profession, vouched that her husband had taken his sister out for a drink, pitying her forlorn and distressed condition, but was completely blank as to where they might have fetched up. 'Cast up' was the phrase she actually used. Lou was from a down-to-earth rural family, and retained the language of the shires.

How long had they been gone? She was vague. Twenty

minutes, maybe? By car it was possible to cross the entire town in twenty minutes. Lamb owned temporary defeat gracefully, and withdrew to begin a fruitless pub-crawl in search of his quarry in the nearer reaches of Braybourne.

At Rainbow Road it fell out somewhat differently, but to the same final effect. Sergeant Wells approached Number 35 directly, and left it to his instincts what line he took when the door opened. It opened, as it happened, upon a nymph of about eighteen, red-haired and buxom, in a trailing corduroy skirt slashed to one hip, and a glittering sweater top with high neck and long sleeves in several beetle-wing colours against a black ground. She beamed through minimal make-up, still steaming from a bath.

'Hi! You *must* be a mistake,' she said. 'There ain't no females here but me, and I'm bespoke. Ten minutes more, and I'll be gone, too. And I haven't put a face on yet, so make it short, eh?'

'Mrs Dutton?' said Wells, deliberately crass. And he grinned at her shamelessly, having seen plenty just as with-it.

'Have a heart!' said the nymph, injured. 'Do I look sixty-five? She's gone round to baby-sit for her niece while she's at a keep-fit class, she always goes one evening a week, but she'll be back around eight, if you're interested? You don't *look* interested!'

'I'm more interested in her art students, actually,' said Wells. 'Would you be one of 'em, by any chance?'

'Not me, I work in the Development Corporation offices. But her other three roomers are all art school types. 'Fraid you've missed 'em all, though. Last one went out on the town half an hour ago. Can I take a message?'

'It's just a matter of roping in as many as possible to enter stuff for the Art Society exhibition,' Wells said airily. 'We've not got much backing up to now, and it looks bad if the show flops. Some of us on the committee thought we'd try and round up the stragglers. How about if I drop in an entry form or two?' He had armed himself in advance, the accumulated literature of the varied events in the Braybourne Spring Festival lay about wholesale in libraries, offices and shops for the taking.

'Oh, sure,' said the nymph obligingly. 'I'll pop them up on the letter-board. I expect the two old stagers know all about it already, but the new boy may not.'

'Oh, you've got a new one?'

'Hmmm! Have we!' she sighed seraphically. 'Dishy, but booked, unfortunately. Pity! He only came yesterday. I had hopes!'

'Sorry I've missed him,' said Wells. 'You don't know when he's likely to be back?'

She giggled. 'Judging by the bird of paradise he went out with, past midnight at the earliest. They were going out to dinner – to start with!'

So that was that. He thanked her, and withdrew to telephone Cope from the nearest box.

'He's out to dinner with a girl, no knowing where. No, definitely not Jess, this one seems to be an altogether fancier bit of goods. The landlady isn't in, no fear of any panic. Shall I sit it out here till he comes back?'

'No point,' said Cope, 'waste of two or three hours, by the sound of it, and I need you here. There's a new development. I've had Leicester on the line, with a queer tale that seems to link up with this lot. Two nights ago they had a break-in at a tobacconist's, and today they picked up an old regular customer on suspicion. Chap by the name of Snuffy Boycott. Seems he produced a cast-iron alibi, proved he was sitting in a pub at the time of the robbery, talking to Alf Jarrett. He says Jarrett came up to offer him a share in a job they were planning here on Cassell and Gulliver, the jewellers in Bright Street. They wanted a good peterman, and Snuffy used to be that, only his mates often found him unreliable if there was trouble. Naturally he says he turned the job down. The barman says they were there all right, but he wouldn't be so sure Snuffy was turning the offer down, it looked to him as if it was a fifty-fifty chance – tempted but not convinced. And what,' demanded Cope, 'do you make of that lot?'

'Looks like Snuffy's given us a straight tale, in which case this chap I'm hunting may well be the substitute. Or else that was the lure they put up to get Boycott down here, meaning to use him as Bastable's stand-in, post mortem – and he ducked from under, and left Jarrett recruiting on the motorway. Neither explains everything. But Alf Jarrett could, if we can get our hands on him.'

'Exactly! Now I want him badly, and at once, and he's gone off somewhere with Mrs B. Lamb's hunting him, and I'm going to put out every man we can spare until we pick him up and haul him in. Come in! I need you! Now we've got to keep a weather eye on Gullivers, too.'

Callie and Willie walked back through the gathering dusk, mildly disappointed. The sky was overcast, and the light passing ahead of its time. Easter had come as early as the calendar allowed. In the brightness of King Street, ahead, cars and buses passed, and the brisk dark figures of people, silhouetted for a moment before they vanished again.

'I don't think he was much impressed,' said Willie.

'I don't know! He did emphasise that you ought to keep under cover,' said Calli thoughtfully.

'Well, naturally he doesn't want them to cotton on to it that I'm still around, and take to the hills,' he agreed reasonably.

'He doesn't want them to have another go at knocking you off, either,' she said firmly.

'It's not that bad. Even if the town's full of accomplices all willing to see me off, there's only one person who knows what I look like, and that's Alf.'

They emerged into the yellow-tinted pavements of King Street, under the sodium lighting that was just fading from its original orange-red to its proper ochreous glow. Diagonally across the street from them, slightly to their left, an old and rambling inn called the *Goat and Compasses* presented its narrow side to the street, its frontage opening on the car-park, which was unpaved earth under old trees, with shrubberies along the house wall. Beyond the inn a second narrow, dark alley split the otherwise uniform façade of a row of eighteenth-century shops. The *Goat and Compasses* had entrances on three sides, from street, car-park and alley.

They crossed the street, and walked along under the shadow of the trees that fringed the pavement, roots splayed along the black, hard-beaten earth of the car-park. From the opposite direction another couple approached the bar door, which shed light down three steps to the street. They turned there to mount and enter. The light from within shone on them, and for a moment outlined every feature.

The girl had long, straight hair that was probably corn-coloured by daylight, but now looked almost silver. She was extremely pretty, though perhaps not quite so pretty as she thought, and certainly not as pretty as if she had worn less make-up. Her lipstick was pearl-textured but dark lilac in shade, and her eyelids were tinted with a similar glitter in a similar colour. She was fairly tall, and had a figure calculated to catch any man's eye, and accidentally well set off by the current fashion wear. She had a long black skirt, a printed silk shirt with extravagantly wide sleeves cuffed at the wrist, under a tight silver jacket, the sleeves of which were very narrow and ended at the elbow. And inevitably, boots, high-heeled and of tooled leather, displayed as she hoisted her skirt to mount the steps. The effect was spoiled by three floating, diaphanous scarves in various shades of mauve. A cross between Ilsa Koch and the Lady of Shalott, thought Calli.

The young man beside her wore grey slacks and a darker roll-neck sweater, and a tight-waisted suede jacket in a dark green. He was slender, and moved lightly and powerfully, and the light showed up clearly the fine-drawn lines of dark-russet beard and moustache that made a latter-day Mephistopheles of his face. For one instant Calli thought she even caught a flash, brief and blinding, of his tiger-eyes, like those of a true cat.

She stopped dead, while they were still shadowed by trees, her hand gripping Willie's arm. 'That's him! Speak of the devil . . .! There *is* William Banks!'

'Where?' Willie froze, following her gaze.

'Just going into the pub. With the blonde.'

It was only the last glimpse of them Willie caught, the long drift of the girl's hair, and the skirt of the green coat, then they vanished into the bar.

'You're sure? That's the chap you saw at Mrs Dutton's?'

'I'm sure.'

'Now there's a piece of luck,' said Willie with enthusiasm. 'Come on, what are we waiting for?' And he set off with new verve along the pavement.

'What do you mean? What are you going to do?' demanded Calli, trotting beside him in some consternation.

'Take you in for a drink, and get a better look at them, of course. We might never get a chance like this again.' He had the bit between his teeth now, and no mistake. She hadn't been prepared for quite such aplomb.

'You make an inventory of the girl, accurate descriptions are always a help, even if we don't pick up much more. And with a bit of luck we'll do better than that.'

'Don't forget he's seen me. He'll know me again.'

'So what?' said Willie cheerfully. 'Even colourists' saleswomen have a right to get taken out for a drink by their boy-friends in the evening, haven't they? In a crowded bar he'll never notice you, and if he did, what can happen among a crowd? With that girl looking on, he daren't try to make a pass at you if he wanted to.'

'All very well,' said Calli, mildly offended, 'but it was *you* who told me off for sticking my neck out by going near him in the first place.'

He halted on the steps to give her an astonished look. '*I'm* with you now, aren't I?'

'True, true!' said Calli, dazzled, and emitted an uncharacteristic giggle. 'All right, lead on. But it's going to cost you a Campari soda. I've always wanted to taste one.' There are more ways than one, she thought, of getting swept off your feet. One is suddenly being dragged along at speed by a runaway St Bernard that was always quiet and docile before.

It was still early in the evening, but the *Goat and Compasses* had a cook who rated well above many pretentious chefs, and a reputation for excellent and reasonably cheap meals, and thus could fill its bar with pre-dinner drinkers as early as seven o'clock. The loud and cheerful noise enveloped Calli and Willie as they entered, and the drifting smoke of many cigarettes. It was a real bar, too, with a brass rail and no fixed stools, the panelling was dark and old, and the floor tiled and slightly uneven, so that half the tables had one or two or three beer-mats inserted under the feet to keep them steady. No peril from dart-players, either, the board was accommodated in the snug. Altogether a very proper pub. The clientele was a mixed bag, a few regulars tucked into their own corners, a lot of young people, and several couples who looked likely diners. Stan Bastable and his companion were leaning on the far end of the bar, their drinks just being set before them. Calli found herself a corner of a settle near the door, and was willing to remain unnoticed. Willie pushed his way to the bar, and came back with her Campari and a half of mild for himself. Standing, he shielded her partly from view, but did not cut off her view of the quarry.

'Well?'

'I made no mistake,' she said. 'That's Stanley Bastable.'

'Wrong! It's Willie Banks, art student, remember? You think that could possibly be his wife?'

'Not a chance in a thousand,' said Calli positively.

'No, she doesn't look much like Alf, certainly. And anyhow, if his wife's spent the afternoon with the police, she isn't likely to come near her husband immediately afterwards, like this, in public, is she? They might be tailing her to see what she does do, if they're in doubt.'

'She wouldn't,' said Calli, fascinated by the blonde's eyelashes, which were black and impossibly long, 'unless she's got wind of this one. Then I wouldn't bet!'

'This one's pretty good cover, actually. So spectacular nobody's going to look at him. Do you think he's really thinking of ditching his wife and going off with this one? If he recovers the money, I mean?'

'I should say the chances are pretty good. It's said his wife's older than he is. And he has an eye for women. Even saleswomen,' she added, between distaste and satisfaction.

'Hullo!' said Willie, pausing with his tankard at his lips. 'They're going into the dining-room. They're going to eat here. Look, there's a horde of others off through the same door. They must have just started serving.'

Half the population of the bar melted away rapidly, but enough were left to keep the barman busy. 'I suppose we might as well go,' said Calli.

'No, don't be in a hurry. Let's just have a look . . .' Willie strolled to the open dining-room door, and stood peering interestedly within. The room was narrow, but long, all along the car-park side of the building, with one central gangway, and tables on both sides, couples on the left, more ample fours on the window side. The door to the car-park was three-quarters of the way along on the right, and at the far end two doors separated by the width of the room led, on the right, to some rear corridor and the cloak-rooms, so the door on the left must be to the kitchen. A very plain room, with checked table-cloths, pale flowered wallpaper, slightly scuffed serving tables, and plastic flowers. Evidently here the food was the draw. That, and perhaps the absence of pretence. The lights were full, honest lights by which you could read a handwritten menu in English. There weren't any candles in smoky glasses, or genuflecting waiters, just a brisk middle-aged woman and a bright-looking girl, in nylon overalls.

'I like this,' said Willie, aloud. The barman heard him, grinned and approved.

'You'd be OK here, chum. The grub's good.'

'It must be. Do you know there isn't a solitary table left?'

'I should worry! They share tables here, if you can spot a pair left at a four.'

'I can,' said Willie with deep satisfaction, 'I can!' He drained his half of mild, set down the tankard, and turned to Calli, who was watching him doubtfully. 'Come on, let's! We shan't do any better than this.'

Calli put down her glass and got slowly to her feet. At that moment it dawned on her distantly what he was up to. She came to his shoulder, through the fine smoke and vociferous gaiety of the bar, prepared for anything. Just beyond the door to the car-park, at a table for four beside a mirror on the wall, sat Stanley Bastable and his blonde, already drinking soup. The smell, incidentally, was decidedly alluring. There didn't seem to be any smoked salmon or caviare, but if the soup came up to the aroma, nobody would have chosen them in any case.

'Hungry?' asked Willie, hugely grinning, and took her

hand and towed her all down the narrow strip of carpet-protector that unrolled along the gangway.

Almost neutrally she said, into the ear he inclined towards her: 'Now what are you up to?' As if I didn't know! she thought, with serene resignation. One Campari soda couldn't have done this to her, it had to be Willie. She had discovered a booster drug of unparalleled force, and there was nothing she could do about it, or even wanted to do about it.

She was never sure whether it was two, or three, unfilled tables they passed by to reach Stanley Bastable and his girl-friend. Certainly they arrived there brisk, pink and apologetic, armed with any amount of well-heeled confidence, and an equal amount of well-bred diffidence. Beaming down into one pair of astonished and interested blue eyes rimmed with lashes like black-widow spiders, and one pair of green-gold, tiger's-eye irises with a black dagger-point for each pupil, Willie said wooingly: 'Excuse me, but are these places free? They do seem to be rather full up this evening.'

The long, mobile mouth in its sketched framework of beard opened to repel these unwanted boarders, either with a flat, uncivil objection, or more probably with the customary cold pretence that the two free places were being saved for friends. No doubt whatever, from the look in the tawny eyes, of his intent. But Calli beat him to it. Fetching up a little breathlessly at Willie's elbow, she beamed down at the incumbent of the table with a mixture of embarrassment and pleased surprise, and before he could get out a word she was saying, in a clear, guileless voice:

'Why, Mr Banks, fancy seeing you again so soon! I expect you're getting nicely settled in already, aren't you?' And without waiting to be welcomed, she sat down in one of the empty chairs, and settled her handbag by its shoulder-strap over one arm. If he had the gall now to tell her to get up and push off, he would be attracting to himself a kind of notice he could hardly be courting. He didn't. He scowled, but he said in a tight voice:

'Oh, it's you!' Which could be interpreted however one wished, and struck a slightly dubious note with his companion. 'Quite a coincidence,' he said drily. 'Not on duty tonight?'

Calli giggled, and spread her skirts comfortably. 'You know each other?' said the fair girl, with no enthusiasm at all. And beaming at them both as though they had extended the most affable of welcomes, Willie sat down in the fourth chair. The two girls were side by side. Two black shoulder-bags, of roughly comparable size and both bulging, swayed together and nuzzled each other.

'The lady sells artists' materials,' said Stan. 'She called on me at lunch-time with samples, but I haven't yet had time to know what I need.'

'I guess I was a bit too eager,' Calli admitted, 'but I like to make the round as soon as the term opens. Then at least, even if new students don't buy at once, they know about us, and where to get all the things they want. My name's Francis,' she offered expansively, 'and this is my friend Tim Jones. He works at our place, too.' Brightly and cheerfully and without even a fraction of a second's pause for thought, or the quiver of an eyelash. She hoped Willie appreciated it. It did occur to her, with mild sensations of pleasure, that he had taken her alertness for granted, and would have been immensely surprised and shocked if she had let him down.

'Nice for you,' said Stan, and returned to his soup. He did not volunteer his companion's name in return, though that had been the object of the exercise, but the lady did not relish being left out. She said with condescending interest and a local accent glossed over with too careful polish: 'Oh, you must be at Forbes and Wrighton's?' And when

Calli happily agreed that she was: 'I don't paint, myself, but I do some modelling sometimes for the life classes. Not often, though. I do fashion modelling mostly, for magazines.'

'You needn't tell me the pay's better,' said Calli heartily, accepting a menu from the girl in the nylon overall. 'I've been two years and more in the art materials business, it isn't all that profitable for the painters or the painted. *We* do best out of it. Haven't I seen your picture in *Mode*? I can't just recall the name, but I'm sure . . .'

'It's Crystal Cavendish,' said the fair girl magnificently, and ignored a flash of the tigerish eyes at her left, between warning and scorn. 'That's my modelling name,' she said with dignity. This time an undoubted sound proceeded from her companion, very soft and apparently aimed at no one, but located between snort and sneer. He looked from her to Calli, and appeared to do a little weighing and measuring in his own mind, of which the results did not show. Calli got the impression that wherever he found himself in company with two reasonably presentable females, the same process would inevitably be set in motion.

'It's marvellous to get into *Mode*,' said Calli, pleased with her success. 'Especially so young!'

No snort issued from Willie, but she could feel his amusement, caginess and almost alarm sending out waves in her direction for a moment. Don't overdo it! She seemed to be tugging the St Bernard along now. Better revert to the subject of food, perhaps. A couple of minutes' conversation between enforced partners at a table is almost a necessity, but after that the thing is to leave the other pair alone, and see and hear nothing that is not specifically intended for you. She conferred with Willie, found herself hungry, and ordered the soup of the day, and home-made steak and kidney pudding to follow. Willie chose fish. When the waitress had gone they settled back in their chairs and made a little muted conversation of their own, and she remembered to call him Tim. It didn't suit him, though. He was a Willie if ever she'd met one, but he was also having a subtle influence on her conception of what a Willie should be. It was changing constantly, and she wasn't sure where it was going to fetch up.

'You ever do any modelling yourself?' asked Stan unexpectedly.

'Me?' she said, startled. 'Goodness, no! I never thought of it.'

'You could. Better worth it than plenty who do.'

'Watch it!' said Willie amiably. 'Don't forget there's a chile amang ye taking notes! I'm the one who's supposed to pay the compliments to my girl. Not that I don't want her to be appreciated, mind you, but there's a limit.'

He had the most innocent effrontery, of a kind that parried Stan's blunter presumption beautifully. Over his soup he mildly inspected the liver and onions that had just been deposited in front of Miss Crystal Cavendish, sniffed appreciatively, and opined that he might have made a mistake, choosing the fish. The curious moment of menace, if that was what it could be called, passed without harm. They all returned to their food. But the fair girl was not pleased. The black-widow spiders she wore attached to her eyelids flicked this way and that, blue darts from beneath them transfixing Stan and narrowly examining Willie. Calli was afraid one of the adornments would be propelled into the liver and onions if she lashed them about much more.

Willie sat back as his soup plate was removed, and in resettling himself contrived to move his chair round, so that he faced more towards the wall, where the mirror hung. It was a full-length glass framed in ebony, no doubt acquired at some auction, since it matched nothing else in the room. It took Calli a few minutes of calculation to work out that he had placed himself in a position from which he could cover the entrance from the bar, and watch everyone who came in. Calli began to feel a charmed admiration, as if she had discovered a hitherto unrecognised talent.

And Willie talked. Not too much, not too little, not subsiding constrainedly into private mutterings to exclude the other pair, not at full stretch to impress or ward them off. Not a particle of doubt, he was very good at it. There wasn't a word he said that they couldn't overhear and record if they wanted to, and there wasn't a word that was meant to assert itself in their hearing or present a façade to them. Then, of course, one layer below that, was the reality that the whole performance was meant to impinge upon their hearing and produce precisely that impression. Calli wondered how she was doing. She wouldn't have felt so confident with any other partner. Would he? Something seemed to be going on here besides their combined assault on Stan and his girl-friend.

'Will you excuse me?' said Willie smoothly, just after the plates had been removed. And he rose and walked away towards the right-hand rear door, without any haste. The back view of him was curiously more impressive than the front view. He had nice, large shoulders, very straight and well-set, and his neck rode on them lightly and serenely. One hand in his pocket, the other gently swinging with his stride. He pushed the swing door, and vanished into the corridor behind.

Calli, looking after him, was blessedly unaware of the tornado bearing down upon their table, for she could not see what Willie had seen in the mirror on the wall. Only when the two pairs of solid feet thumped down towards them did she realise that something of perilous importance was happening. She heard the vehement approach, she saw Stan rear himself tall in his chair, with flaring eyes and set

jaw, and the girl sat back in hers in blank wonder, be
holding the assault of a Nemesis of which she understood
nothing but its visible menace.

It wouldn't have been politic to notice their consternation, or anticipate the storm to come. Calli devoted herself
to her steak and kidney pudding, and let the thunderclouds
surge and rumble round her. If the lightning started flashing
she might have to admit to a mild interest, but so far nothing had happened, nothing but a prickling sense of a large,
firm, scented body looming at her back, and Stan's golden
eyes transmitting murderous maledictions from a perfectly
mute, controlled face.

'So there you are!' said the voice that belonged to the
body, a voice dripping with honeyed venom, but equally
under control. If the next table heard anything, and sensed
something constrained about the tone, the words would still
defy criticism. So far! 'You might have left your loving sister word where to find you! If your landlady hadn't overheard you say where you were going with your young lady,
we'd have missed you, and that would be a pity, wouldn't
it?'

Stan's lips parted just enough to utter neutrally: 'I wasn't
expecting you.' The eyes said: 'I'll break your neck for
this!'

Calli turned her head just far enough to get one good
look at Jess Bastable, solid body bulging the demure navy-
and-white ensemble, superb erection of hair thrusting
towards the ceiling, and almost flattened in a coil of plaited
hair-piece on top, like a caryatid. The face wore a wide,
ferocious smile.

'I know you weren't,' she said. 'I had to come to
Braybourne unexpectedly. Family business! But I couldn't
miss the chance of seeing you, now, could I? I like to keep
an eye on your interests when I get the opportunity. Won't
you introduce me to your lady friends? Taking 'em on in
twos now, are you?'

Calli pushed her chair back gingerly, not to impinge upon the abundant bust behind her, and made to get to her feet. 'Look, it will be much more comfortable for you if I move to another table.' She gave Jess a fleeting, polite smile. 'I'm here with someone else, actually – there wasn't an empty table when we came. You have this chair . . .'

'Sit still!' said Stan unexpectedly, and with such flat, assured authority that in sheer surprise Calli obeyed. 'My – sister – will only be staying a minute, she doesn't want to disturb you.' And to Jess he said, in the same tone: 'I'll see you in an hour, at Alf's.'

Nobody had noticed the lady's companion much until then, certainly Calli had hardly realised he was present. Now, seizing upon the name with sudden enlightenment, she turned and gave him a frankly curious stare. Built like the woman, broad, compact and powerful, but without the opulence. A rough, weathered, cleanshaven face, a bent nose, and eyes wrinkled at the corners. He looked both wary and unhappy at the moment, and was plucking at his companion's sleeve, but she took no notice of him.

So that was Alf-with-the-van, who had collected from some expert friend up north a timed fire-bomb, and failing to collect the arranged victim to go with it, had picked up Willie Banks on the motorway to take his place. And this was certainly his sister, who was married to Stan Bastable. It was a revelation that neither of them looked at all like a killer, or indeed a criminal of any kind, yet this man had been happily prepared to send an unoffending fellow-creature, selected at random, out of the world by a terrible route, and the woman, at a slightly more decorous distance from operations, had seen nothing wrong with the arrangement. The prick of reality made the short hairs rise on Calli's neck.

'Yes, come on, Jess,' Alf was saying persuasively. 'We'll wait for him at home. He's said he'll come.' He tended to whisper, a mistake the others hadn't made. It didn't convey words to those around, but it did convey tension, and some people at nearby tables were beginning to look round covertly to see what was going on.

'We'll sit and have coffee with them,' said Jess firmly, 'and then we can all go together. They're as far as the pudding now. Pull me up a chair from that table, Alf.' And she unbuttoned her coat, and prepared to make herself comfortable.

Alf hesitated, his eyes swivelling from Stan to Jess and back again. Having given her order, Jess ignored him. 'I'd like to get to know your young lady better,' she said to Stan with vicious sweetness, 'if she's going to be one of the family.' And she made a rapid and acute survey of Miss Cavendish's petrified and bewildered face, dismissed her as of comparatively little interest in herself, and then swung back to her in the kind of double-take that went out with silent films, but persists in real life.

'Hey, I *do* know you! I've got you now. You're one of Jim Brogan's lot, I used to see you years ago when we came visiting Uncle Fred, round by the canal. You lived in the end house of the same row, and your mum took in laundry for the boatmen who had no women aboard. Beattie Brogan – that's it! Come on in the world, haven't you? Won the pools, or something?'

'I'm afraid you have the advantage of me,' said Miss Cavendish-Brogan in a desolate squeak. 'You're making some mistake. I don't know you.'

'I'm making no mistake, love. I know you, all right, if you have changed a bit. Your dad never did a hand's turn in his life, he was usually propping up the betting shop or the boozer. But that's nothing against you. I don't blame you for poshing yourself up a bit and starting out on your own. But you want to be careful who you let pick you up, a pretty girl like you,' said Jess, grinning ravenously. 'There's wolves around. Men that'll swear they're single and mean business, and promise you a fortune and a wedding ring, when all the time they've got a wife and kid shoved away somewhere and left to shift for themselves. You wouldn't believe what goes on behind some of these nice open faces.'

The unhappy Alf, by this time, had got as far as borrowing a chair, and was hovering behind Jess with it in a helpless way.

'Put that back,' ordered Stan, through lips barely parted and teeth almost audibly gritting together. His face had burned to a dark, coppery glow of rage, without any disintegration in its granite features. His eyes were now the colour of pale lemon marmalade, but with a white-hot fire burning behind. From across the room he must still have looked quite normal. From across the table he looked terrifying. Calli, a mere spectator, was fascinated.

'Get out of here and go home,' he said in a chill, calm undertone, and he closed one hand on the plump one Jess had laid on the edge of the table, and clamped it tight with a ferocity it hurt to see. Without a word or a sound, Jess removed from her lips the cigarette she had just lighted, and ground it out on the back of his hand. He gave a violent but quickly suppressed start, and swallowed an oath as he snatched his hand away. And then, before he could retaliate, even supposing he had been as willing as Jess to get involved in a scene in public – and pretty certainly Jess was gambling on it that he wouldn't dare! – everything seemed to happen at once.

The older waitress, worried about this knot of people partly blocking the gangway, started towards them with her deprecating smile poised, pretending to take them for normal customers in need of service. The door from the bar opened, and a big, fair, husky-looking young man shouldered his way through it with his hands in the pockets of a light poplin coat, and began to saunter slowly down the room, surveying and dismissing the diners at the various tables as he came. He was about a quarter of the way towards them when Stan saw him, and froze into absolute stillness for a moment. Then, gingerly brushing off the ash Jess had left on his hand, he felt in his pocket, apparently failed to find what he wanted, and leaned across Beattie to reach the handbag that swung on the arm of her chair.

'Got a tissue in there?' His long fingers flicked one out and clapped it to the burn. But Calli was sure his hand had been closed when he reached across, only thumb and fore-finger twisting the catch open. Now he had nothing in his palm but the scrap of yellow tissue. He had put something in Beattie's bag. She hadn't noticed, perhaps she was used to his making free with her tissues. But Calli knew what she'd seen, and was almost certain she'd heard something, too, a faint clink of metal against metal. Stan had disposed of something, something he wanted off his person. And he had done it the instant his eye fell on that big, fair young man now lounging towards their table with an amiable smile and a cold, measuring eye.

Now the door from the car-park also opened, and another man came in by that way. He wasn't smiling, he didn't look as if he ever achieved a real smile. A lightly built, silently moving man with a lean face and a mouth like a trap-wire. He, too, approached without haste, and he, too, had his hands in his pockets. It had never occurred to Calli before how menacing that could look.

Jess was the first to see Slitter McGoy, but Stan was only a second after her. This one they both knew. Moreover, his presence made Jess look round quickly over her shoulder, and then she also saw Sam Copper bearing down upon them in slow motion from the bar.

'Hullo, Stan!' said Sam Copper with his vast, expansive smile. 'Hullo, Mrs B., nice of you to lead us straight to him.'

'Hullo, Stan!' said Slitter McGoy, looming up from the other door. 'Been looking for you.'

Calli caught a light flurry of movement outside the window, where the deepening dusk and the closely planted shrubs made a premature darkness. How many of them were there prowling about the hapless *Goat and Compasses*? Two inside and still one more on the watch outside. Or wasn't he one of theirs? He was peering in with deep interest, parting the bushes cautiously before a long, lugubrious face. And his eyes, mild in surprise, satisfaction and – yes! – eagerness, were fixed upon Stan. Stan, whom everybody was looking for, and at this moment most of them seemed to have found.

'Aren't you going to say hullo to an old friend?' said Sam Copper, injured.

Stan, sitting quite motionless in his chair, both hands out of sight under the tablecloth, suddenly hoisted the whole table and heaved it over in Sam Copper's direction. Dishes, water-jug, glasses, plastic flowers went flying. Calli leaped aside too late to evade the flood of water from the jug. Jess got the tangle of plastic flowers in the towering erection of her hair and cursed like a trooper. Beattie uttered a squeal of hopelessly confused and resentful fright, receiving down the front of her silver jacket the sticky remains of her apple pie and custard, and sat down abruptly on the floor, as Stan pulled her down from her chair beside him. One of her false eyelashes did fall off then, and clung miserably to the custard-soaked end of one of her filmy scarves. Miss Muffet and the spider! Stan flung himself flat, reached forward to Sam Copper's ankles, and fetched him down on his back with a crash.

It was all splendidly farcical and ungovernably comic – until you realised that the thin man with the unsmiling face had lunged forward at Stan just as Stan ducked behind the shelter of the table, that Alf had made a dive to intercept the lunge, and that what the thin man was now whipping out of his pocket as they wallowed among the wreckage was a knife.

The whole room was just rising to them, with indignant, panicky cries and the fluttering uncertainty of ordinary people confronted with the extraordinary, when all the lights went out.

Among all the panting and exclaiming and fumbling about that seemed to fill the whole room, the absurdity of would-be helpful people bumping into one another, and dropping things, and falling over things, one person at least moved with pre-gauged accuracy and force, charging silently out of the rear premises straight into the confused mêlée near the door into the car-park. A hand closed firmly round Calli's arm. 'Come on!' said Willie's voice in her ear, and he lugged her towards the door.

She held back for a moment, just long enough to lunge across towards where the arms of her chair and Beattie's still nuzzled each other. She touched another hand in the dark, groping like her own, found the strap of the bag she wanted, and jerked it free. She stepped on another hand and produced a horrifying string of oaths from its owner. She hoped it was the nasty little man with the knife. Then she was hauled away, stumbling over the doormat, and the chill air of the night and the piney scent of the bushes met her. She was out in the car-park, and running, being towed along into the deepest shelter of the shrubbery. Behind them the dark windows and the invisible uproar receded. Willie didn't halt or slacken speed until they were safely in the deep shadows of the alley.

Calli pulled away from him for a moment, panting, and turned about to stare back from cover towards the *Goat and Compasses*. 'Look!' A big, cream-coloured Jaguar wheeled across the car-park at speed, slowed for a moment by the kerb to pick up a running man, and surged away along King Street and out of sight.

'That's this other mob! Whoever *they* are! And I bet you Stan and Beattie were no more than five seconds after us through that door. She was fumbling about after her bag, the same as me, and he was trying to pull her clear.'

Calli was shivering, partly with excitement and reaction, partly with the chill of the evening air. All the front of her skirt was soaked with water from the jug. 'I've simply got to get home and change,' she said, her teeth chattering. 'I'm drenched!'

She didn't tell him, then, that she had another reason for getting back as quickly as possible to the safety and privacy of Nelson Court. That she was wet and miserable, and showed signs of catching cold, was quite enough for Willie. He hurried her along solicitously by the nearest way. Almost at the flats she exclaimed suddenly, in horror: 'Oh, lord! We haven't paid!'

'Yes, we have. I left two pounds on the service table at the back. It's all right.'

One crime less, anyhow, she thought. But they're going to have a lot more than two pounds' worth of damage to make good.

'I'm sorry if you thought I'd walked out on you, like a heel,' said Willie contritely, when they were safe inside the flat, and the catch secured on the outer door. Calli was in the bathroom, stripping off her wet clothes. Presently she came back into the living-room, still dishevelled but no longer shivering, huddled into a thick woollen dressing-gown.

'I didn't think you had. I knew why you'd taken yourself off, as soon as I heard them call that man Alf. He'd have recognised you. There wasn't anything you could do but vanish.'

'He didn't spot me, then? It would have blown the whole thing if he had,' said Willie, relieved. 'I hated leaving you to cope with them alone, but they didn't know you, and if

I'd stayed you'd have been in the soup with me.'

Calli stood holding the bulging black shoulder-bag before her, and looked at him over it long and thoughtfully. 'All right, you don't have to apologise. I got the idea right away. But we've got some notes to compare. You first. What did you actually *do*? It must have *been* you.'

'There's a corridor back there, with the lavatories, and then a back lobby with a door through to the snug. There are hooks all along the wall, and a lot of coats hanging. I kept watching how things went in the dining-room until they got too complicated, because after all, we might pick up quite a lot of tips. But when I thought it was starting to get out of hand I just put on a donkey jacket from the passage, and there was a tool-bag somebody'd hung up there, coming off work. Plumbers' tools, actually, but the bag looked pro. And I stuck my head in the snug, and said: Where's the fuse-box, mate? And somebody told me. They do, you know, if you sound as if you are on a job. It was in a closet off the passage there. So I put the coat and bag back, and threw the main switch.'

'Just like that,' said Calli, impressed.

'Well, there wasn't anything to it, was there? And then I made a dive for you. I almost left it too late. How did you make out?'

She told him. 'The girl's real name is Beattie Brogan, according to Stan's wife. She used to know the family. Beattie must know about Stan – I mean who he is, what he did, and that he's married – but I don't think she realised she'd ever seen Mrs Stan before, or knew her when she walked in. I get the impression Stan can't keep off the girls, and none of them can be sure of him for long, and Beattie's been told enough about a rosy future together in the money somewhere, to make her want to hang on to him now. But I don't think he'll have told her anything about where the

110

money is. I still think there's only one person knows, and that's *him*.'

'I suppose,' said Willie, studying the question critically, 'he would prefer, if he can get away with it, to take Crystal Cavendish away with him rather than his wife, wouldn't you say? After all, she *is* rather spectacular, besides being easier to manage, by the look of it. But what's in it for her? I mean, he doesn't exactly cherish her, does he? And nobody could find *him* comfortable to live with, not for long.'

'Money,' said Calli roundly. 'He's her meal-ticket for life, or so she thinks. And even if she knows he'll walk out on her later, she can get her hands on a nice piece of change in the meantime. And I daresay she thinks him no end glamorous, the big bank robber who's led the police of the world by the nose for three years, and is all set to live the rest of his life like a millionaire. Anyhow, I think Beattie will put up a fight for him.'

'And what about this other mob? Where do you suppose they come in? And who are they?'

'I don't know. But Stan knew those two men, all right. As soon as he spotted them he took the trouble to get rid of something he was carrying. So that if by chance he wasn't able to get clean away from them, it shouldn't be found on him, and they shouldn't get it. He did it very neatly,' she said. 'I don't think Beattie noticed anything. But I did. He put it in her bag.'

Willie, bright-eyed with eagerness, instinctively looked down at the bag she was holding so squarely between her hands, the worn shoulder-strap swinging. He sighed. 'What a pity that isn't her bag you're hugging there.'

'It is,' said Calli simply. 'I swiped it.'

His eyes rounded respectfully. He swallowed. 'You mean that? My God, and I was dragging you off, and wondering why you pulled back! You ditched your own bag to get that one?'

'Not willingly,' said Calli wryly, 'but lucky I did. I meant to collar both, they were hanging there side by side, and I wasn't thinking very clearly. But I went for this one, to make sure. Naturally she was grabbing for hers, as well, and she got the one that was left. Just as well! Now, with luck, she won't look at it until they get indoors somewhere. They're not really so much alike, the design's different, but they're much of a size, and black, and overloaded, and scruffy – I reckon it won't occur to her anybody would deliberately snatch the wrong one. Lucky for us,' she said, 'I always carry the key of the flat in my pocket, never in my bag. I can never find it if I do, without emptying the whole collection on the doorstep.'

'How about emptying this one?' said Willie, and swept everything off the table to make room for the contents.

It looked like a jumble-sale. There was one paperback romantic novel, a copy of a weekly paper with a knitting pattern, much thumbed, two plastic knitting needles with the beginning of a lilac sleeve in a lacy design, a worn leather purse, a small wallet with a photograph of Miss Cavendish (definitely not Beattie Brogan!) inserted into a transparent envelope, a powder compact with a very dirty puff, a couple of tiny pots of eye shadow, four lipsticks in varying shades and stages of use, a crumpled lace handkerchief, a sheaf of multi-coloured tissues, a comb, several hair rollers, a handful of hair grips, two jewelled clips to hold long hair, and quite a collection of stray blonde hairs accumulated in the corners of the bag. There was also a combined pocket corkscrew and bottle-and-can opener, a crumpled head-scarf, a small kewpie doll in a feather skirt, and a miniature pack of cards. There were no letters, no owner's label inside, no rent book, no means of determining who the proprietor was, or where she lived. There was a normal Yale key in the wallet, but no means of knowing where it fitted.

There were also two other keys, on a ring. One of them was plain, heavy and old-fashioned, a door-key to a door surely a century or more old. The other was small, bright and apparently unused, never a scratch or a tarnish on it, but its pattern was elaborate to a degree, a work of specialist art.

'That's it,' said Calli, gazing. 'It must be. All the rest of this junk is pure Beattie. And I heard metal touch metal when he planted them. This is what he couldn't let the hijackers get their hands on. I don't know where they fit, but these are the keys to Stan's hoard.'

CHAPTER SEVEN

In the *Goat and Compasses* the lights went on again only after an unnecessarily long interval, owing to the general stupefaction, which had prevented even the most level-headed from living up to their normal style. It was somebody from the snug, unaffected by the hysteria generated in the dining-room, who remembered the young fellow who had stuck his head in and asked after the fuse-box. The same somebody, without bothering to inform anyone else, went sensibly with a torch to have a look, and found the main switch turned off. He remedied the fault. The *Goat and Compasses* emerged positively bathed in light, just as the police car arrived.

A uniformed sergeant and constable walked in to find the dining-room studded with dazed and blinking survivors frozen where the light had found them, and in one corner, by the open door to the car-park, a table overturned, broken crockery spattered several yards around, and Jessamine Bastable sitting in the middle of the chaos beside the apparently lifeless body of Alf Jarrett, who lay flat on his back, sprawled across the fallen tablecloth, with a knife in his ribs. She was cursing monotonously but fluently, the flat tone belying the miraculous invention displayed in the words. She was understood to say that somebody called Lou would never forgive her.

The corpse turned out not to be a corpse at all. But it was in such obvious need of care that an ambulance was summoned, and the victim despatched to hospital, accompanied by Jess, before anything else was undertaken. The knife, withdrawn from its lodgement with great care under police supervision by the young doctor who arrived with the ambulance, was reverently enclosed in a napkin loaned by the establishment, and left in the charge of the constable.

The sole casualty removed, the sergeant proceeded to get statements from all those remaining in the dining-room. A lot of what he got cancelled itself out, but he was quite accustomed to that. What he did get that intrigued him was as follows:

Prior to the lights going out, four people had been seated at the table where the incident occurred. Two couples, because one pair had arrived after the other, and asked if the places there were free. And just before the other characters involved started to appear, one of the young men, the later comer, had gone off to the Gents. Then these others, the casualty and his companion, had arrived and started bandying words with the remaining couple. The other girl didn't seem to be involved, except that she happened to be sitting there. And then, quite quickly – was there a suggestion that one arrival followed the other of intent? – these two men had appeared, one from either door, and converged on that table. And as soon as they got there the table had been tipped over, some sort of fight had started, and then the lights had gone out. He got descriptions of all the people concerned, but they varied considerably, especially of the two latest comers, in whom he was most interested, since they seemed to have precipitated the actual scrimmage.

The real luck came later, when they were prospecting outside in the car-park and the street, just in case. The car-park was an alluring playground for the relatively deprived young of the district, having trees, bushes, lights and shadows, and a fair amount of space. And there were plenty of young in the district who did not go to bed at eight o'clock, having parents who regarded them as harassments to be got from under their feet after work for as long as possible.

Some of these sprats were bright as buttons, and dead keen on cars. The nine-year-old who emerged from the shrubberies to offer his observations had a notebook nearly as big as himself, filled with car numbers collected on this spot, and scrawled descriptions of the vehicles concerned. He was also hot on accurate times, having been given his first watch at Christmas, and guarding it like a diamond.

'I seen 'em,' he said firmly. 'They went off of here about three minutes after the lights went out. That was just around eight o'clock by my watch. A man came scooting out of that door and across to a big cream-coloured Jag, this number I got down here, see? He got in and started her up, and druv her round to the way off, and this other chap come running out of the bushes and got in the front with him, and they shot off that way, towards the town. Like a bat out of hell!' he added hopefully, having seen that line produce a highly satisfying reaction on telly.

The sergeant was cool, cagey but encouraging. The child was stung, and reached for further revelations, but being basically a truthful and uninventive being, offered only what his retentive memory suggested:

'About a minute after that, there was this old Mini took off after it. A quiet sort of chap come walking across, I din' see where he come from, I was watching the Jag. He got in and started his car and went off the same way. I guess it wouldn't really be a minute. He was getting into his car just when the Jag was pulling off down King Street, he could have been following it.'

Naturally the child also had the number of the Mini. Sergeant Bryan noted it down without comment.

'Did you see two young couples come out and make off? Or anybody else come out of that door?'

The child thought for a moment and shook his head, thought again and demanded, enlightened: 'You mean walking? No cars?'

'As far as I can see, no cars.'

'If they din' have no cars,' said the child with sad reasonableness, 'I wouldn' notice 'em, would I?'

That being unanswerable, Sergeant Bryan confided the car numbers to Constable Downes to be whisked back to the office as quickly as possible. 'I want a couple of owners, fast. And get the desk to let Sergeant Wells know that this woman who's gone off to the hospital with the chap who was knifed is the same Jess Bastable he had at the morgue this afternoon, identifying her husband's remains. He'll be interested. Either these Jarretts and Bastables are getting suspiciously accident-prone, or else there's a link-up here that will bear looking into. And when you've done that, you can go and check up at that hospital, and get a proper statement out of her if she's in a fit state. Before they sedate her out of this world.'

But when Constable Downes eventually reached the casualty ward of the hospital, it was to find that Alf Jarrett had already been rushed into the theatre for repairs, and Mrs Bastable, in no need of sedation, had taken herself off in quite competent order.

'As soon as she was told the damage wasn't critical, and he was in no immediate danger,' said the Sister, 'she said she must go home, because his wife didn't know anything about it yet, and she'd rather tell her in person than by telephone. Which is reasonable enough, especially as she could also tell her now that it isn't as bad as it looked. The knife just missed all the vital bits, but it's a nasty gash, and he bled a lot. We'll be pumping blood into him all night, but he'll be OK. What did you want her for? There wasn't any suggestion we should detain her. And she did say you had her brother's address, and you could always find her there.'

'That's right,' the constable agreed. 'She did give us a statement of a sort, back at the pub where it happened, but she wasn't very coherent at the time, we may get something more useful out of her once the shock's worn off.'

Or we may not, he thought privately. Shock can be a very useful state sometimes, if you want to be protected from having to make statements too soon, before you've had time to think. According to Jess, to date, she had merely gone with Alf for a meal, and he'd stopped to talk to some young fellow he knew, and then these others had muscled in and all hell had broken loose, and she, personally, hadn't a clue what it was all about. Alf, she opined, might know something. But Alf couldn't be questioned tonight, or perhaps for several days. Which might be very convenient for someone. Even for a number of people.

Though this account of hers diverged somewhat from those given by other witnesses, by and large it held together. Nor was it very odd, after a nasty scuffle like that, that the other young couple, the bystanders, had hurriedly dropped two pound notes on the serving table to pay for their meal, and fled. People prefer not to get involved. There was, however, the mysterious business of the young man who had stuck his head into the snug to enquire for the fuse-box, a few minutes before the lights went out. Somehow he didn't sound like one extra and freakish character in the affair. He sounded like one of the 'Other characters played by members of the cast'.

'How did she seem,' asked Constable Downes, 'when she left? Pretty steady?'

'As a rock,' said the Sister definitely. 'If you ask me, most of what she was shaking with was rage, not shock. I gave her some good strong tea, and offered her some tablets, but she didn't take 'em.'

'She say anything interesting?'

'Not to notice. I said to her: Do you know you've got a plastic anemone stuck in your hair? And she yanked it out and gave it a very funny look, and said: That's not all that's got in my hair tonight, not by a long chalk! And then she looked at her watch, and said she'd have to get home to Lou, before she heard it from somebody else, and the porter called a taxi for her, and off she went.'

'Did the porter see which way they set off?'

'I saw them myself, from the window. Couldn't help noticing, because of the lights. He made a U-turn on the tarmac there, and out at the gate and turned left, towards the town centre.'

'Left?'

'Certainly left. Why, is there something funny about that?

'Interesting, anyhow,' said Constable Downes. 'The Jarretts live in Little Felling, and Little Felling is two miles out of town in the opposite direction.'

The cream-coloured Jaguar swung into the car-park of the *Eagle and Serpent*, and Sam Cooper wheeled it into the most remote corner, shaded by a large chestnut tree which was just coming into lavish bud. Beside him Slitter McGoy mourned softly to himself for his lost knife, as for a strayed kitten dearly loved, but between recriminations he also reported on the black Mini that had peeled off from the *Goat and Compasses* close behind them, and was keeping pace with them along Market Street, perhaps a hundred yards behind.

'He's passed,' said Slitter. 'We were wrong. Just happened to be leaving then, that's all.'

'I'm not so sure,' Sam said, backing still more modestly into the corner. The less that was seen of the Jaguar around town, after that episode, the better. And all because of this little runt who could never keep his hands off steel. 'You'd better pray we weren't wrong. We're going to need something to show for the jaunt, after letting Stan slip through our fingers like that. If you've got blood on this upholstery Alec'll have your guts for garters.'

'They don't bleed that fast,' said Slitter, 'not with the blade still in. Good thing gloves are second nature to me. Don't worry, I'm clean. What are we sitting here for?'

'Shut up, and keep well down.' Sam cut the motor, and the big car sat in darkness and stillness. Nothing moved on the car-park. 'Ten to one he comes back. He's just giving us time to get inside.'

'What I don't get,' said Slitter fretfully, 'is who he is.'

'Nor do I, not yet. Got a glimmer of an idea, though. What did I tell you? I thought he was taking a careful look when he crawled past. Here he is back again.'

Across the width of the car-park from them, outlined against the street lights, the black Mini, coming from the square, slid back into view and turned coyly in between the bollards. Slowly it cruised across the open space and came to rest in one of the slots along the wall.

'Come on,' said Sam triumphantly, and was out of the driving seat and across the intervening concrete in a fast lope. Slitter hopped eagerly out after him, and shot along under the trees in deep shadow, to erupt on the other side of the Mini, which had just doused its lights. In the driving-seat a meagre black figure sat quietly as they leaned one against either door. He looked up with the faintest, most resigned of smiles upon his melancholy, aging face, and gently rolled down the window on Sam's side.

'Well, well!' said Sam Copper, drawing a deep breath. 'Denis Sievwright, as ever was. Would you believe it? I had it worked out it had to be you or Collins. Who else was likely to be on the job?'

Sievwright's smile acquired a small gloss of satisfaction. 'Hullo, boys! Had a nice evening? You cut it a bit short tonight, didn't you? Going to buy me a drink inside?'

'The boss might allow you one,' conceded Sam, '*after* he's talked to you. And if you're co-operative. You're coming upstairs with us, Denis, to have a little chat with Alec.

You won't make any difficulties about it, will you? Not that I want any fuss or noise, but we are two, Denis, we are two. So it's through the foyer and up in the lift to the boss-suite where we're holding our little business conference, and no monkey tricks. OK?'

'You know me,' said Sievwright peaceably. 'I don't go for violence and I don't carry guns. I manage things in a civilised fashion. Besides, why should I want to make trouble, when I came here specially to see Mr Match?'

'Like hell you did!' said Slitter with a snarl of laughter. 'You were going to have a look round the cars and a poke among the staff to see what you could find out, more like.'

'I hadn't quite made up my mind,' owned Sievwright placidly, 'when you led me here. But I tell you what it is, boys, I'm getting too old to operate against the odds on my own any more. And too cautious. A quiet life and a modest profit is what I prefer. I'll feel safer on your team than playing a loner. Alec's got the resources, I've got some information. Why shouldn't we pool our assets?'

'I believe he means it,' said Sam, after a pause for thought.

'I mean it. Lock the car, boys, Alec won't be pleased with you if you neglect his Jag. And let's get up there and start talking.'

'So I don't get what I asked for,' said Alec Match, more in anger than in sorrow, though his voice was still low and honeyed, and his face still benign, 'and I do get what I didn't ask for. Not that it isn't a pleasure to see you again after all these years, Mr . . . ?'

'Currently Henderson,' said Sievwright tranquilly. 'James Henderson. Of Knutsford.'

'Thank you! Yes . . . a very respectable town, Knutsford.'

'I am a very respectable person,' said Sievwright modestly. 'An accountant.'

'No doubt a very competent one. More competent, I hope, than these apes who're supposed to look after my interests. Not that I expect them to be able to add two and two, but I did think they could do a little job like running Stan Bastable to earth for me, and get him here in one piece.'

'Much chance we had,' said Slitter sourly, 'with all that crew around. and no possibility of using guns. You can't stick a knife in a bloke's gut in the middle of a crowded pub . . .'

'You seem to have managed it,' said Match.

'That was an accident. He jumped me, and the lights went out, and there were five or six of us rolling about in the dark. And then we heard the sirens. What were we supposed to do?'

'Bring me Stan. And you didn't make it. I don't like failures, Slitter, especially failures who whine. You'd better make sure of the next job you get from me. All right, we followed up Mrs B.'s lead, and located him – I had a feeling all the time she was fooling us about that body, but I hand it to her, she's good! It could all have been true. Now that's all wasted, you've lost him, and lord knows where he'll hole up this time. It means finding him all over again, and without any help from her, now she's wise to us. Back to square one!'

'We're one step forward,' Sam pointed out, none too happily. 'We *know* he's alive, now.'

'He's one step forward, too. He knows we're in town, and after the same thing he's after. And we haven't a clue where to look for him.'

'Denis may have,' said Sam.

'So he may.' Match spread his large, soft but shapely

123

hands upon his knees, and gazed long and attentively at Denis Sievwright, who sat at ease with lean legs crossed, and sustained the stare with equanimity. He was showing his age, in the taut, shiny skin drawn close over his cheekbones, and the thin grey hair, but there was nothing the matter with the sharpness of his perceptions, and no tension turned his mild, regretful composure to brittleness. 'You say you came here to pool resources. I've got the men and the means. What have you got?'

'How about a drink?' said Sievwright. 'I talk better, lubricated.'

'Get him whatever he wants, Preacher.'

Preacher Tweddle poised his prayerful, undertaker's hands over the open cabinet of drinks, and raised one thin black eyebrow.

'Scotch, please. No soda, just a little water.'

He got it, and held it to the light, admiring the pale gold colour, before he sipped delicately, and sighed gratefully. 'That's better! I've had quite a strenuous day today, and as you see, I'm not as young as I used to be. Now! First, my demands are modest, and won't penalise any of the rest of you. All I want is a competence that will keep me without worries for the rest of my life. I'm not asking for an equal share-out, I know my limitations. I'll be content with a nice annuity that will see me through comfortably. I could also be useful in an advisory capacity, should you ever need an expert in the mechanical field. And what I'm offering to put into the pool is information.'

'What information?' demanded Match bluntly.

'Three valuable things. I know who the body in the mortuary is – really is, I mean. And I know, if not where Stan Bastable is now, where he's been living, and where all his things are.' A sharp rustle of interest went round the room. Sievwright smiled. 'I don't guarantee he'll even go back there for his clothes before heading for a new bolthole – but he doesn't know we know it, and it's worth trying, isn't it?'

'Where?' demanded Match urgently.

'Am I in?'

'On those terms, you're in. Where is this place?'

'Lodging as an art student with a Mrs Dutton, at 35, Rainbow Road, Norden Common. They picked up some kid named Banks to be the patsy, and Stan took over his lodgings and his name.'

'Banks?' snapped Match. 'That witch told us . . . '

'I know. She told you a chap named Boycott. I'll explain all that. Take it from me, *Banks* is the name.'

Alec Match turned and snapped his fingers in Preacher Tweddle's direction. 'Got that? Banks! Mrs Dutton, 35, Rainbow Road. You'd better go, and take Crummie to drive you. Make it fast, if he does decide to duck out he won't lose any time about it.'

'Wait!' said Sievwright quickly. 'There's one more thing. If he should have a girl with him, tall, slim, a looker, painted up to the eyes, long blonde hair, purple glitter eyelids, lashes three inches long – the lot! – bring her as well. Especially bring her bag – big black shoulder-thing in leather, with everything in it but the kitchen stove, by the looks of it. There's something in it that ought to interest Mr Match.'

'Got that, Preacher? Girl and all!' said Match. 'Make it fast!'

Preacher drained his glass and left without a word, Crummie Best on his heels. Alec sat back with a relieved sigh.

'Get yourself another, Denis. Be my guest, dear Mr Henderson. Now, tell me more. What is this thing that should interest me? And what's it doing in this bird's bag?'

Sievwright settled back in equal relief, and told him all about the uncomfortable but rewarding time he had spent in the cupboard under the stairs at the house in Elmwood

125

Drive, and everything he had overheard there.

'So that's when they mentioned this name Banks,' said Match. 'And Stan still *doesn't know* that this kid somehow got out from under, and it's Collins who copped it?'

'I don't see how he can, nobody's had a chance to tell him yet. She never got around to it at the pub, though no doubt that's what she went there for, to bring him up to date. Your lads put paid to that.'

'Good! Then he still thinks he's safe as houses using the same name. Now what's this about the girl's bag?'

'When these boys here appeared, Stan leaned over and dropped something inside. it. Whatever it was, it was vital, he wasn't risking your bunch getting hold of it.'

'In short,' said Match, licking his lips, 'it might well be whatever we need to get at the money -- wherever he hid it. You don't know what it was?'

'No. But something small, he could hide it in his hand. It was the first thing he thought of protecting. If Copper had managed to bring him back, you still wouldn't have got hold of that. And you wouldn't have known it existed.'

'Yes . . . yes, I see that. Did the girl know?'

'No. Positively not. Dim as twilight, I should say. Of course he may have got it back from her by now, whatever it was. But if you find them both, you find *it*!'

Sievwright's observations had been constant and accurate, as long as conditions permitted. His eyes were as sharp as his ears, they had had to be. But not even he could see, in the sudden darkness after bright lighting, and through plate-glass reflecting the distant street-lights outside that the wrong girl had got away successfully with the right shoulder-bag.

Stan let himself in at 35, Rainbow Road, at about the same time that Denis Sievwright was walking across the foyer of the *Eagle and Serpent*, with Sam Copper on one side and

Slitter McGoy on the other, like a guard of honour. A lot was happening in Braybourne that night, and a lot of inquests were being held in various places.

'Come on!' hissed Stan, bundling Beattie inside and easing the door closed again very quietly. 'Up the stairs, that first door!' There was a dim light burning at the back of the hall, just enough to make the ascent of the stairs safe. Mrs Dutton had to economise wherever she could. 'Get inside there, quick! I don't want her to hear us.'

Beattie was hopelessly at sea, she didn't know what was required of her, or what he intended. Finding he wasn't following, she hesitated on the stairs, and looked back, and he waved her onward and hissed at her with such furious impatience that she fled into his room like a hare, and closed the door.

It was a few minutes before he came, but at least when he again closed the door, with the two of them safely inside, he looked more relaxed and breathed more easily. He looked first at the window, saw she had drawn the curtains, and actually smiled at her. It was a brief, abstracted thing, but it was a smile.

'What kept you?' she said fretfully. 'Why are we in such a rush all at once, and then you hang around down there five extra minutes?'

'Idiot,' he said without venom, only rather wearily, 'I was telephoning. We're getting out of here. I've got a hotel room, a shoddy bit of a place, but nobody'll ever think of looking there for us. You're coming with me. We're Mr and Mrs Banks – got that?' He was emphatic because she wasn't very bright, especially when anyone tried to hurry her. '*You're* Mrs Banks! Hang on to that, and some day, somewhere, we really will be Mr and Mrs. But you've got to stick it out with me.'

'I will,' she said. 'You know I will.'

She sat down on the bed, and watched him with uncomprehending devotion. She'd only known him sixteen days, after quite an accidental meeting in a snack bar at the cinema. She'd been looking her best, and he had looked, and that had been that. He wasn't exactly the first, but certainly the first she'd ever really felt like this about. She also felt very warmly towards all the lovely money he'd promised her.

'What are you doing?' she said.

That was typical. He was, quite obviously, hauling out a large suitcase, hurling open wardrobe and drawers, heaving things out of both in armfuls, and stowing them away into the suitcase. There was no mystery about it. Nobody else would have bothered to ask, though they might have asked why, or what next. He darted into his little shower-room, and came out with shaving tackle and washing kit, shoving these, too, into the corners of the case.

'Getting out,' he said with exemplary patience. 'I told you. How the hell could I stay here now? She'd be on to me in no time, and she might bring all that lot after her. And I've told you what that would mean. You're not baulking about coming with me, are you?'

'But, Stan,' she protested, 'I've got to go to work tomorrow. Ivy's away, I must be there.' Most of the time she worked in the pay-box of what was, since the Bingo boom, the town's only surviving cinema. Her excursions into modelling were not really very frequent.

'Don't be wet, girl! To hell with that crummy flea-pit! Tomorrow, with luck, we'll be on our way. We'll have to, time's getting tight. I've got to try it, at any rate while the fuzz think I'm dead. It's now or never.' He snapped the locks on his suitcase, and looked rapidly round the room. 'That's it!'

'That's why you told the taxi to wait,' she said. He had told it to wait fifty yards down the road, outside another gate, for further insurance.

'That's it, love. Now come on, give us your bag. There's something of mine I slipped in there, when those baboons came muscling in.'

She had dropped her bag at the foot of the bed when she came into the room. She hadn't looked at it since they ran from the *Goat and Compasses*; it fitted her shoulder and the length of her arm familiarly, and the weight felt right, there'd been no occasion to give it so much as a glance. Now she leaned over and hoisted it to her lap, and set her fingers in the usual grip on the clasp. Then she did look at it, in momentary disbelief.

'What on earth . . .! This isn't mine!'

Stan spun round from the doorway of the shower-room. 'What d'you mean, it isn't yours? How the hell could it be anybody else's? Have I ever seen you without that great portmanteau slung on your shoulder?'

'But it isn't,' she persisted in a rising squeak. 'It's like mine, only the clasp is different, look, and the stitching on the strap. I can't help it, Stan, it isn't my fault. We must have got hold of the wrong ones in the dark. They were close together. And what with you dragging me out like that . . .'

'Are you trying to tell me,' he demanded, leaning over her like a thunder-cloud, 'that the girl who sat by you has gone off with your bag instead of her own? With *my keys* inside?'

'Keys?' she repeated, goggling idiotically.

'Keys! You haven't got cloth ears! Has she got the damned bag or hasn't she?'

'I suppose she must have. Well, she couldn't tell, either, could she? Anybody can make a mistake in the dark. How were we to know?' Beattie was dabbling a hand helplessly among Calli's possessions. Stan snatched the bag from her and up-ended it over the bed, and swept furious fingers through the resultant avalanche. The contents were as multifarious as in Beattie's own case, and their sheer quantity just as impressive. There was a hard-cover thriller, a couple of spare library tickets, a mirror, cosmetics, sparse by Beattie's standards, a purse, a wallet bulging with snap-shots, membership tickets, shopping notes, a diary, a small sewing kit, a block of bitter chocolate, a comb, a suede case of hair-grips, a shoe-horn, two or three letters, a folder of stamps, three ballpoint pens, a folded handkerchief, and an opened tube of mints. There were several things there bearing Calli's name and address.

'Francis!' whispered Stan, harrowing the collection with frantic hands, and finding no keys of any kind. 'That's her! Francis, she said her name was.' He stood glaring at Beattie speechlessly, flexing the long, murderous fingers as though they itched for her throat. And in view of the taxi ticking away down Rainbow Road he couldn't even raise his voice, for fear Mrs Dutton should be alerted and start asking questions. All he could do was howl his rage and deprivation in a throaty croak.

'You stupid cow, do you realise what you've done? My God, why did I ever take up with you! I'd have been better off with Jess, at least she's got sense enough to hang on to her belongings. Nobody'd get a bag away from *her*! Our bloody keys to the life of Reilly, and you have to let some scared kid run off with 'em by mistake!'

'How was I to know?' flared Beattie, injured. 'You never said nothing to me about them. It's me that's lost my things, not you. You think I did that on purpose?'

'How the hell could I say anything to you, with two of the Match boys closing in? I thought at least you could keep a hand on your own property. Now you've chucked the whole show down the drain. Unless we can get that bag back, there won't be any sweet life, there won't be any lux-ury hotels, there'll be nothing, not a penny for you or me.'

'Look!' said Beattie, inspired. 'That girl only took it by

mistake, didn't she? You think she was any keener than I was to lose all her own stuff? She'll be glad as us to get the right one back. And we know where she lives – look, Flat 8, Nelson Court, Miss C. Francis.'

Stan simmered down instantly into solid thought. In a moment he said: 'Get all that junk back in, tidily. Quick! Whatever happens, we've got to get out of here. We'll talk in the taxi.'

They crept down the stairs very quietly, and out at the front door. It was still short of nine o'clock, Stan's fellow art students were out, and Mrs Dutton, home from her baby-sitting stint, was peacefully enjoying television in her private sitting-room. Nobody saw them depart.

'Pheasant Hotel,' said Stan to the taxi-driver, sitting back with a long sigh of relief. Safely out of there, and nobody'd know when, and nobody'd know where he'd gone. Nothing to pay, either. If he'd run into the old biddy and had to spin some yarn about his 'sister' bringing bad news, and his mother very ill at home, he might have had to pay her a week's bed and board to get away.

'All right,' he said into Beattie's ear, 'now we've got to get those bags swopped back. That's your job. You'll have to go and look her up at home. Like you said, she should be glad to get the right one back.'

'I reckon she's sure to be at home,' said Beattie. 'She got pretty well spattered, same as me, she'd want to change.' All Beattie had been able to do was to discard her remaining false eyelash in the street, mop the sticky debris of apple and custard from her jacket with tissues, and stuff the clammy georgette scarves into the laundry basket in Stan's shower-room. She felt battered, and in need of new make-up.

'That's it, then. Once we get that straightened out, we're on our way.' He felt forgiving. He even went so far as to put his arm around her. 'At least there's nobody got an eye on us now,' he said contentedly. 'We'll make it to that South Sea island yet!'

At the corner of Rainbow Road, where four roads met and the street lighting was new and good, another taxi was just turning in. The angle of their own turn caused the light to penetrate brightly into the back of the car, and illuminate Stan's head and Beattie's agreeably cheek to cheek against the upholstery. The passenger in the other taxi uttered a muted bellow, and banged on the glass partition until the driver slid it aside and let her vehement voice through to him.

'That's him! That's the chap I want to see, in that cab we just met. Turn in this drive, and go after him.'

'Lady,' said the driver, swinging the wheel nevertheless, 'we don't want no midnight chases. This is New Braybourne, not So-bloody-ho.'

'You needn't catch him. Just don't lose him! You get me to wherever he's going, and I'll see you don't lose by it.'

'At this time of the evening, that'll be easy,' said the driver, and shot away in pursuit towards the town.

It was perhaps ten minutes later when the Bentley drew up outside number 35, and Preacher Tweddle, immaculately respectable, walked sedately up the drive and planted his finger on Mrs Dutton's bell. He favoured the suave approach. He could afford to, having just over half a pound of Spanish Starlet .25 automatic in his pocket, so short and light that it hardly dragged at the severe line of his jacket. There were eight rounds in the magazine, but he wasn't expecting to have to do more than show it. He was in no doubt at all that Stan Bastable would have a gun some-where about him, and with the shapelessness of modern clothing the bulge would hardly matter, being partnered by several other bulges. But Preacher was backing his own longer experience and sharper reputation with guns, and the modicum of sense that must survive in a young man who had evaded the police of the world for three years.

'Good evening!' said Mrs Dutton, reassured at sight of this almost clerical person, and beaming shortsightedly under her fringe, having poor night vision. 'How can I help you?'

'I hear from my sister,' said Preacher Tweddle, politely raising his black trilby, 'that her boy has started at the School of Art here this term, and is staying with you. Banks is the name. I'm in town very briefly, and he isn't expecting me. But if he is in, I should like to see him.'

'I'm so sorry,' said Mrs Dutton, 'but I'm afraid he must still be out. He went out to dinner with a young lady, earlier, and I haven't heard him come in since then. It is quite early, I mean . . .'

'Quite!' agreed Preacher, with an understanding smile that cracked his austere face almost unnervingly. 'In attractive company . . . What a pity! I wonder . . . Might I just see his quarters? His mother – you'll understand! She's been rather opposed to his leaving home, and it would be such a reassurance if I could tell her . . .'

'Oh, please, do come up!' said Mrs Dutton, charmed and sympathetic, quite forgetting the tiger-eyes in this vision of a possessive female thirsting for comfort. 'Let me show you the way. You could wait for him, if you have time?'

Her flow of friendly conversation died abruptly as she opened the door at the head of the stairs. Stan Bastable's room opened before them empty of luggage, clothes, everything, the wardrobe door hanging wide, the bed ploughed and tumbled. In the shower-room nothing was left to remind Mrs Dutton of her vagrant lodger. William Banks was flown, leaving not even a handkerchief behind.

She lamented, her honourable bourgeois soul outraged at this abandonment of responsibilities. Preacher concurred wholeheartedly, mourned the debilitation of modern youth, claimed he had had some doubts concerning his unhappy nephew's character. He also investigated, as it were absent-mindedly, the laundry basket, and dangled from his staid fingertips in disgust the soggy, discoloured georgette scarves Beattie had discarded. The traces of the *Goat and Compasses* were clear to be seen. That decorative bird of Denis Sievwright's had been here. And was gone. No doubt still in company with Stan.

'I feel it most,' declaimed Mrs Dutton tragically, 'for his poor mother. She telephoned me, you know, before he came, she was so punctilious, and so anxious for him. I shall really have to give her a call if he doesn't get in touch and make some explanation tomorrow. For her sake, I must! She confided him to me, you know. Not every mother, these days, takes her responsibilities so seriously. I can't let her down!'

Willie would have recognised this note, and respected while he deplored it. But Willie would never have precipitated it. At that moment he would have been staggered if he had heard the mourning music of his unknown landlady's voice; he had forgotten his mother's existence in the exigencies of the time.

'I do fully sympathise,' Preacher Tweddle soothed nobly. For God's sake, what they didn't need around here was a man-eating mother hunting for her son, especially since that son was, as far as Preacher's knowledge then went, in the morgue in an incinerated condition. 'But do, dear Mrs Dutton,' begged Preacher wooingly, 'leave this to me. I'll get in touch with his mother, and I shall also make it my charge to look for him, and restore him to his true self. Please, you must allow me to reimburse you . . . had he given notice in a normal way, he would certainly have owed you a reasonable recompense . . .'

He got out of it for a fee of twelve pounds fifty, which was not bad, considering the implications. But she had no idea at all as to where her errant lodger could have gone. Her description of the young lady only confirmed Preacher's recollection of Sievwright's sketch.

Back to square one, he thought, beaming with almost clerical consolation upon Mrs Dutton in leaving, and cursing softly but viciously as he walked down the drive. And where the merry hell do we take up from here?

CHAPTER EIGHT

The *Pheasant Hotel* was in the tangle of small, dingy streets and lanes in the upper part of the town, close to where the railway station and the yards had been before the Beeching era wiped them out in the interests of economy. In the interests of economy, twelve years later, preparations were being made to lay a new line into precisely the same district, to give the new town the artery it desperately needed if it was ever going to be viable, even the lavish new road system proving quite inadequate to the traffic accruing from the influx of people and, less enthusiastically, of industry. The fact that all the bridges on the line had been joyously demolished to settle all doubts about its non-future was a trifling detail, considering what the overall cost was going to be, anyhow. However, the interests of economy had been virtuously safeguarded – twice, sparing no cost in the process.

In the meantime, however, none of this work had begun, and since no alternative development was possible because the area was already ear-marked, the Sidings district remained gently mouldering where it had always been, a rabbit-warren of lanes, alleys and yards, of small working-class terraces, minute corner shops, seedy garages and obscure and rather depressed-looking public houses, which owing to their fine cellars kept some of the best-served beer in Braybourne, or indeed in the country. The trendy modern inns that would some day replace them would never touch the standard again. They were not, however, fashionable, which suited their regular clients very well.

The *Pheasant* had a plain, stolid brick frontage on Dolphin Lane, and an unsurfaced and uneven car-park behind, approached by a narrow yard at one side, as well as room for just three or four vehicles on its flagged apron. The lane, like other main thoroughfares through the Sidings, was quite wide enough to accommodate traffic, but because of the buildings that hemmed it in it looked narrower than it was, and because of the sparsity of the street lights round those parts, and the number of dark, short-cut alleys that threaded the quarter, it had a ghostly quietness in the late evening.

Stan paid off the taxi at the corner, and towed Beattie across the road and into shadow. The second taxi, ambling behind at a cautious distance, had no difficulty in driving on past and turning into the next side-street, affording its occupant a good view of the two figures scuttling into cover under the sign of the *Pheasant*, and the large suitcase bumping alongside.

'You wait here,' Stan ordered, flattening Beattie against the wall, behind the rearmost of the three parked cars. 'I'm only going to check in and dump this thing. We're not hanging around here now, time's precious.'

'But I want a wash,' she protested, 'and a mirror. I only need five minutes.'

He knew better than that. If she got in front of a mirror she'd want to put on fresh eye-shadow, lashes, lipstick, the lot, as well as combing out her hair again, and by the time she'd finished they'd have lost half an hour that Stan couldn't afford. It wouldn't help that she'd mislaid her own armoury, there was the Francis girl's make-up in that bag she was clutching, bar the lashes, perhaps, and she'd reckon it fair enough to borrow for the occasion. If she even got inside as far as the cloakroom he would have had it, and who knew what might be happening, meantime, to his keys? That honest, upright young citizen might go and hand the bag over to the police, if she found no name and address in it, and that was unthinkable.

'You'll wait for me here,' he said in a savage whisper, scaring her into obedience. 'Do as I tell you, or the whole bloody thing's off. Twenty minutes wasted could be the ruin of us.'

Stan himself certainly wasted no time. In the cheerfully grubby hall with its scuffed carpet trampled into an indeterminate dark red, he rapped at the glass panel that afforded a view of the office, and by the time the tired and indifferent girl typing in the corner had finished her sentence and crossed to attend to him, he had already reached through for the dog-eared register, and signed in Mr and Mrs William Banks.

'I 'phoned up about half an hour ago for a double room. Banks is the name.'

'Oh, yes, that's right,' she said. 'For how long will you be wanting it?' He didn't look quite like the usual run of small commercials who used the *Pheasant*, and were taken for granted as one-nighters, but you could never be sure what a traveller would look like, these days. If that was what he was, it was a pretty safe bet the Mrs was a temporary arrangement, but that was none of her business.

'Only one night,' said Stan, 'if my luck's in. But let's say one, with the option of staying on a second. I don't think my business is going to keep me here longer than that. I've got to get on with it right now. What's the room number?'

'Eight. It's two flights up.'

'I'm not going up now – I'm in a hurry. Have this case taken up there, though, would you?'

'OK,' said the tired girl, yawning, and went back to her typing. And Stan departed as abruptly as he had come, retrieved Beattie from where he had deposited her, and lugged her away downhill by the maze of dark alleys that cut short the distance to the embankment and the river.

'Now we've got to get these bags exchanged, and quickly. That you'll have to do, without me, but I don't see you having any trouble. And listen, it's all right here, but when we get into the lights I shall drop behind, and you'll go ahead on your own. I won't be far away, but it's best not to seem to be together. OK?'

She was a very spectacular girl, which was what had first attracted him to her, but tonight he didn't want to be seen with anyone as eye-catching, not after that one ill-fated sally. Once he got her away from here, where it was safe, where the police couldn't find them, then she could be as staggering as she chose, and he'd sit back and enjoy it.

'OK,' said Beattie submissively.

Their way downhill kept to the passages he knew well from of old, for here nothing had changed as yet. Only when they hit Market Street, which continued the line of High Street beyond the square, did they emerge into town lighting and the normal social bustle of late evening. There were quite a lot of people around, for the night was mild and windless, warm enough to dawdle and stare among the windows of the expensive shops displaying antiques, fabrics, fashions and furs. That was good, because Beattie faded into the passing show without comment. He held her by the elbow as they came to Market Street. Here they had to cross, continue downhill, bearing slightly left, cross Marley Street, which ran parallel below, and then they would be approaching the flats.

'Not through the square,' he said in her ear. 'Go to the left here, when you've crossed, and nip through the *Eagle and Serpent* car-park.' It spanned the block, as did the hotel, and gave access to two streets, and it was used by everyone as a thoroughfare to cut corners. 'Right, you go ahead as if you're on your own. I'll catch you up as soon as we get to the quiet bits again.'

Beattie stepped out gallantly, hugging the shoulder-bag that was not hers, slipped across Market Street between buses and cars, and walked jauntily along the opposite pavement until she came to the bollards and white chains of the hotel car-park, and the wide entrance with lamps on both sides. The trees, some of them in flower and shedding petals, made a pattern of light and shade across the tarmac. She looked back before she stepped into the dappled enclosure, and saw Stan just setting foot on the near pavement. He was not far behind her. She went on without qualms.

The steel-grey Bentley and the cream-coloured Jag among the captive cars meant nothing to her, except a reminder of how expensive and exclusive this hotel was, the only one of its class in Braybourne. The bedraggled Mini near the portico was more surprising, but she had no eye for cars, and didn't realise how incongruous it was. Nor did she pay any attention to the two men who had just emerged from the lighted doorway and were coming down the three broad steps together. Turning towards the Mini. Turning towards her, just as she came into the circle of the canopy lights.

'He'd been back,' said Preacher Tweddle, reporting, 'and I should say not long before I got there. The old biddy hadn't heard a thing, or she'd have raised the roof. I paid her off. She could sink everything if she called in this kid's mother and blew the whole business. Tigresses I make pets of, but bereaved mums – no! I duck for cover!'

Alec Match, doubled over on his clenched fists and thinking so hard that his eyebrows were crocheted into a continuous line, turned his head for an instant and exchanged a glance with Sievwright. 'Tell him!' said he, too soured to do it himself.

'The real William Banks,' said Sievwright wearily, 'somehow got a message from heaven, telling him not to sleep in strange beds. Not alone, anyhow. What the fire brigade salvaged out of Cromwell Court is still considered by the police to be Stan Bastable. We know it isn't, and we supposed, provisionally, that it was what was left of the said William Banks, who just got dragged in. Not so! I told Alec, after you left, what I'd overheard at Alf Jarrett's. Mrs B. was taken to identify the body. She did, for the benefit of the fuzz, but I heard her telling her brother what she really recognised there. She knew it, all right. It's George Collins, our wheel-man. The Banks boy got out from under. He's still extant. Somewhere! You tell me where, and why!'

'You mean there's two of 'em walking the world?' demanded Preacher.

'Too right!' said Sievwright. 'Two of 'em. As if one wasn't enough.'

'And Stan still doesn't know he isn't the only one?'

'The one bright spot,' said Alec. 'His wife never had time to tip him off. I'd say he's still feeling safe being William Banks, in some other hide-out. That's the only name we've got to follow up now. What chiefly bothers me is, where – and for God's sake, *why* – is the other one? What the hell is he up to? Do we have any inexplicable characters of student age breezing about in our affairs? There's a lot been going on!'

'He has a managing mother,' said Preacher Tweddle consideringly, 'whom I suspect he wants to ditch. Not viciously, you understand, just to get away from her claws and get going. There's many a potential top-liner been hampered by feeling a certain duty to a hell of a mum. This could have been a heaven-sent opportunity.'

'If he had that much nous,' said Alec, brooding, 'he had enough to smell a number of rats. And if he had that sort of frustrated enterprise, gentlemen, then he had the guts to stick around with trouble when he smelled it out, for the sake of the experience. You tell me the answer to what I asked! Where's the young fellow around twenty, and green the way grass is green – never under-estimate grass, it bursts paving-stones and plays hell with concrete! – who's surfaced somewhere in all this run-around, and chucked a spanner in the works every time? Think about it! Because he wants watching just as much as Stan Bastable does.'

'There was this young couple,' said Sievwright slowly, 'the ones who shared Stan's table. The place was full, mind you, I don't guarantee there's anything in it. But they were the right sort of age. Only in that case where did the girl get in? He was supposed to be a newcomer here, so I gathered. Then just when Mrs B. and Alf showed up, this lad got up and went off to the Gents. Odd he should vanish as soon as Alf appeared.'

'And he didn't come back until the finish?' demanded Match.

'Not until after the lights went out. When the girl bolted she was hand in hand with a bloke, who else could it have been? They beat it ahead of Stan and his piece, the lac-quered lass. I wonder,' he said, musing, 'where the fuse-box is at the *Goat and Compasses*?'

'So do I,' said Alec heavily, 'so do I! This original William Banks I would like to see. That sort of talent I could use. And what about this girl? Not even a name, nothing! Where did he pick her up?'

'And where,' demanded Sam Copper bluntly, 'do we go from here? That bastard's got away with clean heels, and nobody's got a clue where. What if he hits his jackpot and gets away with that, too?'

They kicked it around a little longer before Sievwright

got up to go, but they had made no advance. 'I'll drop in here again early,' he offered without much hope, 'and keep an eye on the Elmwood Drive place, in case, but I doubt if he'll go near anywhere his missus might be. About time I took the Mini off the park, it shows up those bangers of yours, Alec.'

Crummie Best went down in the lift with him, and out to the portico. He was never consulted in conferences, and they frankly bored him. He came into his own only when there was action. But he did feel sufficiently protective towards his boss's interests and his own to watch Sievwright off the premises. So it happened that the two of them emerged from the doorway and came down the broad steps side by side, and turned towards where the Mini was parked.

There was a girl, a tall girl with flowing fair hair and a lot of bizarre eye-decoration, coming across the car-park from Market Street, and as they watched her advance she entered the lighted circle about the doorway. The elaborate paint-job was slightly chipped here and there, the black-widow eyelashes were gone, leaving only fine lines of black round her eyelids, but Sievwright knew his lacquered lass again. He stopped in his tracks.

'Talk about luck!' he said in a joyful whisper. 'That's her! The very girl we need! And with her bag on her shoulder still! Come on, come and help me net this bird for your boss's aviary.'

They opened their ranks, causing her to pass between them. She was unaware of ever having seen either of them before, and thought nothing wrong until they closed in alongside, one at either elbow, and took her quite gently by the arms.

'You'll excuse me, miss,' said Sievwright in her ear, 'but there's a gentleman inside here who's dying to meet you. I'm sure you can spare him ten minutes of your time.'

Beattie shrank and held back, flashing affrighted glances from one to the other, opening her mouth to cry out, and then turning her chin wildly on to her shoulder to look for Stan. But Stan was nowhere to be seen. He should surely have reached the entrance to the car-park by now.

'I don't know you,' she said shakily. 'What do you want? Take your hands off me, or I'll scream for help.'

'I shouldn't do that,' said the voice in her ear chidingly. 'My friend here has a gun, for one thing, and he doesn't like screamers, and for another thing, it's quite unnecessary. Nobody's going to hurt you if you act sensibly. It might even be to your advantage. All we want is a little talk with you. You'd be a silly girl to start things off on the wrong foot, wouldn't you?'

Between them they had turned her towards the door of the hotel, and were walking her slowly to the steps, though she held back with all her weight, still straining towards the distant lights of Market Street, and the lamp-lit entrance where no Stan appeared.

'But I've never seen you before, why should you want to talk to me? I don't want to come with you. Let me go! But Crummie Best had jabbed a hard finger-tip into her ribs, making her think of all the short black barrels of all the nasty little hand-guns in all the films she'd ever seen, and Beattie did not scream.

'Now, my dear,' purred Sievwright, 'you're going to walk in here with us, cross the foyer and get into the lift, and you're going to do it convincingly, as if you were our guest just arrived. As you are! Make it good, and you'll soon be going home none the worse. Make a hash of it and you may not be going home at all. Got that?'

Beattie cast one last despairing glance over her shoulder. No one stirred in the dappled spaces of the car-park. Then she knew that Stan had deserted her, had seen her accosted and left her to her fate.

As soon as she knew she was on her own, her mind began to work again. Maybe she wasn't very bright, but she was bright enough to realise that she would be safer inside this well-lit and populous hotel than out here in the dark. 'All right,' she said sullenly. 'I don't know what this is all about, but let's go and see this chap, whoever he is. The sooner the better he realises he's barking up the wrong tree, then maybe I can get on home.'

They held on to her, all the same, but with every appearance of reverent attention, as they ushered her across the foyer and into one of the lifts. For all her fright, she looked about her with kindling interest, never before having been inside these palatial doors. The vision of the luxury she had been promised brought home the baseness of Stan's desertion. She clutched at the bitterness of her resentment as at a lifeline.

Sievwright tapped at the door of Match's suite, and it was opened by Slitter, whose mouth fell open in sheer astonishment at the sight of Beattie.

'What on earth . . .' began Match, turning from the drinks cabinet with a bottle of Scotch in his hand.

'This,' said Sievwright, 'is the young lady I told you about, the one with the magic shoulder-bag. As you see, she's still hugging it. Pure luck! She was just passing when we went out. I thought you'd like to meet her.'

'I would! I would indeed! Nothing could give me greater pleasure.' He came close, still holding the bottle, and inspected Beattie appreciatively from head to foot, his large brown eyes open wide, and his head cocked to one side. 'Well, I'm damned! Talk about one door opening as another shuts! My dear, I'm very happy to see you.'

'That's all very well,' said Beattie, reserving her options, 'but I don't much like being hustled about like this, when I don't even know what's going on. I didn't want to come here, these men made me. I don't think that's very nice.'

146

'All done in zeal, my dear! You'll find it makes sense. I'm sorry, I don't know you name?'

'It's Brogan,' she said, sensibly abandoning Crystal Cavendish. 'What about it?'

'Just putting everything on a correct footing. Sit down! What would you like to drink?'

'Gin and lime,' said Beattie. She might as well get out of it whatever was going.

'Sam – do the honours! Now, Miss Brogan, not to waste your time, please hand over that bag you're carrying.'

She did so, without a word. Nobody had explained anything to her even when she asked, why should she do any explaining until at least she was asked? Besides, it gave her time to think. She watched Match open the bag upon the round glass coffee-table, and tip out its contents bodily, just as Stan had done in Rainbow Road. Looking for the same thing. Only Stan had known what he was looking for, and from the careful way this man surveyed all Calli Francis's possessions, and the doubtful look on his face when he had examined them all, it was plain to her that he didn't.

'This is where you can be helpful.' He looked up at her over the collection spread out on the glass. 'We know you were with Bastable this evening, we know he put something in your bag for safekeeping. All right, which of all these blameless bits and pieces *doesn't* belong to you?'

'None of them do,' said Beattie, and enjoyed saying it. If he knew so much already, why tell him one fact more than was asked?

'I shouldn't play games,' said Alec Match, gently and chillingly. 'It's too late in the evening. What is it he put in here? Open up, I want to know all you know about it.'

'I'm telling you,' she insisted. 'If you look at those letters, you'll see the name isn't mine. Because the bag isn't mine. If you know so much about where we were tonight, you know how it ended up. You should, two of these fellows came in there and bust the whole place up. I was sitting by this girl I've never seen before in my life, just they came and shared the table, and when Stan grabbed me and we got the hell out of there I reached for my bag in the dark, and this is what I got. Hers! And I was just on my way down to that address you've got there, to see if she's home and get my own bag back.'

'You don't say,' said Alec Match, studying her closely with narrowed eyes, but perforce believing her. 'Maybe we should have waited. Or then again, maybe it's as well we didn't. Are you sure you haven't got Stan Bastable hanging around somewhere biting his nails, waiting for you to come back with the right one? Do tell! I'm sure you know where he is.'

Beattie had only a split minute to decide how much she should admit to knowing about Stan. She owed him nothing – hadn't he just thrown her to the wolves to save his own skin? On the other hand, even if she'd finished with him, she didn't really want to hand him over to these thugs.

'Listen!' she said vehemently. 'I'm done with Stan Bastable, after what's happened tonight. I only met him recently, and I never knew he had a wife until she came roaring down on us this evening. Oh, I know, I had a pretty good idea what he was, and when he told me he had all this money tucked away I guessed it wasn't come by honestly, but I liked him, and having the cash wasn't any drawback, either. But he never told me he had a wife!' She was thinking very hard and very earnestly now, and for her rather more clearly than usual. These were obvious professionals, and plainly successful, not afraid to drive around openly in big cars, the proceeds of their coups, not hiding under assumed names in holes and corners, but putting up at the biggest hotel in town. If those keys Stan had raved about were really the key to a fortune, then Stan was not the only one capable of turning them and opening the box. It began to appear to her that he was not even the best bet, not with these gentry around. She wouldn't stick them on to him, but letting them in on his cache was a different matter. Hadn't he just left *her* to her fate?

'I'll tell you all I know,' she said, making up her mind. 'I never saw what it was he'd hidden, I didn't know he had until we got to this place where he was lodging. But I do know what he *said* it was, when he lost his temper and started raving at me for coming away with the wrong bag. "My keys", he said. He said they were the keys to what he was after, and he had to have them.'

A concerted sigh of satisfaction went round the room. 'So that's it – keys!' said Match, eyeing her intently. 'You know what I think, sweetheart? I think Stan's sent you to see this girl and get the other bag back, keys and all. And you know just where he's waiting for you.'

'No,' said Beattie firmly, 'I don't.' It was almost true, because he surely wouldn't stay at the *Pheasant* now, having seen her dragged in here by this lot. Would he trust her not to give him away? She wasn't going to, but he wouldn't know that, would he? 'I'll tell you,' she said. 'Back at that lodging place, when he found what had happened, he went wild, and we had a flaming row. It was coming, anyhow, because I was mad as hell about him kidding me along when all the time he had a wife. We had a real fight, and I made up my mind to finish with him and get out from under, while the going was good, but you don't tell things to Stan, not to his face, it isn't safe. Sure he wanted me to go get the right bag for him. So I said all right, and we came back into town, but I never meant to go through with it, not for him, not after the things he's said. So I said I had to go to the Ladies first, and we went into the *Little Brown Jug*, by the bus station, but the minute I was out of his sight I slipped out by the back door down the passage and ran for it. And that's the last I've seen of him, and the last I ever want to see. I came straight down here and left him sitting waiting for me.'

'You weren't afraid he'd cotton on fast and get to this girl before you?'

'How can he?' said Beattie reasonably. 'Even if he's got windy by this time and sent somebody in to look for me, what can he do? He can't just go to the door and ask her for it. If he'd been sent, even, he'd have to have the other bag, wouldn't he? He might try breaking in to look for it, but he won't just go and ask.'

'And what,' asked Preacher Tweddle curiously, 'were you intending to do with these keys of his, when you did get the bags swopped over? Not knowing where they fit? You sure you *don't* know where they fit?'

She knew she was still walking a tightrope. One minute they inclined to believe her, the next they reverted to disbelief.

'I don't know, and I don't care,' she said sturdily. 'I don't want the keys, it's all my own stuff I want. I should probably have dropped 'em down a drain, just to spite him.'

Alec Match noted the tense, and smiled at her, at once wittingly and unnervingly. 'But you wouldn't do that now, would you?'

'No,' she said with deliberation, 'I wouldn't do that now. Not when there's somebody else wants them – somebody I don't have any reason to spite.'

'Excellent!' he sighed smugly. 'I think, Miss Brogan, you should complete your errand. Sam, here, will go with you, and make quite sure you get there safely. And relieve you of the weight, like a true cavalier. Tell me now where you live.' She complied, afraid to unsettle so precarious a compact. 'Now, listen! When you get the bag, you will hand it to Sam intact. Stan may have planted more than just the keys, I want to see everything that could possibly have come from him. Then you will go straight home, and

150

keep well out of sight, for your own good. If things turn out all right, you shan't be the loser. I'll get in touch with you, and you shall have your cut. But you won't try any tricks of your own, will you? I wouldn't recommend that at all. You'd be a foolish girl.'

'Why should I?' said Beattie, shovelling Calli's belongings back into the shoulder-bag. 'You seem to be my only ticket to profit around here. Foolish I may have been where Stan was concerned, but I'm not fool enough to cut my own throat.'

She slung the bag, and looked round defiantly at Sam Copper, who was just shrugging into his light poplin coat. 'Come on, then,' she said, 'and let's get on with it.'

On closer examination she found she had been awarded a well-set-up and flattering escort. 'Sam . . .' she said tentatively, and smiled at him.

CHAPTER NINE

The last of Calli's bath-water was just swirling away down the plug-hole, and she was wriggling into slacks and a thick turtle-necked sweater, when the door-bell rang. She stiffened to listen, her arms still raised and one eye obscured, then silently pulled down her sweater and let herself out into the hall. Willie wouldn't answer the door, she knew. This was, after all, a respectable bachelor-girl's flat, and even if the late caller was someone as innocent as the girl from the floor below, wanting to borrow a packet of soup or the evening paper, still he had better not be seen or heard. He was standing on the alert in the kitchen doorway, and he exchanged a long, significant glance with her before he withdrew inside, and drew the door to after him. There was a built-in spy-hole in the outer door of the flat, he knew Calli could examine the caller before she opened.

The shoulder-bag that belonged to Beattie Brogan lay in the middle of the studio couch, all its multifarious contents again packed into it, rather more tidily than before. All but one item. The linked keys were carefully rolled in a clean handkerchief, and reposed in Willie's pocket. They had already agreed that there was nothing for it but to make another trip to Central, and hand them over to Chief Inspector Cope, just as soon as Calli had changed into dry, warm clothes. It began to look as though she had lingered in the bath just a few minutes too long for safety.

What she saw through the magic eye, however, apparently reassured her. Willie, hovering intently behind the kitchen door, heard the latch snapped back.

'I'm so sorry to bother you at this hour,' began Beattie in

a high, nervous voice, 'but I think you took my bag by mistake . . .'

'Oh, it's you!' said Calli. 'I'm so glad, I was hoping you'd get in touch. I didn't know where to find you, you see there wasn't any name and address. I am sorry you've had to make this special journey.' She turned, leaving doors wide open behind her, and caught up the bag from the couch. They stood one on either side of the threshold, gazing at each other with mild, embarrassed smiles, each holding a large bag between her hands, their movements duplicated like those of mirror images. 'Wasn't it wild? I still don't know what happened, not really. Tim dragged me away so fast, I never realised till I got home what I'd done.'

'Just the same with me,' said Beattie with a shaky giggle. 'I even started looking inside it for something, and couldn't make out why I couldn't find it.'

The two bags changed hands, in an almost ceremonious motion.

'I'm very relieved. I was wondering how I should be able to find you.'

'Yes . . . good thing you're tidier-minded than me! I never seem to have my name in anything. I'll put it in everything, after this.'

'Good idea! Well . . . thanks awfully for bringing mine back.'

'Thank *you*! Goodnight!'

'Goodnight!'

Calli closed the door, and stood listening to the clop of Beattie's platform soles descending woodenly. At the first landing she thought she could catch the sound of a quieter but heavier step joining the trot of little hooves. She waited until all sound had ceased, and then turned and went back into the living-room. Willie, with a face of grave resolution, was advancing upon her with her coat held ready for her.

'You heard that? That was Beattie. Not alone! I'm nearly

154

sure there was some man waiting for her just down the stairs.'

'I heard it,' agreed Willie. 'Come on, we're getting out of here fast. Not down the stairs, either – out the back and down the fire-escape.'

She stared, astonished. 'We are? But why?'

'If you're right, and there was a man waiting for Beattie below,' said Willie positively, 'he wasn't waiting for her kewpie doll, or "The Ward Sister's Wooing". And if he doesn't get what he's waiting for – and he can't very well, can he? – then he's liable to come back and ask for it in person. I think we'd better not be here. And I think we'd better not go out the way he's watching, either.'

'You could be right!' said Calli, and dived into her coat.

Sam Copper stretched out his hand authoritatively for the bag as soon as Beattie came down the stairs and drew abreast of him, where he stood in deep shadow, invisible from above. He hadn't trusted her far. She supposed they didn't trust anybody in this business, and on the whole she thought they were right. She loosed the sling from her shoulder, and let him take it. They went down one flight together without a word.

'I'll need some money to tide me over,' she said quietly, as they emerged into the court before the flats. 'You've got all my ready cash in there. The lot, he said! You can guarantee I haven't so much as opened it. The lot is what he's getting. But I need bus fare and lunch money for tomorrow.'

'All right,' said Sam, and reached into an inside pocket for his own wallet. 'You played fair enough. Here, here's five singles. You'll get the bag back, and everything in it, except what matters to Alec. Come on, I'll see you as far as the lighted street. You got far to go?'

'We live round by the canal,' she said, remembering

Jess. That was a sour laugh he wouldn't appreciate. 'No, it's not far. I don't need transport.'

They came into the lane, sparsely lit and running between high walls, that led up towards the town. A lighted street crossed their view ahead.

'OK, kid, take off! Go home and know nothing. He'll get your stuff back to you, and a nice bonus on top of it. Just keep your mouth shut tight, and wait for the windfall.'

'That I've been waiting for all my life,' she said. 'Here I go, then. So long, Sam!'

She headed for the lights, glad and relieved that she was going home, not back to the *Pheasant*, or even to the unfamiliar splendours of the *Eagle and Serpent*. The terrace house on the waterside smelled like sanctuary to her. She wasn't going to be in any hurry to hitch up with another handsome underworld type, either, even if he did have tiger eyes.

The shadow that had followed them from Nelson Court, slipping from darkness to darkness, using the young, discouraged but gallant flowering trees, lurked invisible under the high wall that blocked off the last mercury lights installed with the flats. I'll murder the bitch! he thought, I'll cut her heart out! But it was only the shivering hysteria of the night talking nonsense in him.

He'd let her drop with a sickening thud, back there, what could she do but try to stay alive and immune? He had that much sense left.

It wasn't Beattie he had to see off, it was that bastard waiting there for her to move out into the street, into the clear. He was the one who had the bag, he'd taken it from her before ever they reached the ground floor. Stan knew that, because he'd been lurking there in the cleaners' cupboard, the only thing nobody bothered to lock.

From where he stood in deep shadow, flattened against the gate-post, he could see a faint line of light that silhouetted Sam Copper's big, easy body, motionless as he watched Beattie on her stacked wooden hooves clopping along the alley towards the street lighting. He wouldn't move until she was gone. Even then it was doubtful if he'd follow by the same way. There was a whole maze of runways here on the slopes above the river, ramps and stairs and little cobbled lanes by means of which you could work your way all round the south side of the town and never come under a modern lamp, nothing but the occasional dim bracket high in the wall. Copper would stick to the dark ways. That suited Stan very well. There wasn't an alley down here he didn't know as well as the tom-cats that haunted them hideously at night. Nothing here was changed apart from the erection of those incongruous blocks of flats.

You can't mug a man in a well-lighted street with dozens of people still around. Stan fixed his eyes hungrily on the bulge in the pencil-line of light that showed where the bag was securely slung under Sam's arm. He had to have it! And Sam Copper was bigger than he was, and probably carried more gun than he himself possessed. There was only one place for it, and that was down here in the dark, and time was running out with every distant echo of Beattie's footsteps. And there was only one way, and that was to be the first to shoot, not the second. No coming to grips, no struggle, no noise, nothing to delay the getaway. It was a perfectly respectable tactic, these days. The pre-emptive strike, they called it!

There'd be the report, of course, and at this stage of darkness the flash, but between these high walls there'd be nobody to see the flash, and the ricocheting echoes of the shot would seem to come from all directions and almost any distance, a backfire somewhere, down on the embankment, up in the square, anywhere. And he'd be gone. There wouldn't be time to go groping around after the expelled case, even in so narrow a field, but when they found it, it wouldn't tell them much. The gun in the inside pocket of his natty suede jacket was a Webley and Scott automatic of the type once in general use by the Metropolitan Police, .32 ACP, barely six inches long and weighing little over a pound, and since it had been stolen from its original owner, and not by Stan, it was unlikely to be traced to him. Even if he hadn't been lying dead in the morgue, as he fervently prayed the police still believed. You can't be charged with murder when you're dead, can you? And you can't charge somebody with murder when you're dead. All he'd have to reckon with was the rest of the Match Boys. With luck the killing might even be attributed by the police to one of Sam's colleagues, since rogues do fall out. Who else was so likely to own an M.P. Webley and Scott?

He extracted the pistol from his pocket with care, and thumbed up the safety catch behind the trigger on the left side of the receiver. He was possibly sixty feet from where Sam stood, he needed to get nearer than that. He was a fair shot, but there had to be certainty. The last thing he wanted was a delaying struggle, chaotic and obscene, to keep hold of the sling of that shoulder-bag.

Beattie had reached the slight bend in the alley that partially obscured the view of the lights in the street. The flat echoes of her footsteps were cut off at once, before she actually emerged on to the pavement. And at the same moment Sam Copper hitched himself erect at leisure from his leaning stance against the wall, and walked gently on. Not after the girl, but turning right after a few yards into Clare's Shut, to work round in darkness and solitude. That was one thing guessed right, and a good omen. Stan took off instantly from his hiding-place, not sauntering like his quarry, but at a fast, silent run, long-stepping on rubber soles. Only a few yards along Clare's Shut there was the only bracket lamp in all its sombre length.

He reached the turn and peered round just as Sam

Copper drew almost abreast of the light. Its grubby yellow patted his fair hair, and slid down into the nape of his neck, then lower, flowing down the shoulders of the beige poplin coat. The timing was perfect, and the distance less than thirty feet. With the light now full on the large shoulders and back, Stan even took time to draw a deep breath, and steady himself in a sidelong stance, before he levelled the gun, lined up the sights, and squeezed the trigger.

He knew he couldn't miss. Sam Copper was so big that he almost filled the narrow passage from wall to wall. But the flash and the crack, in that shut-in place, seemed blinding and deafening, and caused Stan to leap and tremble in a paroxysm of jarring nerves. Sam seemed to be shoved forward sharply but not violently by a poke under the left shoulder, then as abruptly jerked back upright, where he hung for a fraction of a second motionless. Then with no movement of his arms, no attempt to break the fall, he pitched forward like a dead weight on his face. It was as if some bored child had thrown down a rag doll. If he moved again at all, Stan never detected it. Not that he waited to find out. The instant he could make his legs go, he leaped forward in a wild run, caught at the sling of the shoulder-bag and yanked it away from under Sam's left arm, which waggled helplessly and fell back limply to the ground. A dark stain was spreading steadily under the left shoulder-blade. No need to worry about Sam, he was out, he'd never lifted his head. Even if he lived to talk he wouldn't know who'd shot him.

Stan tucked his prize under his arm and ran like a hare, doubling and weaving through the maze of lower Braybourne, to emerge at last well along Market Street. Before he came out into the lighted ways he halted, leaning in darkness, to regain his breath and his composure. The Webley and Scott he had thrust into the bag, after re-setting the safety catch, in preference to returning it to his pocket, and for a moment he was tempted to hunt through Beattie's random possessions then and there, by feel, to comfort himself with the touch of his keys. But his nerves were too short, he could have fumbled, dropped something betraying, lost too much time. No, he had to get this thing and himself safely back to the *Pheasant* at a reasonable hour, and behave as if all was normal and ordinary. Beattie knew nothing about what he'd just done. Since Sam had sent her off alone, she must have been told to go home and keep her nose clean. Going back to the *Pheasant* was a risk, but what wasn't, and he couldn't believe she'd told them where to look for him. It would look fishy if he moved off again and cancelled his booking at this hour. No, he wouldn't bolt unless there were clear signs of the hunters lying in ambush.

Only one little snag, and he could see his way round that very easily. There wasn't going to be any 'wife' arriving, after all, to share the room with him. Any excuse would do for that – whatever he said, they'd simply take it that his temporary home comfort had let him down, and grin behind his back. As if that mattered! He wasn't the first, and he wouldn't be the last.

Stan squared his shoulders, passed a hand over his mane of hair, and stepped out boldly across Market Street, clasping Beattie's shoulder-bag lovingly against his side.

At the *Pheasant* he prospected every approach with care, but all was dull and quiet and commonplace. His instinct had been right, she hadn't told on him.

He leaned down to the reception window and rapped for his key. That was the first shock.

'The key's upstairs already, Mr Banks,' said the languid girl, opening the glass panel. 'Mrs Banks asked for it, soon after you went out.'

He hoped she had not noticed the blank, shocked stare he

gave her, shaken out of his stride just as he had recovered it. Probably she didn't think anything about him one way or the other. She'd delivered her message, and was back at her knitting, a good deal more interested in the lace pattern she was perpetrating in hectic pink than she was in him.

'Oh, good! Thanks!' he said inanely, and made for the stairs, racking his mind for the meaning of this development. Maybe he should have considered the possibility. And maybe it wasn't so bad, after all. He could hardly blame Beattie for playing it very cautiously when she found herself in the hands of the Match Boys. She'd gone along with them as far as recovering and surrendering the bag was concerned, but damn it, what else could she have done? And she'd made off when she was told. But what if she'd rushed straight back here to warn him, to explain, to make excuses and cling to her rights in him, even to help him in his struggle if she could? It was a possible and a flattering thought. A pity it was spoiled by that flabby girl downstairs saying: 'Mrs Banks asked for it soon after you went out.' Beattie had been detained on unavoidable business of one kind and another for a good hour after they left the *Pheasant*. Or was that just casual talk, meaning no serious reference to the time?

He drew a deep breath on the landing, suddenly aware that if Beattie was really back here, and had managed not to give away where he was hiding, they were back on course again. She wouldn't know it yet, but there it was. She had him, and he had her, and they had the keys again. No need to tell her how he'd recovered them. The plans could go ahead. He could get the cash, and they could get out together, as far and fast as possible, out to some island in the sun where there was no extradition, and no wife and child round his neck. He began to hope it was true. By the time he opened the door of the room he was practically convinced, so that he opened his mouth to say something kind and forgiving, before she could remember that it was he who had turned tail and left her to the wolves, and she who should be doing the forgiving. Then he stopped dead. The door, released, closed itself behind him with a gentle click.

On the faded taffeta cover of the double bed Jess was lying comfortably propped with pillows, her shoes off, her ankles crossed, reading the evening paper. She had taken down the magnificent but by this time somewhat groggy temple of her hair, and stopped being a caryatid for the night. The voluminous hair-pieces that were not quite a match for her own tresses lay coiled on the dressing-table like a sleeping Pomeranian. Her own luxuriant crop flowed over the pillows and her shoulders. She looked up at him without moving, looked him over from head to foot, and said caustically: 'Well, well! Come down to bag-snatching, have we?'

She was the second shock, and a bad one. He stood glaring at her, unable to speak for a moment, so desperate were the implications. In a voice thick with menace he got out: 'How did you get here?'

The funny thing about Jess was that she never seemed to notice any menace in him. On the occasions when they'd fought, she'd been at least as stimulated by the exercise as he had, and appeared to enjoy it, and somehow, whether by reason of her own undoubted prowess or some unsuspected inhibition in him, she'd never really got hurt, and sometimes had even emerged the winner on points. She never batted an eyelid now, but answered simply: 'By taxi,' and went back to the evening paper.

'Don't come any games,' warned Stan, 'not tonight. You know damn' well what I mean. How did you find me? How did you know where to look? If you could make it here, so could others.'

'Take it easy,' said Jess soothingly. 'The police aren't looking for you, they don't even know what you look like now. As far as they're concerned, you're dead. I saw to that for you.'

'Maybe, but Match and his lot *are* looking for me, and after that botch-up tonight they *do* know what I look like, and they know I'm alive and kicking, not on any slab in the morgue. If you've led them here . . .'

'If I had,' she said coldly, 'you'd have known it by now, wouldn't you? You don't think that bunch stand on ceremony? I've given away nothing, stop shaking.'

'Who's shaking?' he said furiously, aware that indeed he was. 'And how *did* you run me to earth, then?'

'As soon as I came from the hospital I took a taxi straight to those digs of yours at Norden. Just in time to see you and her leaving! Don't think I don't know who Mrs Banks was supposed to be, I'm not that green! I had the driver follow you, and you led me here yourself. And after you'd gone off with that little floosie I gave it ten minutes, and then walked in and asked for your key. It wasn't any big deal, the register was there wide open, if I'd been in any doubt about the name. So here you are, complete with wife, all according to schedule. What are you grumbling about? Nobody's going to ask any questions about the other one, nobody inside here saw her, did they? I don't mind asking one myself, though,' she conceded thoughtfully, 'now I come to think of it. What have you done with her?' Her eye travelled shrewdly over his person, and the bag, which had come unfastened and was gaping partly open under his arm, showing a bluish gleam of metal. 'Shot her?' she suggested with mild interest.

A chill convulsion passed through Stan's body, and emerged in a horrible but muted curse. The *Pheasant*'s walls were old and fairly substantial, but you never know how sounds carry, or how nosy the fellow next door may be. She had nearly made him shriek aloud, putting her finger on the quick of truth so devilishly.

'You'd better not say things like that,' he said through his teeth. 'If I have, you don't think I'd stick off at you, do you?'

'That's the gratitude I get,' said Jess, pleased at his discomfiture and quite unalarmed by any threats, 'for keeping my mouth shut, keeping my head, keeping your secrets, and keeping the police certain you're dead and out of their hair. And what do you do for me? Get poor old Alf knifed – oh, no, he's not dead, he's going to be as good as new – and try to ditch me for a daft little cat without two wits to rub together. A long way you'd ever have got with *her*! But don't think you're going anywhere without your ever-loving wife – not this time. What *did* you do with her, any-how? And what, for Pete's sake, are you doing with her bag, if that is hers?'

He didn't answer that, though he was grateful for the reminder that he held the joker, after all. It had been a bad evening, but he'd come out of it the winner. Alive, not like that big hulk down in Clare's Shut. Had anyone stumbled over the body yet, and raised the alarm? From the Sidings the sirens of police and fire in the town centre and the lower town hardly disturbed the immemorial peace. And he had the keys right here in this feminine bag that was tantalising Jess so much. He hugged it to his heart, like a balm for all aches and pains.

'Move over,' he said, 'and I'll show you.' And for the second time that evening he up-ended a bag that didn't belong to him, full of the trivia of femininity, and tipped its contents on the bed. No tremor of apprehension went through him at the repetition, no sensation of getting caught in a treadmill that would have him endlessly repeating the same pointless movements and getting nowhere.

Jess swung her feet to the floor, and sat looking on mildly, as at the antics of a not very bright child. He held

164

the empty bag upside-down, and shook it. Incredulously he eyed the tumbled collection of Beattie's treasures.

'I now declare this jumble-sale open,' said Jess, yawning.

It wasn't possible. Not twice! He stared and counted, pawed through the dusty debris, clawed in the corners of the bag.

That was the third shock, and the worst. His legs gave under him, and he sat down beside Jess in a flurry of Beattie's spilled powder. He uttered an almost soundless howl of anguish, and began simultaneously to curse in a monotonous undertone and to cry tears of pure rage, squeezed out without his knowledge from the tawny tiger-eyes.

'*Now* what?' demanded Jess with disgusted resignation. 'All right, what is it that should be there and isn't? I've got the idea.'

'My keys! The keys to everything, if you want to know. Damn it, they *had* to be in the blasted bag, they weren't in the other one, I know that. My God,' he said, shaking with hate, 'all that for nothing! *For nothing!*'

'*Your* keys! To where the money is? You wouldn't be in this state over anything else,' she said, needing no answer. 'They're that important? You can't get at the stuff without 'em?'

'I could – maybe – if I'd got all the time in the world, but I haven't. I've got practically no time at all, with the Match Boys breathing down my neck already. Not that you'd know anything about that,' he said, with venomous self-pity.

'You'd be surprised what I know. You'd have been a hell of a lot cleverer and safer if you'd got in touch, and given me a chance to tell you what I know, instead of fooling around playing art students with that little bitch. All right, so you've got to have these keys, they're that important. So how come you let 'em out of your hands in the first place?'

'Idiot, I had to! Damn it, you were there, you saw those two closing in, suppose they'd cornered me with that lot in my pocket? I ditched the keys in this bag of hers, and I got her and myself out of there intact, too, if it was touch and go. And then the daft little nit had to grab up the wrong bag in the dark, and land me in all this trouble. I could wring her neck!'

'Then how'd you get this bag back again?' demanded Jess, eyeing him narrowly.

'There was an address in the other one. She went and took it back and asked for this one.'

Her eyes flashed dangerously. 'You've still got her hidden somewhere, then? She's still dangling round you?'

'Is she hell! If you want to know, she ditched me. As soon as she got hold of this she handed it over to one of Match's lot – the big, fair bruiser, Copper – and I had to jump him to get it back. And all for nothing!' he repeated, shaking again at the recollection. 'The bloody keys aren't there, after all that!'

'Then Copper took 'em out and pocketed 'em before you got to him. What else?'

'No, he didn't, I'll swear to that. I was watching him the whole time. He never opened it.'

'Then she's smarter than you give her credit for, and she nicked 'em herself before she handed over.' She said it reasonably and thoughtfully, but without conviction, because she had just conceived of another and more interesting possibility.

'She never did. She'd be too scared, and anyhow, he was keeping an eye on her, as well as me. No, I reckon it's those damned kids have got 'em. The girl who went off with Beattie's bag, and that lad who was with her . . . But *why*?' he asked himself and her and the fates who ran things so badly, without justice or logic. 'Why should they pick out that one thing, and hand over the rest? What could they want with 'em? What could they know about 'em? Nothing! It makes no sense!'

Jess was thinking that it did begin to make sense. 'Let me get this straight,' she said. 'That girl who was at the same table with you – she did say she was with somebody else, but I never saw him.'

'He went off to the back just when you and Alf came in,' said Stan abstractedly.

'Yes, so it seems. Interesting, when you think about it.'

'Why? I'd never seen him before, he was just her boy-friend. She sells paints and things for some shop in town, she came hawking 'em round the lodgings, that's the only time I've ever seen her, either. Just plain accident they shared the table.'

'Accident my foot!' said Jess flatly. 'Maybe *you'd* never seen that boy before, but I'd lay anything Alf had. That's why he made off as soon as he saw us coming. We'd been wondering where that lad was, and why he was lying low and saying nothing. I'll tell you his name, if you like. It'll shake you! His name's William Banks.'

He stared at her open-mouthed. 'You're raving. The Banks kid got himself incinerated, remember? Alf picked him up when Snuffy Boycott failed to show up. Or are you one jump behind, and still with Snuffy nominated for the body?'

'No, love,' said Jess acidly, 'I'm one jump ahead, as I'd have told you earlier this evening if you'd given me a chance. I identified that body as you, and as far as the police are concerned it *is* you. But as far as you and I are concerned, my lad, it's neither you nor William Banks. It's George Collins! Coming to keep you company closer than a brother till he got his stake, only he picked the wrong night and got grilled instead. Oh, Alf's boy delivered the parcel, all right, but he didn't stay to go up with it, and he didn't go to his lodgings, either, or to the police, when he heard the news, or any of the places a nice, innocent lad should have gone. God knows how he picked up the girl, but after that, you think she just turned up peddling paints by chance? She was checking on you. You think they just blundered in at the pub by coincidence? Not a hope! They were on to you. You think she got the wrong bag by accident? That nobody saw you palm the keys into it? I'm betting *she* did!'

'But it's barmy,' he protested, clutching handfuls of his hair. 'They don't even know what they've got, where it belongs, what to do with it. Why should they want it?'

'They know the one thing that matters. They know it's the joker. Why else should she blandly hand over the bag with all this stuff, but without the keys? They're no innocents! You're up against two gangs, not one.'

'You needn't sound so bloody pleased about it,' he said, stung. He passed his hands wearily over his grey face, and said miserably: 'I shall have to go down there again, and get in after the damned keys. If they took 'em, and they must have done, then they're somewhere in that flat. I've *got* to have them – if I have to lay her out to get 'em.'

Jess didn't answer that at once. She sat thinking, jutting her lower lip aggressively at all the problems that loomed between them and wealth. Also going over the words he had used, and recollecting how easily he had slid past the point where he jumped Sam Copper. Sam, the big, husky type, built to cope with Stan one-handed, and as if that were not enough, with more experience in guns than Stan had, and certainly with no more scruples. Casually she put out her hand and picked up the M.P. Webley and Scott, lying among the wreckage of Beattie's beauty aids. She sniffed at it delicately. No need to slide out the magazine.

He watched the act without a word, and looked her in the eye.

'All right,' he said. 'So what? Her, too, if I have to. And that green boy-friend of hers. I'm not letting anybody stop me now.'

'Where've you left him?' asked Jess, with no note of disapproval or alarm, or indeed of anything but the desire for accurate data before she made a decision. It was queer how the initiative seemed to have passed into her hands. He was just too tired to fight.

'Under the lamp in Clare's Shut.'

'And you reckon you're OK? Clean?'

'Clean as a whistle.'

'And where exactly is it this girl lives? Close?'

'Nelson Court – Flat 8.'

'Too close,' she said decidedly, and got up as if that settled it. 'It's long odds the alarm's gone out by now, that quarter down there will be swarming with coppers. You can't go back there tonight.'

'But I've got to! If I don't, it means another day.'

'Another day lying up here isn't the end of the world. But if you go down there now, with a murder hunt beginning, and this same gun on you – breaking and entering five hundred yards from where the cops are operating – that will be the end. Look,' she said reasonably, turning about with her best navy dress unzipped and one round, pale shoulder out of it, 'stay put, and they're still not looking for you. Go and get spotted somewhere, and they will be, and there'll be no stops they won't pull out. Sure the Match Boys want you, and want the keys, too, but they don't know where you are, or where the keys are. Beattie Brogan may know, but my guess is she'll be lying low and saying absolutely nothing, not for anybody on either side of the law. She'll be looking after Number One. Especially when she hears about Sam Copper. No, you'll stay right here and keep quiet till tomorrow night, because you don't have any choice. With any luck they'll have cleared out of the district by then, and nobody'll expect lightning to strike down the same alleys the next night. And once you've got your keys, for Pete's sake get straight after the locks where they fit, and let's get out of here for good.'

He wasn't best pleased at taking advice from Jess, but he had to admit it made sense. Accepting it, if only for want of an alternative, also allowed him to relax into the nervous tiredness that he had been fighting off all this time. It had been a hell of a day, the thought of a long, undisturbed night was very pleasant. With her hair down like that, and half undressed, she wasn't a bad old bird, either. Not Beattie, of course, she hadn't Beattie's youth, and she never had had Beattie's looks, but she had plenty of guts and sense when it came to the point – both qualities that were not conspicuous in her rival. Still, once out of England with the cash safe in hand, with a new name and identity, was he going to need a lot of brains in his woman? Stan drifted, too drained to be capable of making a choice. The main thing was, Jess was right here.

'I shall have to sleep in my slip,' said Jess, and giggled. 'I'll buy a nightie tomorrow. You've got nothing to worry about, is my guess. If you want an excuse to stay out of sight all day, you can be having a cold and stay in bed, I'll see nobody bothers you. Might even have a scout round by Nelson Court myself, and see what's stirring. And I tell you what, better get rid of that bag. In the morning I'll take it out and sink it with a couple of bricks off the foot-bridge. Then there'll be nothing to link you up with it. Come on, get all the junk back into it. I want to go to bed.'

It had been a strenuous day among the Braybourne C.I.D., what with the arson and murder at Cromwell Court in the small hours of the morning, and the affray and knifing at the *Goat and Compasses* in the evening. Even when he came with possible good news, the desk-sergeant at Central Division tapped almost apologetically on Detective Chief Inspector Cope's office door.

'Couple of new items, sir. Just got a fix through on those car registrations the kid noted down on that car-park. The two that took off in a hurry after Jarrett got knifed. The Mini is registered to a James Henderson, with an address in Knutsford. No form or anything. The division say he's a perfectly ordinary middle-aged chap, works as an accountant. Been at the same address about three years.'

'Probably an innocent citizen getting the hell out of a situation he didn't like the look of,' said Cope resignedly. 'I could certainly do with an eye-witness of that affray. Luck isn't exactly blowing our way, is it? When we do finally pick up Jarrett, it's unconscious, with a knife in his ribs. And they have to let his sister slip through their fingers before I so much as hear about it. What about the Jag?'

'Ah, that's more interesting. Matter of fact, I ought to have thought of it myself, but of course there are quite a number of cream-coloured Jags. And I wasn't expecting that mob to be operating up here.' The desk-sergeant was within a few years of retirement, and had been wafted away from London to supposedly more peaceful fields after a nasty encounter with a minor gang on a shop hold-up, which had left him intact and fit enough for sedentary duty, but not up to the rough stuff. 'The Jag is well known in city circles, and they can't have intended any bloodshed this evening, or they wouldn't have been using one of the boss's own cars. It's the property of Alec Match.'

'You don't say!' The Match empire was of the modern kind, composed of two-thirds legitimate businesses – at least as far as anyone had ever been able to ascertain – plus one-third decidedly illegitimate concerns, which no one had so far been able to prove. Occasionally a minor officer of the unit had been cornered and put away successfully for minor offences, but none of the muck had ever been made to stick to the upper ranks, though a lot of people, in and out of the police, knew quite positively of a great many criminal things which were going on. Enough money can buy a long run of immunity, not because the police are subornable, but because they are limited, hog-tied and hampered on all sides by regulations, provisions, benevolent societies, malicious busy-bodies and vested interests, all operating on the side of the criminally suspect, and money can buy the professional skill to manipulate all these to the best advantage – sometimes even making public money pay the costs of people who ought to be behind bars, and are at large only because law, not justice, is operative. 'So we've got the Match Boys in town, have we?' said Cope dubiously. 'No doubt at one of the four-star jobs?'

'Yes, Sir. The *Eagle and Serpent*. I just checked. All open and above-board. Something must have gone sour. I should guess Alec wanted an interview with someone who didn't want to be interviewed – presumably Jarrett – and Slitter McGoy let his fingers run away with him, as usual. But the knife isn't going to tell us anything, if that's so. You'd never catch Slitter without gloves. No word of anything much going on there, not tonight. They'll be lying low, with a good story all ready.'

'That we can be sure of,' agreed Cope sourly. 'I don't suppose it will make the slightest difference if we let 'em stew until tomorrow. But it looks as if they've smelled money – a lot of money.'

'They never fetch up anywhere for anything else,' said the desk-sergeant. 'But there's this other development. . . . That young couple who were in here earlier today – they're back again. Asking to see you. They say they've brought you a piece of important evidence.'

'I wouldn't put it past 'em, either,' said Cope, between

hope and resignation. 'We chase it all over Braybourne, and they walk out of here and start falling over it, I shouldn't wonder. All right, bring 'em in. Maybe they'll change our luck for us.'

CHAPTER TEN

Chief Inspector Cope sat staring at the two keys, which lay on the unscuffed leather of his desk, Willie's handkerchief unwrapped and cradling them gently in its clean, austere folds. He had wanted an eye-witness, and now he had two, and there was no getting past their evidence. Stanley Bastable was still alive and kicking. Nor was there the slightest doubt that if these keys were as important as that to Bastable, then they had to be the open sesame to that bank haul he had salted away. That was what he'd come back to get, that was what Alec Match had brought his private army to hijack.

And I missed the chance of leaving Wells to keep watch on his lodgings, thought Cope bitterly. Not much point shutting the stable door now, I'm afraid, there won't be any horse inside after that fright!

However, he did what had to be done, though he knew it would merely confirm that the pseudo William Banks and all his belongings had disappeared from Rainbow Road. After finding the entire Match gang on his heels, it was a foregone conclusion that he wouldn't still be where they might know enough to look for him. No, Stan would have taken off at speed, and gone to earth in some even more obscure spot.

Mrs Dutton, unused to receiving calls so late, fluttered aggrievedly until she grasped that she was being asked about her decamping lodger, and then became wide awake, voluble and self-righteous. Also avidly curious, for it was very difficult to reconcile these goings-on with the anxious mother who had confided her boy to a landlady's tender care with so much gratitude. For her comfort Cope went so far as to hint that she had been made the victim of an impersonation, the character she had entertained being, in all probability, a known con-man, and that she was lucky to have got rid of him without losing anything of value.

'You mean that young man may have been a *criminal*?' fluted Mrs Dutton, her fringe quivering with emotion. 'Now that's interesting, for you know what happened afterwards? How I found that he was gone? This gentleman came to the door, he said he was Mr Banks' uncle . . .'

With her mind on a grievance, she produced a most life-like portrait of Preacher Tweddle. Cope's knowledge of the various characters involved in the Match entourage was sketchy, but he noted the particulars carefully to try out on the desk-sergeant, who put a name to them without hesitation.

'That's him! Looks like a super-fashionable undertaker, Alec's got a cast to fit all situations. Preacher would be the one he'd send to reassure an art school landlady.'

'So *they've* lost him, too,' said Cope.

The next thing was to try and locate Mrs Stan again. Alf was in a hospital ward, not yet out of the anaesthetic, and although he was going to be as good as new after two or three weeks, he certainly wasn't going to be interviewable for a day or two. Jess owed them a couple of hours of her night's rest. But he doubted if she would be found at Alf's house, however anxious she had been to go and comfort his wife. If she was that worried about her own marital and economic rights, most likely she was hanging on to Stan tooth and claw – if, of course, she had managed to locate him again. Everybody looking for Stan Bastable now, and nobody finding him.

Cope called Alf Jarrett's number. Lou pounced on the telephone at the third ring, by this time very anxious, but still wary. Clearly she knew nothing at all about what had been happening during the evening. Cope told her, ambiguously in the character of a policeman charged with the notification of accidents, and such distressing duties, of her husband's injury, operation, and present hopeful state. He was in good hands, and in no danger. That made a good beginning. It was no problem after that to ask if she knew where he could contact Alf's sister. Was she, by any chance, there with Mrs Jarrett?

She was not! Lou's voice shrilled into indignation. Jess had gone out with Alf, and nothing had been seen of her since.

So that was that. Both missing from where they might just have been expected to be, the odds were they were together, or the one in close pursuit of the other. The trouble was that to date nobody knew where. The girl Brogan wasn't on the telephone. Such amenities scorned any approach to the canal-side terraces. Somebody would have to go down there. Somebody was going to be hauled out, by the look of it, just as he was shedding his tie and kicking off his shoes.

The chief inspector went back to his innocents, the only people around who appeared to be as fresh and alert as if they had just got up. The sergeant was just gathering up their signed statement.

'I bet he wasn't there,' said the Banks lad, not smugly, but so regretfully that Cope forgave him.

'He wasn't. You may as well know, seeing how much you know already. William Banks has decamped from his lodgings without paying his bill.'

'Oh, help!' said Willie disgustedly. 'My name'll be mud. The poor old girl, I shall have to pay her off.'

'And Mrs Bastable is not at her sister-in-law's house, where she should have been, and hasn't been seen or heard of there since around six o'clock or before. Both missing. Hypothetically, they could be together.'

'They didn't show much sign of getting together earlier,' said Calli dubiously. 'At least, he didn't. He was doing very nicely with this Brogan girl, and not at all pleased when his wife showed up. I was taking it for granted it was him, waiting just down the stairs for Beattie, when she came to the flat to swop bags with me. But I suppose you can find that out from her.'

'You're sure there was someone?'

'Ninety per cent sure. It sounded like a man's tread, very quiet, but weighty. Anyhow, we were sure enough to beat it out of the block by the fire-escape instead of the normal way.'

'Well, whoever he was,' said Willie with satisfaction, fondly eyeing the keys, 'he didn't get 'em.'

'Perhaps I ought to tell you,' said Cope probingly, 'that Mrs Bastable has actually identified the body from Cromwell Court as her husband.'

They weren't in the least thrown by that. They looked back at him with large, alert eyes and confident smiles. 'Yes, she would, of course,' said Willie agreeably, 'otherwise it was all wasted. We had the advantage of knowing that it wasn't me, of course. But I do wonder if she knew who it really was, once she'd seen it. And whether it really is who we decided it must be.'

'And who would that be?' asked the chief inspector with interest.

'Well, it had to be someone closely connected with Bastable, and most likely one of his partners in the original job, coming to look after his interests. The one seemed too old to match up. There are ways of judging approximate age, I believe, even in a calcined body. We thought it must be Collins, the younger one. Is it?'

He asked with such aplomb that Cope almost found himself answering as directly, and giving away the simple fact that up to now, in spite of his natural scepticism concerning anything Jess Bastable swore to, he had been inclined to believe her identification. George Collins was a highly interesting candidate for the vacancy created by Stan's proven survival.

'We're keeping an open mind on that,' he said cannily, 'until the experts have reported. It would certainly account for her rushing straight out after her husband, to bring him up to date. He was operating on half the facts, always a dangerous thing to do.'

'I think she also came to boot Beattie out,' said Calli bluntly.

They were rising to leave, almost reluctantly, when the desk-sergeant burst in again, so precipitately that his very step was news, even before he was through the door.

'Emergency call just come in from down the riverside district, sir! Man on the beat reports finding a body in Clare's Shut. Big chap around thirty, natty dresser, fair hair. Face down, shot in the back.'

'Who's the man on the spot?' demanded Cope, already on his feet.

'Hartley. He's sound. He says the chap's dead, and not long ago. Cartridge case lying close by him. Nowhere for it to go between those walls.'

'OK, get the Incident Squad down, we're going to need the big lights. I'll got straight down there, you get Inspector Lamb and Bryan out after me as fast as possible, and have the doc and the rest of the show alerted. We're going to need 'em. This is a lot too apt, practically on the doorstep. What are the odds it's all part of the same case? Doesn't sound like Bastable, though, does it? Tall, yes, I wouldn't have said big. And nobody's mentioned a bleach job.'

'No,' said Willie, all ears, 'dark, reddish brown.'

'But it does sound like one of those two who came busting into the *Goat and Compasses* after Stan,' said Calli. 'He was big and fair, and rather smart. . . .'

179

'Could be one of Match's boys,' said the desk-sergeant. 'Alec's right-hand man – Sam Copper . . .'

'Come on!' said Cope, clapping a hand on Calli's shoulder and turning her towards the door. 'We'll give you a lift back home, Miss Francis. It looks as if everything's moving down into your locality. You'll be able to sleep in peace tonight, there'll be police losing their own night's sleep all round you.'

On the way round to the embankment and the approach road to Nelson Court, Willie sat in the back of the police car, studying the nape of the Chief Inspector's well-barbered neck, and thought so intensely that his braced silence in itself had a disturbing effect.

'Chief Inspector,' he said insinuatingly at last.

'Well?' said Cope cautiously, without turning.

'If this *is* the big, fair bloke who came to fetch Stan, and if he actually is this Sam Copper, and belongs to this Match gang, then it looks as if *he* was the man on the stairs, doesn't it? I mean, that was no face-to-face encounter, from what your sergeant said. It was a shot in the back. It's the competitor who *hasn't* got hold of the loot who shoots the other fellow in the back, isn't it? Two parties in opposition, after the same thing. The one who gets it makes off as fast and furtively as he can. The one who hasn't is the one who comes up behind, fires the gun, and snatches the prize. The two parties in this case seem to be Bastable on the one side, and the Match people on the other. So Stan fired the gun and got the handbag, but he still didn't get what he expected. He's close around, somewhere, and he won't go away without his loot if he can help it. There's just one thing will fetch him out of hiding, and that's the keys. And you've got them.'

'Proceed!' said Chief Inspector Cope, with slightly grim irony. 'You interest me.' Sergeant Wells, at the wheel, gave him a sidewise look, and said nothing.

'But it would be only half a success, wouldn't it, to get Bastable but fail to recover the bank money? And then there's this other lot, maybe they could be hooked with the same bait and let themselves get caught out in some real crime, so that you can land them in gaol, too. With a bit of luck you might get the lot of them, *and* the money. But it would mean somehow getting the keys back to Stan, wouldn't it, because he's the only person who knows where they fit. Getting them back to him and then watching every step he takes. You could lure him out of hiding to get them, and then run him in, but then you'd never get a word out of him about where the loot is. But if you could let him have the keys back in some way that didn't involve you, and didn't scare him off, then he'd lead you straight to the place where it's hidden. And if this Match chap cottoned on to the idea and also followed along, there'd be at least a chance of catching him out, too.'

'It sounds quite a procession,' said the Chief Inspector sardonically. 'All right, that's the strategy, now let's have the tactics.'

'At present they all seem to be snatching bags from each other, on the grounds that because Stan put the keys in there, they must still be there. But suppose the keys had fallen out of Beattie's bag in the street, somewhere close by the *Goat and Compasses*? On the car-park, even? And been found by somebody later on, going to drive off for home? I don't think that would surprise Stan all that much, or make him smell a rat. People advertise things they find or lose in the local evening paper. You could get it into the noon edition tomorrow with luck, they have an all-night recording service. I know, I had nothing to do all morning but read last night's paper, and I always look at the small ads. So do most people. If you gave a nice address that has nothing to do with the police, one you can stake out easily, and then follow up whoever comes to claim them. . . . And they would. A nice, private deal like that, between citizens, why should they hesitate?'

'Too many people might turn up to claim them,' said Sergeant Wells.

'Anybody who could describe them would be straight from Stan, and lead you straight back to him. Nobody else, except we two, and now you, has had hold of them. Everybody seems to have been grabbing and missing. Even if they know by now that it's keys they're after, they don't know what they look like.'

He added, happily unabashed by the heavy silence that hung over the two in the front seat: 'And it would set a lot of minds at rest about Calli and me, and take the heat off us. By this time they're all thinking terrible thoughts about our interfering, and knowing too much, and having designs on their loot, and all at once they find she just took the wrong bag by honest mistake, and handed it over just as she found it, and all the time the keys had been dropped in the car-park. There were they blaming us, and getting scared of us, and all the time we were completely innocent.'

'Oh, sure!' said Chief Inspector Cope in a slightly stunned tone. 'Yes, that I do see. Innocent as babes unborn!'

He dropped them off at the entrance to Nelson Court, with strict instructions to forget the whole thing and stay out of all future proceedings. He did not caution them not to leave town, but Willie assured him helpfully that they had no intention of going anywhere while this case remained open. Nor did the Chief Inspector say that he would have a constable keeping a casual watch on the block for their protection, but it was one of the first things he did when his reinforcements arrived. The other was to draw Sergeant Wells aside, and commission him to make certain arrangements on his behalf.

•

'You think Molly Hamilton would loan us her place for a fishing expedition? What have we got to lose?'

'She'd jump at it,' said Sergeant Wells.

'Well, ask her. And if she agrees, hash up the ad to fit. You know all the details. As soon as we get this cadaver on its way we'll confer on ways and means.'

'One thing,' said Sergeant Wells thoughtfully, and without a trace of surprise, 'even if nobody reads the lost and founds, and nobody actually shows up, we haven't lost a thing.'

'That's right, at least there's a fail-safe mechanism – we're none the worse off if nothing happens. I bet he's thought of that, too.'

They went to attend to Sam Copper, lying irrevocably dead in Clare's Shut.

The police doctor came, yawning and irritable, pronounced the victim dead, the instrument of death a bullet entering the back, rather obviously in view of the light colour of the dead man's coat and the stain darkening it below the left shoulder-blade, and the time of death, provisionally, as about one hour past. As the cartridge case was still lying where it had bounced from the wall and rolled, close to the right sleeve of the poplin coat, there was not much room for speculation about the type of ammunition. The surgeon packed up and returned thankfully to his bed as the pathologist arrived, leaving them to it for the night. The photography team set up their lights and took shot after shot at all stages. The scientific officer came, and prowled the whole scene with the pathologist, each intent upon his own narrow world of signs and wonders. When they were satisfied that there was nothing to be lost by moving the body, Sam Copper was hoisted into a plastic shell, tucked into a police van, and driven away to the hospital mortuary, the pathologist's car following. The length of Clare's Shut was cordoned off, to wait a further inspection by daylight, and a constable left in chilly charge for the rest of the night. The whole process had taken about three hours.

It was fairly early in this lengthy business that Crummie Best, sent out to prospect for news when Alec Match grew uneasy at his lieutenant's long absence, circled the block of Nelson Court warily, and caught sight of the curious and powerful reflections of lights beaming upwards out of walled darkness among the alleys of the lower town. Very strong lights, trained on some scene on the ground, but ricocheting from light brick walls and making elongated patterns in the upper air. That, and a lot of movements, quiet, purposeful and constant. When he strained his ears, he caught the metallic, boxed murmur of radio-car conversations, from a van parked at the end of a narrow lane before him. He didn't care to go any nearer, when he realised it was a police van. But he found himself a refuge among the bushes of a rather tired and litter-strewn strip of garden beside the embankment, and watched. Obviously this was the nearest the van could get to the lighted scene. Cars had probably been able to negotiate at least a short run of lane and approach more closely. Whatever was eventually coming out to the van would have to come out this way.

His eyes were well accustomed to the dark by the time it came. It was a stretcher. And quite a lot of police top brass and rankers, and a car driven by a brisk civilian, who hopped out to watch the load being put aboard the van. The nature of the load there was no mistaking. Its identity, of course, was another matter. But Crummie Best knew of one character who had set off into these risky regions and hadn't come back, and he didn't stop to enquire, not being anxious to be the second. For one thing, he had a gun on him at that moment, and for another, he was the only one of Alec's immediate entourage who had form, albeit of a venal kind. He judged it time to return and report, because

184

if what he suspected was true, they were due to be visited, probably before morning, and they had better all be in their beds and ready with their non-story when it happened.

The *Eagle and Serpent*, having considerable nightlife, had plenty of guests still wakeful and voluble to provide cover for his return. He made his way hastily up to his boss's suite, and through a haze of cigar smoke three pairs of eyes fixed on him, and three glasses were lowered. Crummie – his baptismal names were Oliver Cromwell – closed the door carefully behind him, and kept his voice down.

'Boss, there's somebody met it, down there. It could be Sam. I'm afraid it is.'

Alec sat forward with a jerk. 'What d'you mean? You've seen him? What d'you mean, it *could* be? What good's half a tale?'

'Could I walk up and ask 'em? All that part down the slope by the flats is like a rabbit-warren, all little lanes. It's crawling with coppers, I'm telling you. I saw them load some stiff into a meat-van and take him off, but he was in a shell already, not a chance to see who it was. Lights, they'd got up among the alleys there, doctor, photographers, forensic team, the lot! If I'd hung around I'd have walked into some bluebottle's arms, for sure. I came away. Because if it is Sam, they're going to be dropping in on us any time, and we better be ready!'

'Too damn true, we had!' said Match, slamming down his empty glass. He flew to open the windows, light and fast on his thick legs and small feet, to let out the smoke of their long session and the scent of whisky. 'Everybody to bed, and remember, we know nothing about where he was going, he just went out. Make it about the time it was. We think he may have been meeting a woman, he was a great one for the women. That'll take care of any outsider who noticed him leave with the girl. Ditch the guns anywhere

185

safe for a short while, they won't hunt far until they get something better by way of a fix than just suspicion. Poor old Sam!' he said perfunctorily, like a bystander in the street raising his hat to a passing funeral, and again reverted to his own dispositions. 'Slitter, you're his room-mate, you sleep sound, you were astonished to find when you woke up that he hadn't come in.'

'I'll be more astonished now if he ever does,' said Slitter sourly, stacking glasses neatly on the tray.

'It might be Stan in the shell,' suggested Preacher Tweddle hopefully. 'You never know. Sam's plenty experienced.'

'He'd have been back, and complete with cover. Less the gun, if necessary. No, I'm afraid . . . In any case, this has got to look and sound OK. Scatter!' said Alec, with one sweeping glance round the room.

They scattered. 'Sleep well!' said Preacher Tweddle sardonically as he closed the door.

The windows of Calli's flat looked out over the river. There was nothing to be seen from there of all the purposeful activity going on less than a quarter of a mile away. It looked like any other night, calm, starry but without a moon, and with small, drifting clouds moving above the river. Calli and Willie sat in the kitchen, at the fold-away table, drinking large mugs of hot cocoa and eating comfortably large slabs of dripping toast. The studio couch was already made up for the night.

'Funny thing,' said Willie, 'I've never even seen this famous bank they broke into, and started all this trouble. Where did you say it was? High Street? That's the wide one that comes into the square, and then shrinks a bit and goes on as Market Street?'

'That's right,' said Calli.

'Then we must have passed the bank when I first arrived

here, with Alf, because we came in that way. A lot of rather good eighteenth-century town frontages. Houses originally, I should say.'

'They were. Town houses for the big families of the region. The bank's one of them. The middle one of three all built as one block. They have yards at the back, there's a cobbled lane there where the carriages used to drive in. The one on the right was vacant when they broke into the bank. They got in from there, through the cellars. It's rather a nice antique shop now. They're great on antiques in Braybourne.'

'What about the one on the left?'

'That's the Box Museum,' said Calli, with the oblivious disdain of the native.

'The what?'

'Its proper name is the Box and Locks Museum, really. That's what it is.'

'I never heard of it,' said Willie positively.

'I'm not surprised. Nobody has who wasn't born and bred in Braybourne, and probably ninety per cent of them haven't, either. It's just one of those institutions you can't get rid of, because somebody long ago gave the house and the collection for ever, and left a whacking great trust fund to maintain it. I doubt if the town wants it any longer, but they don't own it, so they can't do a thing about it. It's like this,' she explained kindly, seeing that his interest, so far from flagging, seemed to be rendering him more wide awake than ever. 'Boxes used to be Braybourne's special product. All kinds. Snuff boxes, jewel boxes, the sort of enamel boxes people collect, and useful ones, too, wooden work-boxes, sewing boxes, tool boxes, deed boxes, musical boxes – you name it, they made it here. Painted, carved, engraved, brass-bound, the lot. It died off after everything got to be mass-produced, but the last of the Thomason family, after he closed down the works, turned all his fortune

187

into this public trust, and his house into this museum. The locks came into it naturally because of all the elaborations to the various kinds of box. You wouldn't believe how complex some of them could be.'

'Does anyone ever go into it now?' asked Willie.

'Oh, a few, I suppose. Some days probably nobody.'

'It can't be very profitable.'

'It doesn't have to be. There seems to be money enough to keep it going for ever, even if nobody at all visits it. But it's awfully neglected, I'm told. There's a pretty ancient kind of custodian who sits and drowses in his box there, he's all the expense there is. Those houses were built to last more or less forever. I wouldn't mind betting the fund grows instead of shrinking. Some day the trustees are going to get together and wind it up, and say the money should be put to better use.'

'It's awfully difficult to kill off a foundation like that without getting into legal trouble,' said Willie wisely. 'I wouldn't like to be the one to take on Mr Thomason, alive or dead. So that's it! No wonder nobody heard any activity in the night, with an empty shop on one side, and this mausoleum on the other. And good solid outer walls.'

One more question he asked, as they were washing up the mugs. Calli was a great believer in always washing up immediately, and never falling into the weak error of leaving things in the sink till morning.

'Where's the local newspaper office? Are people allowed to consult the files?'

She gave him a slightly dubious look, but told him where to find the offices. 'Don't forget we've been warned off, will you?' Because she was going to have to go to work as usual in the morning, and he would be left to his own devices, and she was beginning to have a fair idea of how wide-ranging and unpredictable his devices could be.

'Sure, but they can't object to my reading up the facts,

188

can they? I shan't be getting under their feet. I wonder,' said Willie dreamily, 'if they will?'

'Will what?'

'Put that advertisement in tomorrow's noon edition.'

'No,' said Calli crisply and discouragingly, 'they won't. It would be a form of gambling, and I don't think policemen are allowed to gamble. Not with evidence, anyhow!'

'I know,' he said, 'but only two of them heard me suggest it, and I have a sort of feeling that they work in harness together a lot, and— Well, wouldn't you say it's possible even policemen cut corners now and then? Honest corners I mean, of course. After all, it's a kind of race, isn't it? They're in it to win. And even if nobody takes the bait, there's nothing lost, they'll still have the keys.'

Chief Inspector Cope had been right. Willie had thought of that, too.

'Keys,' Willie was saying sleepily to himself as he put out the light and slid into the studio-couch bed, 'keys . . . keys . . .' Somewhere at the back of his mind, before he feel asleep, a conditioned echo insisted suddenly: 'Locks!'

CHAPTER ELEVEN

Willie got up first in the morning, and had tea and toast on the go before Calli was awake. He tapped at her door with a cup of tea, and she opened her eyes abruptly, disorientated and alarmed for a moment.

'Can I come in? It's me!' Always the most helpful of reassurances!

Calli said: 'No!' instinctively, and then, recollecting the kind of established partnership they had somehow achieved without noticing it: 'Yes!' It was a bit late to start standing on ceremony. Willie came in matter-of-factly, sat on the edge of her bed, and nursed the cup until she was sitting up and ready to receive it. Then he simply sat there as one having rights, and admired her.

'This was a blessed idea,' owned Calli, noting the time. 'I'm late waking up. Your fault for keeping me up half the night.'

'You look smashing, awake or asleep,' said Willie heartily. 'I'll do you some scrambled eggs, if you like? They'll be ready by the time you are.'

They were dished up and ready to be whisked on to the table when she came into the kitchen washed and dressed and polished for the day. They seemed to have drifted into a kind of domesticity that reversed the usual roles. She could even leave the washing-up to him, and did, without a qualm.

'I feel like the family bread-winner,' said Calli with swaggering pleasure as she put on her coat and reached for her bag.

'You won't always be,' said Willie, without the least

intention of being cryptic, since to him the situation already appeared perfectly clear and mutually acceptable. 'If you'll come home for lunch I'll cook it for you. I can. What do you like?'

'There won't be time, sorry. But I'll see you around six, OK? And you won't do anything I wouldn't do, will you? Look,' she said, turning back from the door with a serious face, 'if that ad *does* show up in the first edition, you won't go near the stake-out address, will you?'

'Not on any account,' he assured her firmly. 'They know how to do that sort of thing. I'm not butting into anything I might mess up for them.'

But when she was gone, and he had put away the crockery and his bedding, and tidied the flat for the day, he sat down to consider exactly where he could butt in without damage. It was still his affair, after all, since he had been the intended victim in the first place. Of course he wouldn't go and prowl round any address used by the police for baiting their trap. Nor would he go roaming about Clare's Shut, uselessly detecting where others had detected usefully, he hoped, before him. Nor try to satisfy his curiosity by visiting the bar of the *Eagle and Serpent*, later on, to get a close look at the opposition. He didn't need to be told that too many people taking obvious interest could only clog up the works. But there was nothing to prevent him from doing some quiet reading on his own, and a great deal more quiet thinking. Thought is free. And never really wasted.

'. . . Mein Mädchen, dabei
Die Gedanken sind frei!'

sang Willie softly to himself, and let his own thoughts out of the flat before him. He had Calli's spare key, and fully intended to be home before her and have a meal ready when she came in at six o'clock. He felt a slight sense of injury at the length of the day without her. All the more reason for making sound use of it.

At the offices of the *Braybourne Evening Journal* they were accustomed to people consulting the past files. He read up everything he could find in the three-year-old records of the great bank robbery. The saga naturally went on over a period of at least a month, and from day to day the coverage tended to contradict itself, to announce sensational details one day only to temper or withdraw them the next.

When he had waded through everything he could find, Willie went off to the public library with his notes, to the study corner where he could sit and think in peace. What stood out was the sheer speed of the coup. The getaway car had been discovered abandoned only fifty miles away, at first light. So how much time had they had to stow away the loot, clear up the evidence, and cover that distance, thence splitting up and vanishing? Only one day later came the first reported sighting of Stan Bastable in France, walking along a street in Amiens, and again vanishing utterly.

'He didn't go far with it,' said Willie to himself, with conviction. 'He simply didn't have time. He had a place all ready for it very close to the bank.'

Stan himself had pin-pointed this town as the place where his treasure was, by coming back here to recover it. Willie boldly narrowed the field still more, to a small circle drawn round the bank. Somewhere there those keys fitted. He even went out and bought a town plan, but it was less useful than it should have been, because naturally it was of the new Braybourne that was only half-made as yet, and took in several square miles of surrounding country, whereas what he wanted was a larger-scale plan of the old Braybourne. Still, he drew his ring, representing perhaps a circle with a radius of a quarter of a mile, its centre at the bank. That was still too generous, he considered, its outer rim need be taken into account only in the last resort. He drew another ring inside it, just covering High Street, part of the square with its gardens, and sections of two or three smaller streets behind the bank. That was more like it.

Now he could still eliminate, if he gave his mind to it. Stan Bastable was born and bred here, and knew the town well. He would be holding a fortune in his hands, and finding the strength of mind to deposit it somewhere and leave it, really leave it, for a matter of years, until the heat was off. Therefore he would put it somewhere that wasn't likely to be changed or interfered with, or the centre of a lot of activity which would be likely to reveal the secret. Take that one step further! Stan was here to retrieve it now, and still biding his time and cherishing his keys after he had certainly surveyed, as his first act, the security and sanctity of his hiding-place. Ergo, his judgment had been sound, the place where he had put it had not been disturbed in any way. Willie could walk round the streets in the circle he had drawn, and write off everything that had been demolished and rebuilt, or had new shop-fronts put in, or extensive face-lifting of any kind, during the last three years. That might eliminate a great deal. Come to think of it, in the turmoil of a new town Stan must have been very, very confident of the timeless nature of his hiding-place. How many buildings, how many lanes, churches, statues, gardens are a hundred per cent safe in such circumstances? To be accurate, none at all, but some stood a better chance of survival than others.

By the time Willie had worked out all this, and strolled round the square and the back streets on that side of the bank, it was noon. The newsagent's shop in the square had a new *Journal* poster in its wire holder, parochial in defiance of new towns in general: 'Norden Beauty-Contest Winner for Carnival Queen'. The new edition was out on the streets. Willie bought a paper, and took it into a snack-bar to read over a coffee and a sandwich. Half the pages consisted of small ads. It took him a few minutes to find the 'Lost and Found' heading among so many, and gave him time to consider philosophically how improbable it was that Stan should ever see the bait, even if it was there. This made it easier to accept the fact that it almost certainly wouldn't be there.

But it was there, at the head of the few items in the column, and so artfully spaced and lettered that it could hardly be missed:

'FOUND in the car-park of the *GOAT AND COMPASSES*, King Street, KEY-RING holding two ornate keys. Owner please apply: Hamilton, Willows, Chapel Crescent, Greyfriars.'

A shocked Alec Match went himself, with Inspector Lamb, to identify the body of Sam Copper. He mourned his loss all the way. An excellent partner – not without his weaknesses, of course, but who is perfect? Women – women were Sam's downfall. It had to be admitted that he did tend to find himself a girl in every port, and sometimes his enthusiasm had led him into little contretemps – but now this!

The same record had been played, with varying degrees of volume and tone, by all the survivors of the Match Boys early that morning, leaving the virtuoso part to Alec. And though the car was there to be seen, it was a foregone conclusion that not a speck of betraying blood would be found in or on it, or any item of Slitter McGoy's natty suiting. Yes, he had gone out to the *Goat and Compasses* earlier in the evening with Sam; Sam wanted to meet a girl there, and she'd promised to bring a friend. Nobody knew how Sam found them, but he always did. Yes, they'd spoken to the people at the nearest table as they came in, but only to say good-evening. The fight that had broken out just then had been strictly between the people already there – 'everybody'd tell you, we were barely inside the door.' Then the lights went out, said Slitter, and they had decided that was no peaceful place to eat, and got out. Knife? Good gracious, no! Why should he carry such a thing? Someone got knifed? Dear, dear! They hadn't even known that!

Then Sam got on the blower to the girl, and made some fresh appointment with her, and later on he went out to keep it. And that was it. All they knew. After all, Sam was over twenty-one, nobody told him when to come in at night. And how was the poor fellow who got stabbed? Not serious? they hoped. Going to be all right! What a relief!

The girl's name? Nobody knew. Slitter doubted if Sam had known it himself. He always called them all 'Honeyrose'. Nothing as common as 'baby' or 'gorgeous'. Maybe that was what fetched them. He always knew their 'phone numbers, but not their names.

And what was the purpose, exactly, of Mr Match's visit to Braybourne? Alec became very confidential.

'I'll tell you, Inspector, but it's hush-hush at the moment, if you don't mind. We came up to look the ground over, see how this new town thing is coming along. These are the places where there's going be money to spend on entertainment. I figured this might be the right provincial town for a new club. That's one of my lines, you know. Haven't made up my mind yet whether it's quite what I want, but I've got some locations in mind for if I do decide on it. The boys do the leg-work for me. I'm not as active as I ought to be. Besides, it impresses when I bring the whole circus with me.'

It could even be true, Lamb thought as he drove back to Central. Only too surely it could true, they'd have to watch out for it. He reported back to Chief Inspector Cope, who had come in after a few hours' sleep bleary-eyed and short of speech, to collate what information there was. Wells had arrived with him, after a similarly unsatisfactory rest, ready to go on vigil at Willows, Chapel Crescent, Greyfriars. No need for him to set off until the first edition was on the counters, he had an hour or so to catch up with developments.

'Not a chance of pinning the knife on McGoy,' said Lamb. 'Not a glimmer of a print on it, and nobody saw it until after the lights came on again. And there's nobody up here knows the man and can attach the thing to him. As for Copper, pretty clearly they don't want to bring Bastable in, they want him for themselves, but I'd say they're dead sure it was him. Copper's written off as unavoidable expenses.'

'I wonder how thorough Match is about reading the local paper,' said Cope moodily, 'if he's so keen on opening up his interests here? Who knows, he might blow his own cover, yet! What did you get out of the girl, Bryan?'

Sergeant Bryan had got surprisingly little out of Beattie, considering she had no criminal record or experience, and should have been (probably was, but not of the police!) easily frightenable. She wasn't as dim as she let on. She'd make some crook quite a useful wife some day. It must be natural genius, a sense of self-preservation not altogether dependent on brains.

'She swears she only met this Banks yesterday, and that's the only name she knows for him. He made a big production of it, she was the one girl – you know! When she went out to dinner with him, this woman showed up and started acting as though she owned him, and Beattie was a tramp, and after the show broke up he admitted it was his wife. The girl claims she left him flat, then and there, and went home, and didn't realise until she got there that she'd got the wrong bag. She insists she simply went to Nelson Court to exchange the bags, the other girl's address being inside, and as she was leaving Copper jumped her and snatched it from her. She claims she didn't recognise him, she took it for a simple opportunist snatch, in a fairly isolated place like that. Says she ran for home like a hare, glad to get away alive. Just about what you'd expect.'

'Damn it, it sounds as if she was coached,' said Cope, exasperated.

'No, just natural camouflage. After all, she's dodging two separate menaces outside the law, as well as us. She *has* to keep her head well down,' Bryan granted generously.

'Well, her we could probably bust if we have to. She's known our Stan rather longer than one day, and known him as Stan Bastable, too. If she's thinking herself well out of that, that could be something gained, at any rate.' Cope reared his head, hearing the unmistakable but undecipherable bawl from the corner of the square, fifty yards away outside the window. 'That's the first edition. Fetch us one in, Bryan, lad.' Cope knew what he was going to find in it, but even so he wanted to see how good a job they'd made of it.

'So long!' said Sergeant Wells, recognising his cue, and not waiting for the confirmation. 'I'll be on my way over to Molly's.'

Mrs Dutton, briefly visited to confirm what she had already testified over the telephone, brooded all the rest of the morning. She acknowledged that the police were now in charge of events, and had no wish either to stand in their way or usurp their privileges. But the young man who had come into her household with his disquieting vigour and his golden eyes was shown up as a dangerous pretender, the uncle who had come looking for him was an impostor, and there remained, somewhere unknown, nobody knew in what straits, the innocent whose mother had cared enough about him to get in touch with his prospective landlady and talk to her as to a sister. And what was happening to him

198

nobody seemed to know or care. Mrs Dutton cared. She was a prim, narrow, eminently ridiculable middle-class pseudo-aesthete. She was also a kindly, childless woman, who felt responsibility for all the hapless young who were not her own, and all the doting mothers who worried about them in absence.

Towards noon Mrs Dutton could not shelve her duty any longer. She dialled the distant number of Mrs Banks's house, forty-five miles away.

'Mrs Banks? This is Iris Dutton here, in Braybourne. Dear Mrs Banks, I feel I must speak to you – about your son . . .'

Stan Bastable slept most of the morning, in pure – or perhaps, rather, impure – exhaustion, after the strain of yesterday and the feverish consolations of the night. He wore the halo of a semi-invalid, victim of the 'flu germ in which everyone automatically believes, whenever it is promulgated, however improbably. There is always, at absolutely any time of year, a lot of it about! Jess had had no trouble at all.

Thus released, Jess had already disposed of Beattie's bag, not without satisfaction in watching the river swallow it, brick and all. It wasn't difficult. The only foot-bridge over the Shelma had a casual and sporadic clientele. On the way back, close to lunch-time, she bought a paper. Over her solitary meal in the dining-room, having fed Stan upstairs, Jess read her way solidly through the noon *Journal*.

She took it up to him afterwards, and showed it to him in silent but majestic triumph.

'You and your bloody capers over that idiotic bag! I might have known! Talk about the devil looking after his own! Come on, now, draw me a sketch of those keys, guards, wards, the lot, if you know them so well. I'm going to have to prove I know what I'm asking for. You think they'll hand them out to the first claimant, without any proof?'

'How the hell was I to know?' complained Stan, busy drawing the designs that were etched on his mind in deep and acid strokes. Complaining and exulting, both at once. My God, it showed you you should never jump to conclusions, never despair. They just fell out! Just like that, while he was rushing her away, that kid – she never knew she'd had them! After all he'd suffered, all he'd done, last night, they were just lying in the car-park, waiting for some innocent car-owner to pick them up and start virtuously hunting for the owner. Hadn't he himself noticed yesterday that the clasp of that bag wasn't a hundred per cent reliable? And the girl was just what she seemed, after all, just a little paint saleswoman, dragged in by accident.

'Finished?' said Jess, picking up the sketch. 'All right, give me five minutes to memorise, and I'm off to Chapel Crescent to collect. And you can go back to sleep. You might as well, if you're going to be any good on the job tonight. And you'd better be!'

The trouble was that after she'd gone, setting off all newly-made-up and trim as a canal barge, he felt remarkably wide-awake and restive, quite restored by the relief of knowing that he might very well hold the keys in his hands again within an hour or so. All the stresses and anxieties of the previous night were easily shed. One more night, and he'd be on his way with the goods, and this time for ever. No need ever to see this crummy town again. His mind drifted off into the sunny dreams of yore, islands in the tropics, himself sun-tanned and idle, lying on golden sands with a gorgeous girl beside him wearing practically nothing. Drinks on tap and fast cars on order, the sweet life!

That brought him back to Jess, who had certainly proved useful after her fashion, but who didn't look her best in a bikini, and who would – why blink the fact? – be past it in ten years or so, and on her way out in the youth and beauty stakes long before that. If, indeed, she had ever been a runner. Last night he'd been glad of her, yes, but last night he hadn't had much left to hang on to, had he, and anything salvaged was a relief. Today was a different kettle of fish.

Beattie, now – Beattie was much more the ticket when it came to lying around elegantly on beaches and perching on bar stools in elaborate Caribbean hotels. She might not have much up top, but then, he wasn't going to need any Brain of Britain once he was well out of Britain and set up for life somewhere safe and warm.

He lit a cigarette and lay and thought about it, and the outcome of his thinking was that there was no need to cut off any of his options at this stage, if he played his cards right. The Globe cinema ran continuous performances, and would already be open with the matinée house, and there was a telephone in the pay-box, and this early Beattie certainly wouldn't be busy. Stan put on a dressing-gown, and went down the stairs to the telephone box in the lobby, and called the cinema's number.

'Hullo?' said Beattie's voice, with the slightly scared and defensive tone of those who have grown up as strangers to the telephone. 'This is the Globe cinema. Can I help you?' She was wearing her high-society accent, and sounded determined to apply herself humbly and devotedly in the station to which fate had called her. That wouldn't take much undoing.

'Beattie, doll, it's me – Stan. I've been waiting on thorns till I could call you. You know there's no way I can get you at home. Bea, love, I don't know how to make up to you for last night . . . I don't know if I can make you understand . . .'

'I understand all right,' said Beattie bitterly. 'You made it pretty plain. I know when I'm ditched.'

'It wasn't like that, don't take it that way – don't cut me off! Look, I know how you felt, but there wasn't anything else I could do. I wasn't deserting you, I was doing the one thing I could do to preserve *our future*. For God's sake, what had I got to offer you if I let that slip through my hands? I know it was awful – for me as well as for you, knowing how it would look to you! But, Bea, we've made it! It's all on again, just as we planned it. It'll be tonight! I promise!'

'Don't think you're going to sweet-talk me into sticking out my neck for you again, after last night,' said Beattie fiercely, but with a note of enquiry and interest in her voice none the less.

'It won't be necessary. Absolutely nothing risky for you to do any more. And no more slave labour for life. We'll be on the merry-go-round together, everything laid on, nothing to do but enjoy. Don't back out on me now, when I've gone through more than you know to get this gravy-train back on the line, and all for you . . .'

She'd been a pushover the first time, she hadn't learned much even now. The lure of easy living puts everything else out of people's minds, at least when there's as little room in the mind as in Beattie's. She tried once or twice to hold him off with reminders of his treachery, but she was already sold. Maybe she had something to shove into the background, too, considering all the events of last night; she might well come round gracefully, if he was willing to do the same.

'Look, girl, I need you, I really do. You're in all my plans.' She was eating out of his hand by this time, he didn't know what he was wasting time for. 'I want you to do something for me, but this time it's simple and safe. You know the Crown Car-Hire place? I want you to go there tonight and hire a drive-yourself car, just for one day. Have him bring it to the car-park by the bridge about nine o'clock, and leave it there. I'll join you there as soon as I can. And I won't be empty-handed. Bring a case, but not too much. Once we're away, you'll be able to buy what you like.'

'You haven't told me,' she said, feebly resisting, 'what's happening? Have you found your keys, then? Honestly, I don't know what's going on.'

'I'll tell you everything later. Will you do it for me? Will you?'

'I didn't tell them where you were, or anything,' she said, 'but, Stan, do be careful! They're awful people, they may get on to you, somehow, they may be clever enough to find you and follow you.'

'I'll be careful. Will you do it for me? Think, down there by the bridge we're practically on our way out of town. Will you?'

'Yes,' she said. 'Oh, yes, Stan, I will!'

Stan hung up complacently, and lit another cigarette on his way back upstairs. The girl from reception met him in the corridor, and asked if he was feeling better.

'A lot better, thanks,' said Stan truthfully. 'By tomorrow I reckon I shall be on top of the world.'

Molly Hamilton had quit the police force to marry and raise a family, but retained a passionate interest in police affairs, and was game for any small extra-curricular ploy that might come her way. Since her married name had never entered into prominence, and her husband was a pleasant and hard-working but quite obscure sub-manager in a supermarket, she could lend her round, cheerful face and unremarkable figure whenever her old colleagues needed a housewifely front. Moreover, her house was in a crescent-shaped service road, with a lunette of public gardens, full of shrubs and flowering trees, between the front gates and traffic, so that there was no problem about having a station-ary car further along the loop, ready to pick up the trail of a vehicle if required, and also a foot follower or a cyclist lounging on one of the seats in the gardens. A cycle has the merit of being faster than a pedestrian, but also able to go through all the narrow lanes of Braybourne, either ridden, where legal, or pushed, where riding it is forbidden. Detective Constable Jones, however, preferred a moped, with the same advantages but more power, being naturally lazy, as well as gifted with a phenomenal ability to be invisible. He was nearly thirty, but still looked barely twenty, he wore his hair down to his collar, affected gear just outrageous enough to be drearily normal, and even his gait had the shapeless nonchalance of modernity, just short of a slouch. When he was out on the town with a girl – he had a long and creditable string of girls – he could look quite different, as if he had switched on the lights inside his own personality.

Wells waited inside the house with Molly, a precaution she derided. He had a private bet on with his hostess that no one would show up. This was his form of insurance against disappointment, since he habitually lost his bets. But it was barely half past one when he emitted a low, pleased whistle, and beckoned Molly wordlessly from the kitchen. Jessamine Bastable, on foot, was coming along the pavement that fringed the service road. Her stride was firm and jaunty, her formidable tower of hair erect. Jess was not called upon, in this act, to present the mourning widow. She was merely the housewife who had dropped her keys, and was coming to claim them.

'That's his wife, is it?' said Molly curiously. The caller turned in at the front gate, and advanced up the path. 'You owe me a quid,' said Molly, and went to open the door, while Wells retired into the kitchen.

'Mrs Hamilton?' said Jess, all winning, grateful smile. 'I've called about the keys you found. I think they must be mine.'

'Oh, yes – the keys!' said Molly brightly. She was pink

and white and blonde, and in a flowered nylon smock looked like an up-to-date dairymaid. 'I should never have noticed them if I hadn't dropped my own car key when I went to start up and drive home. When I stooped to pick it up I saw this ring lying under the bush, and I thought, there, somebody's going to be worrying about those. So I thought the best thing I could do was put an ad in the *Journal*. I mean, you could as well come to me as to the police, and it seemed the quickest way.'

Jess declared herself immensely pleased and grateful at having them restored, and allowed herself to be invited into the hall.

'I suppose you can describe them?' said Molly deprecatingly. 'You mustn't mind, but when one advertises something found, there *are* people who wouldn't scruple to claim them – I mean, if they thought there was any value involved. And keys are immensely valuable, I always say. I'm sure you really are the owner, but if you wouldn't mind . . .'

'You're so right!' said Jess heartily. 'I'm very lucky it was you who picked them up.' And she provided a detailed and convincing word-sketch of the keys.

'You know,' said Molly, half laughing and half ashamed, as she handed them over, 'I doubt if I know the wards of my own front door half as well. There, I'm glad you've got them back so soon. It must be a load off your mind.'

They parted with ceremonious exchanges, Jess trying to insist on at least paying for the insertion of the advertisement, Molly refusing to hear of it, protesting that it was nothing, that Jess would have done the same for her. Molly won.

The square, solid figure marched away down the path and along the pavement, clutching the bag that held the recovered keys. The young man lounging in the public gardens folded his comic into his pocket, languidly mounted his moped, and rode in the opposite direction, round the lunette of grass and trees, to come about and follow along the main road. Since she had come on foot, either she had come from somewhere close by and would walk all the way, or else she'd make for the bus-stop. The stationary car in its turn started up, after a short interval, and took off in leisurely pursuit. The stage was set. Sergeant Wells picked up his cap and took his leave.

'How about my pound?' said Molly.

'Cheap at the price,' said Wells, and paid up without protest. 'Now if those two between them can hang on to her, we've really started something.'

'Good luck! Let me know how it goes.'

Willie was never sure, afterwards, whether he had had the Box Museum in mind as the ace all along, and saved it for the end of his general survey, as optimists save the tops of their cream cakes for last, or whether the idea only came to him as he completed his methodical round and stood on the pavement of High Street, opposite the tall triple frontage that had once been three Georgian houses. Three storeys, attic windows in the roofs above, and a semi-basement below. Lofty sash windows, pleasant russet brick, and stone quoins and cornices. The whole block had the civilised grace for which good conservationists would fight to the death. Not much fear of those premises being flattened to make space for a tower block. To the right of the three, a cobbled alley gave access to the rear, the yards and the service lane behind. The right-hand house had been made over discreetly, by the insertion of a single show-window, into a dignified antique shop, and it seemed to Willie that the work had been done quite recently. Surely since the bank robbery, because this was the then vacant property from which the thieves had made their way into the bank.

The bank itself was the middle house, and had preserved

206

the exterior intact, only its sign, nicely styled in wrought iron that went with the basement railings, proclaimed what it was. And the left-hand house, untouched and sturdily maintained, nevertheless looked dowdy by comparison because its paint was a few years older. The same short flight of stone steps, bordered with curved railings, rose to the front door, which stood open upon a long entrance hall and a massive staircase. The faded sign, painted darkly on grained wood, might have been a century old, probably was. Willie couldn't read its modest lettering from across the street, but he knew already what it said.

So there it was, on offer if he was looking for somewhere impregnably safe from interference or change, somewhere full of containers of all sizes, rarely visited, of interest to very few, if any, of the citizens of Braybourne. It couldn't be done away with, because of the trust; the building that housed it couldn't be commandeered on a compulsory purchase order by the development corporation, because it was of genuine historical and artistic importance, and part of a street frontage of which the same could be said. And it was next door to the Regional Assurance Bank, and both had yards at the rear, dark and quiet by night.

Willie crossed the street and climbed the steps. The wooden tablet beside the doorway said:

THE BOX AND LOCKS MUSEUM
This collection was made and dedicated to the
artisan public of Braybourne by Henry Barclay
Thomason, Esq., of Long Hay in this town, to be
open to the populace for ever.
Opening Hours: 9.30 am to 6.00 pm.
Sundays excepted.

Even close up, it was not easy to read all of it, the background having darkened with time, while the lettering had faded, so that everything ended in a monotony of dull brown. There was another, smaller notice below which said proudly and meticulously:

2007 Boxes of all kinds.

Now supposing, thought Willie, that there turn out to be two thousand and eight? Anybody could add one, who would notice? He cast a glance at the ground-floor window, which appeared to be hung inside with heavy velvet curtains. The room within looked empty. A soiled cardboard square pinned to the wall inside the doorway of the hall pointed a hand-drawn red arrow up the stairs. Willie climbed. The place was obviously regularly aired, by the very conditions of its endowment; it was solid and dry, but it had an air of dust about it, as though he breathed its ancientness and abandonment. The staircase was noble, and made two turns before he reached a short landing, and found himself face to face with a double doorway, both leaves standing open, and came into a great room that ran the full depth of the building to two huge windows looking out, as he guessed, upon High Street. This had surely once been two rooms, the only thing changed here.

Just inside the doors, on his right, was a large Regency table, with a pipe and a pouch of tobacco on it, an open Oxo tin, and a role of dim blue tickets. On the left, a very old man was just backing out of a plain door, with a broom in one hand and a duster in the other. He wore a leather waistcoat, spanned by an old-fashioned watch-chain, and a baize apron round his meagre hips, and he had obviously had it in mind to do a little desultory cleaning to pass the time, but at sight of Willie he looked completely astonished, and quickly put his tools back in his closet, and came to the table.

'Five new pence, if you please, sir. And very good value,

though I do say it. You won't find another museum like this, not in the Midlands, no, not in London, neither, I shouldn't wonder.'

Willie agreed respectfully that it was unlikely. Perhaps not another in the world. He gazed before him, and there they were, all down the great room, the tiny ones in glass cases, the middling ones on shelves and stands, the big ones – there were some very big ones – on the floor. Boxes. He could well believe there were more than two thousand of them.

'More upstairs,' said the ancient custodian, reading his thoughts, or more likely uttering his usual encouragement to the visitor. 'All the jewel-boxes and some of the snuff-boxes up there, and a few that was made for special occasions – making of freemen of the borough, and presentations to prominent citizens, and one little casket that was made for a wedding gift to Mr Thomason's daughter by the work-people, but the young lady died before her wedding day.' He spoke of her and her tragedy as though he had himself experienced it. Maybe he had, he looked old enough. He was very brown, in spite of his indoor occupation, brown and seasoned and gnarled like a walnut, a compact little man with a tonsure time had given him, but a lush fuzz of grey hair round it, and a smoker's orange-stained moustache.

'Did you work for one of the box firms?' asked Willie.

'I did, as a young man. The trust always has a box pensioner as custodian. Enamels, I used to do. There's one or two of mine upstairs, among the collectors' pieces. There's a list of all the curators here on the wall, see. From the founding. All box men!' He made for it like a homing pigeon for its loft, and Willie was in courtesy bound to follow and study it with him. It wasn't a long list. The old men who inherited this sinecure lived to be very old indeed, like the present incumbent, who looked good for his century.

His own name was there, of course, outlined like that of a living author in some literary *Who's Who:*

'Thomas Penfold, 1965– . . .'

There was another Penfold, too, his predecessor. He didn't fail to point out this family entrenchment.

'Ebenezer Penfold, 1950–1965.'

'Me uncle, that was, me father's youngest brother. Very good at the historical bit, he was. But there was more people came in them days. You'd be surprised how lively it was sometimes, what with all his grandchildren in and out here. Me, I never married. Not as I mind, mark you, I'm very comfortable with my little bungalow and garden in the Haven, and my job here. Four sons, my Uncle Ebenezer had, and one daughter, but all the boys moved out later, when the last firms closed up. Mary stayed here, though. Married a Bastable she did, her man was in work in a hardware shop. But she's dead now, poor lass, her and her husband both.'

Just like that! Married a Bastable, Mary Penfold did. And all those grandchildren in and out here!

Willie was eighty per cent sure from that moment that he was on the right track.

'Well, sir, you'll like to have a nice, slow wander round. Plenty of time, sir, you've got till six o'clock.'

'Fine! I'm going to have a thorough look round,' said Willie, aiming to please, 'but I don't suppose I shall need to stay as long as that.'

Famous last words!

CHAPTER TWELVE

He had no idea what he was looking for, all he felt sure of was that it was here, somewhere, how disguised, how indicated, he couldn't guess. So he began by making his mind a blank, a trick he'd cultivated in the office at home, whenever the law seemed to him more of an ass than usual, convoluted and barren, whenever he got to the point of fortifying himself privately with his own special joke: You can be had up for soliciting! In that condition he made the entire round of the Box Museum.

He hadn't known what he was letting himself in for. Viewed without benefit of detection, simply for what they were, the contents were fascinating. He was reminded time after time what superb craftsmen, artisans, artists – where do you draw the lines in this delicate progression? – had lived and worked unhonoured and unsung in the provincial regions of England, maybe throughout recorded time. It was quite true that there was dust everywhere but on the open glass of the cases and the front range of exhibits on the shelves, and that the metal hasps and bindings were tarnished, the beaten silver in some of the work-boxes blackened, that bits of the inlays had fallen out, and other bits were bulging ready to fall, the vagaries of temperature and humidity having treated them badly. It was true that some corners were piled too high with comparative junk, and that he got excessively grubby ferreting around where other visitors seldom bothered to penetrate. But the fact remained, this neglected place mouldering behind its rotting velvet curtains was full of marvels of patience, taste and skill. He saw how the locks had got into the title. Whoever makes unique boxes probably also involves in his plans unique locks. Some of the keys Willie saw were so dazzlingly complex that he could not work out how they could possibly be operated to disenchant a lock. There was no other word but disenchant. Only 'Open sesame!' occurred to him as a parallel.

He walked round and took a general view. The big room on the first floor held all the larger items, which ranged from metal-bound sea-trunks to leather coffers elaborately tooled and coloured. Besides these there were the glass cases, with their carved, moulded, painted and engraved comfit-boxes, powder-boxes, ring-cases and musical toys. Upstairs, by another flight continuing on from the first but shrinking as it climbed, the original two rooms remained, and there most of the very tiny goods were displayed in low, glass-topped tables on dark-coloured hessian. Narrow shelves lined the window-embrasures, where the light was good, and contained other small, fine works, including the enamels Mr Penfold had mentioned. Willie could only suppose that the actual market value of these pieces was less than he would have thought, otherwise it would have been infinitely easier and more interesting to make away with all the best items from the museum, rather than tunnel arduously into the bank for mere money. There were one or two tiny works of art that he would have liked to possess himself, though not to sell. The decorations were diverse and imaginative, traditional country scenes, domestic interiors, trees, birds, butterflies, flowers, shepherds and shepherdesses, sentimental animals. Apparently they hadn't appealed to Stan, who perhaps, if he really had run in and out here with his cousins as a child, felt towards them the contempt bred by familiarity. If Willie was thinking on the right lines, Stan hadn't extracted anything from these rooms, but added something.

So the next thing to check on was whether anything had

visibly been added. Everything he saw looked as if it had been there, and on the face of it undisturbed, for years. He could even believe that the figure of two thousand and seven was accurate and sacrosanct, but to make sure he went down and consulted Mr Penfold, who was sitting behind his table doing his football pools.

'Two thousand and seven it is, to this day,' said Mr Penfold. 'Not a one been added since that was put up, and never a one took away. I used to think it might grow, when they started this new town caper, but not a bit of it, they've got no interest. Pressed plastic it is now, for everything. Nobody's going to need a lot of those, you can't get rid of the old ones.'

Willie thanked him, and went back resolutely to his research. There was plenty of time. He began to count the boxes, slowly making the round again, and this time poking and peering where the exhibits were piled high, to make sure he missed none. Inevitably, when he was halfway round the first floor, he lost count. It was the tinies in the glass cases that dazzled the eyes, and left him in doubt whether he had missed one or counted one twice. But Willie with plenty of time in hand was not going to be so easily discouraged. He began all over again, and this time checked off the tens on the back of an envelope as he counted, and noted down on a scribbled plan the location of the cases and the numbers in each one. Then back again to the two rooms upstairs, with the downstairs total already secured. And this time he made it. The count, which it took him some time to achieve, was precisely two thousand and seven.

That was that. Nobody had risked adding an extra box.

Next, the consideration of sheer bulk. That much money must take up a lot of space. Willie, never having imagined such a sum, could not with any precision imagine its displacement, but he knew it would need a very large suitcase

213

or a cabin trunk, or something equivalent. That put out of the running every single item in the smaller rooms on the second floor, and everything in the glass cases down here, as well as quite a large part of what remained. Willie prowled in corners, studying the sea-chests, the family trunks, the massive tool-boxes, clothes-chests, blanket-chests, old-fashioned nursery toy-boxes, everything of impressive size. Thomas Penfold studied his pools form and chewed his ballpoint behind the table, in a glazed half-sleep, the state in which he probably spent half his time. There was nothing to interfere with Willie's investigations.

If there was indeed a box here that contained what had not been placed in it originally, there were two things absolutely certain: that box would be locked, and the key would not be in the lock. And that was interesting, because this was the Box and Locks Museum, and invited attention to the intricacies of lock and key just as much as to the boxes they secured. Willie, being a well-behaved citizen, was accustomed to treating museum exhibits as not to be touched, but only inspected visually, and until this moment it had not even occurred to him to try if some of these items deployed before him would open. Now it seemed logical to suppose that they would. He tried the nearest one, and the lid rose in his hand. The key was in the lock.

That was encouraging. Obviously his logic was not far out. He began to go round them all, to see if they were consistent, and now that he came to look for that precise detail, he observed that all the keys were there, and turned effectively when he tested them. If he found one that was locked and without a key, then he would begin to believe he was on to something.

It was nearly a quarter to six when he found it. It was at the window end of the room, tucked away in a corner between two graduated stacks of wooden boxes, and standing upon another bigger than itself. It was not too ornate, not too plain, a barrel-topped leather chest bound and studded in brass, not quite so large as a trunk, rather recalling the sort of chest that used to feature in illustrations of *Treasure Island*, full of gold moidores and pieces of eight. Very appropriate, that, if this should turn out to be what he was looking for. It had loop handles of brass at either end, fashioned like ropes and tassels of gold braid. The lock, also of brass, was elaborately engraved, and the keyhole surprisingly small for the size of the chest. Willie tried to recall the exact size of the elaborately chased key, the smaller of Stan's pair, and it seemed to him that it could fittingly belong to this lock. He lifted tentatively at the arched lid, but it didn't budge. Gingerly he raised the handles, and tried lifting it. It stayed where it sat until he exerted the force appropriate to hoisting a sack of potatoes, and as soon as he felt it lift he lowered it precisely down again, not to shift the dust-edges, if they showed no variation already. Then he looked around for another box of comparable size, indeed rather bigger, to be on the safe side, and equally solid-looking, looked inside to make sure it was empty, and lifted that. It rose like a bird, by comparison with the other. Not much doubt about it, the one locked and keyless coffer in the room was anything but empty. Perhaps another box, an alien here, was stowed inside it, full. Perhaps only the money. But on the whole probably a second box to contain it, brought along on purpose, because time had been the governing factor, and to dump one box inside another and turn the key on it takes only a matter of seconds.

And there it can stay, looking exactly as it has always looked, undisturbed, unsuspected, in a place where nothing ever changes, until you come back at leisure to collect.

He stood and thought about what he ought to do. If Stan's smaller key belonged here, and the large one, presumably, in one of the doors of this house, then if those keys had gone back successfully into Stan's keeping this afternoon, the whole show was due to end here, and tonight. The last thing the police wanted was for the bait to be removed; hopefully it was going to help them to catch Stan red-handed, and possibly some of the other gang, too. But what he must do was pass on to the police everything he had done and everything he had concluded, and let them handle it.

He went back down the long room, sensible of the fact that it was nearly six o'clock, and little Mr Penfold had inserted his pools form into the envelope, and was shuffling towards his cubbyhole to get his cap and coat. His impressive bunch of keys jangled at his belt, a hint to the single customer.

'Thank you very much, Mr Penfold,' said Willie politely in passing. 'It was very interesting.'

'Ah, so it is, too, but I wish there was a few more as thought so. Goodnight, sir!'

'Goodnight!'

Willie went lightly down the stairs, round the double turn and along the lofty hall. Before he reached the doorway and the light of early evening he halted abruptly, and shot back a step into shadow. There was somebody standing squarely in front of the door of the Regional Assurance Bank, and gazing at it with narrowed eyes, and as Willie watched him, he detached his gaze from the bank frontage slowly, almost reluctantly, and moved on towards the open doorway of the museum.

Willie had seen him only once before, and briefly, but there was no forgetting that lipless mouth, and the cold, malevolent eye, the lean face and narrow, whalebone body. The only surviving member of the Match Boys who would also know Willie on sight, and he had to be thoughtfully casing the scene of the old robbery at this moment! Two minds working on the same problems are likely to cast up at the same place sooner or later.

Slitter McGoy came to the foot of the steps, staring at the tablet on the wall. Willie slid back noiselessly round the foot of the staircase, and crouched under the treads. There was a narrow door in the panelling there, into a cupboard, but a Georgian-sized cupboard that admitted him and let him stand upright in the dusty darkness. Give the mobsman a few minutes, and he'd go away. He wouldn't be let in, for it was closing time. But he had shown every sign of mounting the steps to read the tablet, and the last thing Willie wanted was to betray the fact that anyone connected with the affair – even so tenuously connected as himself – was interested in this place.

So he waited. He couldn't hear much in here, though he did hear little Mr Penfold trot down the stairs, and along the passage towards the back premises. To be on the safe side, Willie gave himself one minute more, assuming that the custodian was making a security round before leaving by the front door, and he could still beat him out of it and arouse no inconvenient attention. He emerged, peeped round the stairs, and knew at once, by the comparative darkness, that the front door was already closed.

It was quite silent. He realised then that he'd given himself one minute too many. The great front door was locked, and the keys had gone with Mr Penfold, out by the yard at the rear. He knew it before he investigated, but investigation confirmed it. Quite a bunch of keys the old man had. The ground-floor front room of the house, that empty, velvet-curtained room, was locked, the door of what had certainly once been the kitchen and staff offices at the back of the house was locked, and the final back door at the end of the corridor was locked. And all the keys had gone with Mr Penfold. The ground floor of the museum was limited, as far as Willie was concerned, to this long corridor and two staircases, the main one at the front, and a little, narrow deal affair at the back. The floors above were all his, a small kingdom full of boxes, and Willie was very securely shut within it.

Calli came home soon after six o'clock, to find no promised meal waiting, and no Willie, She was not particularly surprised, though she did, for want of the lad himself, look round expectantly for a note to account for his absence and set a period to it. There was no note, either. Still she was not anxious. He had agreed that he was not to interfere in the affair planned for today, and if he had not meant it he would not have said it. But undoubtedly he was off somewhere on the same ploy from another, and his own, angle. He wouldn't notice the time.

Calli made herself a pot of tea, and settled down to wait for him.

The procession that formed at the *Pheasant* before dark was composed of a number of components, some of which had hardly expected to find themselves in such company. Detective-Constable Jones, at his most nondescript, which was saying a great deal, and without his favourite but limiting moped, arrived in good time, and got himself into a game of darts in the front bar, with one ear tuned towards the stairs, and the other towards the side door, which gave on to the car-park. By the time dusk fell he knew the layout like the palm of his hand. He had also located Jess, who was somewhat restrainedly imbibing one gin and tonic after another in the saloon bar next door. Before he thought anything was due to happen, judging by the light, he paid up, finished his game, and installed himself in a deep doorway in the factory fence opposite, and waited in the deepening darkness without the slightest impatience or distraction. He was a young man of many gifts.

There was one police car among those in the rear car-park, and one on the frontage, so that exit with transport from either door could be covered quickly and smoothly. Jones was there to pursue on foot, if required, or join one of the cars. From where he stood well concealed, he could see the yard entrance, and the mouth of Dolphin Lane, which ran past the main door of the hotel. Everything seemed to be sewn up very neatly, and in the saloon bar Woman Police-Constable Joyce Myers kept her eye on Jess and waited for a glimpse of Stan, and between drinks relayed all relevant information to Constable Jones. Joyce looked eighteen, and a mixture of senior school-girl and transport-café hanger-on, very pretty, slightly raffish. Actually she was twenty-four, held a black belt, had nine O-levels and three A's, and was engaged to a research chemist. But that didn't inhibit her from going into a fierce clinch with Jones when somebody passed along the road and peered into the dark corner where they stood.

'She's got a suitcase standing in the lobby,' said Joyce, still in the bear-hug, 'and she's paid their bill. I think there's a taxi ordered. He's lying pretty low, but he has been down for a drink. He's wearing the same – dark green suede coat, dark-grey roll-neck sweater. You can't miss him. Just like that sketch they got the Banks kid to make. Hasn't shaved the beard, or anything. As far as he knows, none of us have seen him, not to know him – not since he got rid of the full beard he wore as Smith.'

'I never have seen him yet,' said Jones. 'His missus, yes, I'll know her again any time, front view, back or side.'

'And there's another thing. There's some fellow in the front garden of that cottage nearly opposite the bar door. Keeping well back among the trees, but he's there, all right, casing the pub and waiting. I'm going round to tell the sergeant. He may know him, if it's one of Match's lot.'

Sergeant Wells pricked up his ears at the news, and made a large circuit round from the yard, via a couple of winding lanes, to a point where he could stand motionless in shadow and wait for any sign of movement among the fruit trees in the little garden. Whoever was there was engrossed in watching the *Pheasant*, and in keeping himself out of sight from any of its doors or windows, and had no cause, so far, to expect surveillance from the rear. Ten minutes of patience, and the rustle of grass as he shifted his feet located him. A few minutes more of concentration, and he had a shape, medium height, thin, slight stoop to the shoulders and slight, discouraged curve to the spine. It took somewhat longer, and an accidental moment when the bar door opened and shot a beam of light across the lane, to give him an identity. He withdrew immediately into the shelter of a tree, but for one instant Wells had seen him clearly, the melancholy, elderly face, the longish nose and lined cheeks of Denis Sievwright.

'So, he's in the act, as well,' thought the sergeant, startled. No one had so far mentioned or sighted Sievwright in the affair, as far as Wells knew, but there he was, homing on the loot he had helped to lift, three years ago. Word had got round somehow of Stan's return; his loving partners couldn't trust him as far as they could throw him, they had to look after their own interests. Clearly Sievwright wasn't playing on Stan's team, since he was here in hiding, watching the pub where Stan was holed up. A lone hand, then? Or had he thrown in his lot with Match? If Stan and Jess could spot the advertisement in the lost and found column, so could the Match Boys – provided, of course, they knew that it was keys they were hunting for. And if the police could hang back discreetly, trail Jess from Chapel Crescent to the *Pheasant*, and rely on Stan to lead them straight to the hoard, then so could Alec Match. Sievwright was getting a shade past it for going it alone, maybe he felt safer with a gang behind him. Better put one of the boys on his tail, and hang on to him tight, now that he had surfaced. They'd wanted Sievwright for three years, almost as urgently as they wanted Stan Bastable, he'd be a nice bonus on this evening's hopeful results.

Wells worked his way back to his own station, and sent Detective-Constable Pearce, almost as close kin to the chameleon as Jones, to attach himself to the new entry. It was fully dark, something was due to happen very soon.

The first thing that happened was that a taxi came along the upper street from the Sidings, and turned into Dolphin Lane, to halt at the door of the hotel. Jess came down the steps with a suitcase in her hand, and the driver took it from her, and stowed lady and luggage into the car. They took off down the lane towards Market Street. So did one of the cars from the frontage of the *Pheasant*, after a decent interval. So did another car from inside the yard. Sievwright stood his ground, so did his shadow, so did Jones. Wells, in the second police car with Chief Inspector Cope, drove gently out of the yard, and halted again before the turn, ready to take whichever road was desirable when Stan appeared. Everybody was waiting for Stan, and wondering where he had despatched his wife. But nobody had any qualms about who still held the keys. Jess might be trusted with some lesser job, but never with getting her hands on the money.

It was a quarter of an hour more before Stan emerged. He came loping out of the yard on the heels of two locals who were nothing to do with the case, and so closely attached to their backs that he might have slipped by as the momentarily silent part of a talkative threesome, fresh from a lost darts game, if they had not been waiting for him with such alert attention. Round the corner he went, and off down the lane towards Market Street, and after him went Jones, hands in pockets, and after Jones, some minutes later, the car with Wells and Cope. The action had begun.

The quarter between the Sidings and Market Street consisted partly of small residential properties of the old town type, partly of minor shopping streets, interconnected by a number of pedestrian passages. Stan set out briskly, apparently bound for Market Street, only to turn off to the right into this mild labyrinth along a narrow street of neighbourhood shops. That made it much more likely that he meant to go wherever he was going on foot. Jones kept his distance. There were enough people walking here to provide plenty of cover, and enough shops still open, the fish-and-chip saloon, a tiny café, a local greengrocery, to provide light and make distance feasible. Stan was doing a certain number of tricks, probably second nature to him, doubling and turning by way of the passages, halting to peer in windows, going round a block on his own tracks. Jones stayed with him. Where the car was he could not be sure. At this rate it would have to keep to the street, and Wells would have to look out for glimpses of the quarry where by-streets opened, occasionally making a halt where there was a legal spot to park, in order to keep pace as nearly as possible with the walkers. If they lost touch altogether they would call Central, to make sure no messages had already been telephoned in, and then go there to await news. Somewhere behind him, Jones supposed, was the man Sievwright, another shadow who also had his shadow. Sievwright knew Stan's mind perhaps better than the police did, and that would be an undoubted help.

By this time they must have made more than half the length of Market Street, and be nearly abreast of the square. Stan had halted again at the window of a paper-shop, still open after distributing the last edition, the sort of crowded little family business that plastered up its windows with postcard ads for things to sell, things wanted, and offers of services. Cigarettes, tobacco and sweets filled the shelves and counter within, and the usual stands of girlie magazines reached from the floor to a height of six feet, blocking out Stan from sight until his pursuer found the right angle to view him through a slit between them. He was buying cigarettes, tucking them away in the pocket of his suede jacket. He seemed to be looking for something else, too, moving off to the far end of the shop, where he again became invisible, this time irrecoverably. Jones waited until he became uneasy, and then pushed his way into the shop with a handful of change and picked up a paper from the counter.

Apart from the proprietor the shop was empty. Small as it was, at the end of the counter there was a narrow extension, the tail of an L. Jones took the few steps needed to see round it, and cursed himself bitterly. The extension ended in another narrow door, giving upon a dimly lighted alley at the rear.

He went through in a hurry, and saw that the alley ran parallel with the street and just behind the shops, linking up with several other flagged 'shuts' of the same kind. A boy and girl, arms round each other in a trance, walked along it in one direction, an old gentleman with a Yorkshire terrier in the other. Of Stan Bastable there was no sign, and no immediate way of knowing which way he had run, or into which rabbit-hole of this warren he had dived. Jones made a number of frantic casts to all the nearest corners, to scan as many exits as possible, but uselessly. Stan had shaken off his shadow, and there was no way of finding him again. Disconsolately Jones went to look for a telephone and report the disaster, kicking himself all the way.

It was easier to hang on to the thread, of course, if you happened to be Denis Sievwright, who on occasions had used that same shop in precisely the same way, and whose mind worked at speed when he saw Stan, far ahead of him, turn into it. There could be only one reason. Sievwright immediately dived down the nearest left-hand turn, and broke into a run until he was in the flagged alley, and could see ahead to the rear door of the newsagent's shop, and watch Stan's darting figure erupt from it and plunge away deeper into the maze. Sievwright went after him, running when Stan turned a corner, hanging back as soon as he had a clear view again. And some little way behind Sievwright, and moving in much the same manner, came Detective-Constable Pearce.

The first thing Willie did, when he found himself locked in, was to go methodically round his prison, and consider ways of getting out of it. Afterwards he was not entirely sure that he had been honest or thorough in his efforts, but at least he went through the motions. On the ground floor he had no access to any window, except an impossibly high one above the door, which amply lighted the staircase but was of no use to him. On the first floor he tried the two huge front windows, which ran from floor almost to ceiling, but it was doubtful if they had been opened in years, and at least one of the sash cords was broken. Willie had no wish to be guillotined. Moreover, there was half the basement floor below him as well as the ground floor, and these rooms were very lofty, and then there were the spiked railings fringing the steps and the area below. No, he did not fancy that way out. At the back the windows were smaller and higher, but no more promising.

Upstairs, again, there were the two smaller rooms, plus cloakrooms, but curiously no fire-escape seemed ever to have been fitted, and from there the drop, either into the street or into the yard, was forbidding. No, Willie was well and truly a prisoner. It was very odd, how little the thought disturbed him. After all, all roads were going to lead to this place within a few hours, if the thing worked, and he felt a proprietorial right in the whole affair, and was by no means sorry to know that he was going to see it out. His imprisonment was also his opportunity. Even if the worst came to the worst, he had only to wait here until morning to be released. If things worked out according to plan, there might still be something he could do to make himself useful.

If Stan had duly recovered those keys, the unique key of the leather coffer, and the, presumably, copied key of the back door, then he would be on his way here as soon as it was dark enough. Night is the time for getting as far away as possible from the scene of the crime. When he arrived, he would make straight for his loot, for he would know exactly where he had put it, and exactly there it would still be. The whole set-up had been planned as it was precisely because nothing here ever changed, was ever moved or rearranged. Willie considered the possibility of opening the box, perhaps with another similar key – though he had thought of it as unique a moment previously – but none of the keys he tried would turn. No, the only way of removing the money to a safe place was in its present container, physically. That might cause a nice, useful delay by rattling Stan, and making him hunt around, if he managed to get here ahead of the pursuit. But everything had to look in order, as he had left it.

Willie examined all the leather chests and coffers among the collection, and found one of very similar size and shape. The handles were different, the colour was black instead of dark green, but in twilight or torchlight it would hardly be noticed. He picked up the green one, and carried it down the long room to the broom-closet near the door. The place was small, but big enough; it was unlocked but had its key, and the door was thick and solid. It would do. He deposited the chest there, and went back to put the other one in its place. The line of dust where its edges had rested was thick enough to have drifted and shifted a little, but he set the replacement as neatly as possible where the outline was drawn, and removed the key, leaving the coffer locked.

The light was already fading somewhat, behind the heavy curtains, and it looked satisfactory.

Willie withdrew into his broom-closet with his treasure, locked himself in, and then pulled out the large old key from the keyhole to see how wide a range of vision it would provide him. He was lucky. The door was not quite in the centre of the end wall of the room, and stared straight up its whole length to the tall windows. He could see almost the whole of that end, including the stand-in box. Pleased with his dispositions, he settled down patiently in the gathering gloom on Thomas Penfold's fraying kitchen chair, to wait.

CHAPTER THIRTEEN

Chief Inspector Cope had hardly done swearing over Jones's catastrophe when the telephone rang again. Calli had waited until her uneasiness became a conviction of disaster, and then resolved on action.

'It's me, Calli Francis. I thought you should know that Willie Banks isn't here, and I don't know where he is, and I'm getting worried.'

'Should he be there?' said Cope, only half attentive and still swallowing his frustration.

'Of course he should,' said Calli crossly. 'I expected him to be here when I got home soon after six, but he still hasn't come in, and I think something must have happened to him.'

It was the Chief Inspector's private conviction that Willie was incurably incident-prone, and that it was unreasonable to suppose that an hour would pass, much less a day, without something happening to him.

'He hasn't gone poking his nose into this key business, has he?' he said, irritated. 'I told him to keep out.'

'I know, and he said he intended to, and if he hadn't meant it he wouldn't have said it. But he did ask where the *Journal* office is, I think he wanted to go and read the case up for himself. You couldn't object to that. He might be following up some lead of his own.'

'Anything to make you think so? Or to pin it down, if he was thinking on those lines?'

She thought for a moment, and said dubiously: 'Not really. He did start asking me about the Box Museum, when I mentioned it, but I don't suppose it meant anything special. Just that he hadn't heard of it before, and it happens to be next door to the bank.'

'So it does!' said Cope thoughtfully. 'So it is.' It might, in the absence of any lead whatever until someone recovered Stan Bastable's trail, be worth sending somebody to have a prowl round those Georgian houses on High Street. 'Well, Miss Francis,' he said, 'you sit tight, and we'll get news to you as soon as we can. And you give us a ring if he shows up.'

She promised. But when she had hung up, and was sitting gnawing her knuckles over the situation as it confronted her, she found inaction and waiting very little to her taste. Willie had had no business to go off on a fresh trail without her, and she was damned if she was going to be left out of it. Calli put on her coat, tied a scarf over her hair, and went out to take a look at the vicinity of the Box Museum for herself.

In spite of all the companions Stan had drawn after him from the *Pheasant*, strung out like beads on a knotted string, he arrived alone at the Box Museum. So far his own plans were working. His followers had not been clumsy – except in losing him – and he still did not know whether he had actually shaken anyone, he had merely taken automatic precautions. At the end he had even made a detour round the block, further afield than there was any need to go, in order to arrive in the alley behind the museum by a route which allowed him a final rapid dash into cover which deluded even Sievwright. There were walls and corners between Stan and every other soul in town when he finally made it into the yard, and stood there frozen against the wall, listening. Nothing stirred, no furtive footsteps came by. He was there, and he was alone.

Sievwright was left standing in High Street, in front of the antique shop, uncertain whether his quarry had crossed or doubled back between the shops on the near side of the street. The only person thoroughly satisfied with his performance so far was Detective-Constable Pearce, who stood hidden among the shrubberies at the corner of the gardens in the square, unwaveringly watching Sievwright.

Stan waited in the silent yard for several minutes, to make quite sure there was no one on his heels. It was all right, it was going to work. And he still had all his options open. Beattie would be waiting by the bridge with the Crown hired car. Jess would be the other side of town with the one he'd given her the money to hire from Corbetts, sitting behind the wheel ready for off, in the roadhouse car-park by the roundabout. He could go which way he liked. Not too far to carry the stuff, in either case. He hadn't made up his mind yet, it might even depend on circumstances. But with luck he thought it would be Beattie. Jess had his suitcase, but that couldn't be helped, she'd have smelled a rat if he hadn't sent it off with her. After tonight he could buy everything new. Tonight what he stood up in was enough.

He let himself in at the back door of the house. One thing that was always looked after here was the locks, no betraying squeaks in this lot. Once inside, he needn't even bother to be silent, the walls were solid and soundproof. He left the door ajar, and went quickly up the back stairs, and along the corridor to the double doors of the long room.

Willie on his rush chair in the dark closet heard the door open, heard the light footsteps dart straight across the open part of the floor, weave between the glass cases, and so recede down the length of the room. He put his eye to the keyhole, and after the darkness in which he sat was astonished at the amount of light there still seemed to be outside. Not enough to preserve any colour or any distinct shades, but there were indistinguishable shapes, and small, strange gleams of reflected light from the glass here and there. And

229

movement. Just one shape moving, darting into his vision, between the tall windows that were rectangles of grey against black. Straight for his box. He didn't need light, he knew the layout of the room probably better than he knew the palm of his hand, and he was triumphantly justified in his faith that nothing would be changed. Any instant now he was going to touch that coffer, feel for the keyhole, try to insert the key. He wouldn't take the box away, he'd want to leave it still looking as it always looked here.

What he actually did, however, was to lift it. Not with any intention of taking it away, possibly simply as the quickest way of reassuring himself that it was as he had left it, three years ago. Whatever the reason, Stan took hold of the handles, and heaved strongly.

The shock was terrible. The chest flew into the air, almost into his face. He screamed; there was no other word for it, though it was not a loud sound, only a frightening and tearing one. He reeled, and by the momentary, struggling sound of stumble and recovery almost fell backwards, with the empty, the horrifyingly empty chest on top of him. Frantically he began to hunt along the array of boxes, making little moaning, cursing sounds, then turned back again to the first one, and began fumbling at it with the key, unable to believe or understand that it would not open for him, even though he knew there was nothing, or next to nothing, inside it. Willie could hear his panting breath, the way it sobbed in his throat, and the scrabbling sound of his hands shoving, pulling, heaving boxes out of line to find the one that was not there.

Willie sat inside his dark cupboard on his kitchen chair, his eye glued to the keyhole and a quarter of a million pounds – hypothetically, at any rate – on the floor beside him, and he was almost sorry for the creature at the other end of the room. Now Stan had lost his head, and struck a match to look more closely at some of the possible candidates. He couldn't believe his box had been taken away altogether, they must simply have been moved around, and all he had to do was find it. Then he realised, as the reflection of his tiny light sprang at him from the windows, how nearly he had betrayed himself, and hurriedly blew out the match and dragged the heavy, dusty curtains across the glass.

By then there was a policeman circling the square and patrolling High Street, on the lookout for anything out of the ordinary, but he happened to be facing in the opposite direction when the match flared in the first floor of the Box Museum. Sievwright, on the contrary, was just looking up at the line of upper windows across the street. The brief explosion of light caught his eye, and that was enough. Sievwright made for the telephone box in the square, and called the *Eagle and Serpent*.

'Alec? I've got him! Come on out and make it fast. Yeah, the Box Museum. He's in there now, and I'll be round the back. That's the way he must have got in. But make it fast, he won't hang around. Who've you got there?'

'Preacher and Slitter. Crummie took off after Stan's missus, but he's called in already, I can get him, too. What can you make of it, he's got his wife sitting waiting in a car up the north side of town, on a roadhouse car-park. The *Highwayman*!'

'Appropriate,' said Sievwright. 'What's the betting he's got the other one dangling somewhere else? Get the boys out here, quickly. I'll be on the yard door.'

He hung up, and slipped like a shadow across the street, and into the cobbled passage that led round behind the three Georgian houses. His attendant shade went with him, sliding out of the bushes. When he had made certain where his quarry was bound, and seen him safely to earth there, he nipped back and collared the uniformed man he had already observed wandering round these parts with unusual concentration. The uniformed man went away to telephone, Pearce repaired to the alley behind the bank, and found himself a convenient wall to hide behind.

At the *Eagle and Serpent*, Alec Match and his men piled into the Bentley, and set out by back ways for High Street, with five minutes' start on Detective Chief Inspector Cope, who, with Wells and two more officers, was soon performing the same hasty manoeuvre at Central, complete with the regulation firearms that were so seldom issued, but seemed to be called for at this pass. Crossing the square from Market Street, where a few people still strolled and window-shopped as on any normal evening, Calli Francis fixed her eyes on the tall frontage of the bank and its neighbours, and saw nothing but stillness and darkness, exactly what one would expect to see in such institutions at this time of night. It took her some minutes to realise what was different about the Box Museum. On the first floor the velvet curtains at the two great windows were drawn. She crossed the street, mounted the steps openly, and under cover of studying the notice, closely because of the dim light that reached it, she tried the great front door. Solid as a rock, and undoubtedly locked and probably bolted. No way in there.

Calli set off briskly round the block to the alley behind. It was beginning to be populous round there, though everyone who joined the party was being very quiet and cautious. All roads converged on the Box Museum.

It was hardly necessary to be particularly silent when the Match Boys let themselves in at the back door from the yard, and climbed the stairs, because Stan was making so much suppressed but furious noise of his own that it's doubtful if he would have heard them even without precautions. Willie caught the soft, rapid movement of feet on the wooden treads, though rather as a sensation than a sound, and stiffened to listen more attentively. Stan didn't hear them at all. He was hunting ever more frantically and ruthlessly at the far end of the room, shoving the unwanted boxes out of his way wholesale to get at the larger ones, which he hauled open and discarded again one by one. And all the while he cursed and moaned on a vicious, monotonous note, just above his breath, while the dust flew in clouds round him, and hectic sneezes occasionally broke the thread of his bitter complaint.

He heard nothing, sensed nothing, until they were close behind him. The only light he had dared to switch on, even after drawing the curtains close, was a small candelabrum on the wall, close to the right-hand window-frame, and that lit him but left the room behind him in deep obscurity. Alec Match was not five feet from his back before the hair rose on Stan's back in animal awareness. There was a small work-box lying tumbled and open near his right hand, and for those few instants his body covered the motions of his hands. He had just time to drop his own gun inside the cushioned lining and tip the lid shut, when two guns prodded him in the back. He froze, both hands, manifestly empty, raised to the level of his chest.

'That's right,' said Alec Match, breathing heavily close to the back of Stan's neck, 'spread 'em out where we can see. Now turn round – slowly!'

Stan turned, as bidden. They were all there, all those who were left. Alec himself on the job for once, his plump, well-tended fist full of a Charter Arms Undercover .38 Special revolver. Alec liked a lot of gun when he carried one at all, nothing but the best for Alec, and he seemed to have no difficulty in getting hold of what he wanted. Stan kept his eye on the snub blue barrel, and his hands still. Preacher Tweddle had the second gun, of course, that little Starlet he favoured. Slitter, who hovered dimly but unpleasantly behind them, preferred steel. And there was Crummie Best, who usually left guns to his superiors, Crummie was rearguard, keeping eyes and ears open in the doorway in case of interruption. So who was that meagre shape hanging discreetly back, midway between? Not Sam Copper, for certain! Stan knew only too well where Sam Copper was. Of course! That weed Sievwright liked a couple of men with guns between him and trouble. Trust him to turn up with a bodyguard! He'd thrown in his lot with the Match Boys.

'I might have known,' said Stan through his teeth, 'you'd change over to the side with numbers, you bloody snake.'

'Listen who's talking!' said Sievwright mildly. 'You were going to stage a fair share-out, weren't you? Partners three, all for one, but not one for all! I'm settling for a small divvy, and you'll have to curb your big ideas and do the same. Maybe Alec'll let you live, and give you enough to get out of the country, if you give no trouble.'

Alec said, with chill, malignant calm: 'I owe you a bellyful of lead for Sam, and my finger's got the itch. But first things first. Come in with us, and we'll write the rest off, and you shall have – as much as you're worth to us. And your dirty little life. All right, where is it? Where's the money?'

That was when Stan started to laugh. It wasn't a pleasing sound, being half-hysterical and wholly venomous, but in an agonising way there was amusement in it. They stared at him as if he had gone out of his mind, and the guns pricked up warily, but he made no move, just stood there shaking with the force of his private joke.

'Cut it out!' snapped Match. 'We know you came here to collect, we read the papers, too. Now you can hand over, or else! Oh, sure, I know it was *your* job – but you weren't playing by any rules, either, and where I join a game *I* make the rules. Go over him, Preacher, he carries a gun. Don't we know it!'

But he didn't. Preacher found nothing lethal on him, and nobody looked at the fancy little sewing-box.

'Not tonight,' said Stan. 'Tonight I was getting out for good. *Was!*' he said, and uttered another vitriolic sputter of laughter.

'And what does that mean? What's eating you?'

'All right, I planted the haul here, I came back here to get it. *And it's gone!* Right here, here where this great coffin is, I slotted that case full of dough into a leather chest, something like this one. But not this one! And it isn't here now. Gone, I tell you, box and all. If you're so bloody clever, you find it. *I* can't!'

They drew in on him in a distrustful ring, even Crummie Best moving inward a few yards from the doorway.

'He's lying,' said Slitter. 'Playing it up to get us out of here.'

'Fool!' snapped Stan. 'Why should I want you out of here? What have I got to lose now? If you can find the damned thing for me, I'd thank you, and come in for whatever I get out of it. Can't you see I've been pulling the place apart?'

There was a brief and pregnant silence. Then: 'It's true,' said Sievwright, 'it must be true, look at the mess he's made. If he'd found it he'd have been out of here so clean and quick there wouldn't have been a dab to be found or a snuff-box out of place. What sort of fool would hang around wrecking the joint if he'd got what he came for?'

They were convinced. It was wonderful how they all suddenly had the same interest and buried all grudges. They began to question urgently. Could the chest have been opened and rifled? How big was it? What was it like? Stan had the key, the only key, and he'd picked it for its puzzle quality, and besides, nothing here was ever moved until now, nothing seemed to have been moved when he got here. The green leather chest must still be here, somewhere. If the money had ever been recovered, the world would have known about it next day. No, he believed, improbable

235

as it was, that they'd rearranged some of the pieces for some reason, done a half-hearted spring-clean, and the chest had got tucked away in some corner. So they had to find it. So what were they waiting for?

Willie, peering through the keyhole from his hiding-place, viewed the frantic, obsessional hunt at the far end of the room, lighted by the dusty electric candles on the wall, like one with his eye screwed to some bizarre new peepshow on the pier of an old-fashioned seaside town. There was nothing real about it. They began to dive into the recesses of the museum like terriers, pouncing on every large box, leather chest or no, opening them, slamming them shut, hurling them furiously aside, reaching for more. So intent were they that they even forgot to keep a close eye on Stan, and he was able to recover his Webley and Scott and pocket it again unnoticed. If Crummie Best hadn't been still hovering at the doorway, Stan might even have been able to fade away safely without being seen. Only he couldn't, not even for his life. With every minute piling up the odds against him, how could he go without his money, after all he'd been through to recover it? He had to find it, even if it must now be split several ways, with himself on the loser's end. He couldn't and wouldn't go without it.

In the middle of the hunt Match looked round, and saw Crummie standing idle by the door. He waved him furiously into the search. 'Come on, get in here! What do I keep you for?'

Crummie obeyed without reluctance. One more character surged onto the dimly lit stage forty feet and more away, and plunged heartily into the piles of boxes with the best. At Willie's end of the room it was solitary and quiet. A chill draught blew under the door of the broom-closet. Only about five yards away, to the right, the double doors had been left open.

236

The pantomime scene at the far end of the room suddenly turned right-side-up again in Willie's mind. It wasn't a comedy programme, in which things fell on people, and people fell over things, and nobody got hurt. It was five cold, mean criminals hell-bent after a prize, and capable of shooting down anyone who got in their way. Three of them had guns, and would use them at the drop of a hat. One of them had already killed a man, Willie was virtually certain, barely twenty-four hours ago, and probably the Match Boys between them had ended more than one inconvenient life, and ruined a good many more. And when they had torn apart every sizeable box at the end of the room they would begin hunting in every other possible place, and then it would be too late to make a move. Just now they were all ferreting away in fine style, and down here it was dark, and the door of the big room open, and open access to the stairs, only about five yards away. Even the rearguard had been withdrawn. It was now or never.

Willie set both hands to the big key, and very cautiously and slowly turned it in the lock. It made no sound. He drew the door open a crack, and waited until he was reassured that nothing had been noticed. If he took off now at full speed he could be halfway down the stairs before they heard and charged after him, but he doubted if that would give him time enough to get out of the house, and certainly it would mean going without the chest. Even if he could slip out and relock the door as he fled – which he very much doubted – he would have given the show away, and guns can shoot out locks if need be. No, either he locked himself in again and sat it out, praying for the police to get here in time to salvage him and his prize, or else he took it with him.

It weighed plenty, and it meant using both hands. On the other hand, the door was open, as he knew by the draught, he needn't try to detach one hand to open it. But he didn't believe he could run with the chest without making noise enough, or at least disturbance enough, to be spotted. Fast movement attracts attention more certainly than slow. If he took the money with him, he'd have to inch his way gradually along the wall and out of the door. A sudden move, and he'd have had it.

Praying that they wouldn't run out of boxes, as by the continuing feverish activity they hadn't so far, Willie drew the door of his closet wide open, right back to the wall. No use risking bumping the box clumsily in carrying it through. Then he carefully picked up the chest by its twin brass handles, raising and steadying it at the level of his chest. Thank God for silent rubber soles! He moved cleanly and quietly out of the closet, and keeping his face towards the treasure-hunters, and his shoulders braced against the wall, began to edge his way gingerly along to the right. Once one of the distant figures turned abruptly, and Willie froze, but it was only the end of one pile of boxes, and the figure had turned to resort to a fresh supply. Nobody shouted, nobody fired, the moment passed. Willie moved again. Three yards or so to go.

It was not any sound or movement of Willie's that broke the spell. It was the soft, shuffling touch of feet on the stairs, several pairs of feet, and then, fatally, the sharp creak of a board under a solid weight. Willie heard it, and turned his head involuntarily, his attention deflected for one instant. Alec Match heard it, or sensed Willie's presence by the only sudden motion he had made, and sprang round with a sharp cry. The paw that wasn't holding the gun swept down another switch on the wall, flooding Willie with light, pinned against the wall with the chest in his arms, and for a moment too dazzled to leap for freedom fast enough.

Match let out a bellow of rage, and fired. The coffer suddenly leaped and kicked like a horse, flattening the wind out of Willie and hurling him back against the wall just as he was lunging away from it. His head struck with a loud and stunning crack. He slid down slowly on his back, with the chest on top of him, and lay still.

Crummie Best and Slitter McGoy uttered a double whoop of joy and started down the long room towards the victim and the prize. But Alec Match whirled in fury on Stan Bastable, standing astonished and bewildered not six feet from him.

'You damned twisting swine!' he said in a muted, animal howl. 'Thought you could still get away with it, did you? Had your mate and the goods all ready to skip, while you played us for suckers? Damn and blast you to hell! *That's for Sam Copper!*'

Stan's hand was in his own pocket by then, but the fraction of time it took him to reach the M.P. pistol was his undoing. Match fired first, point-blank, pumping out every one of his remaining rounds. Stan went down among the chaos of boxes in a sprawling, jerking fall, and a couple of tottering caskets slowly overbalanced and fell on top of him. The gun that would convict him posthumously of Sam Copper's murder slid out of his relaxing right hand and lay in the slowly gathering pool of his blood, but to the last his left hand kept its desperate hold on his keys.

The show was over. At the other end of the room the audience, suddenly augmented, stood dumbstruck at so shattering a curtain.

CHAPTER FOURTEEN

The first shot had sent all those stealthy feet on the stairs galloping three at a time up the rest of the flight. Six or seven people came bursting into the room just as Alec Match's last two rounds went into Sam's body. Those two shots, at least, were fired in front of a crowd of witnesses and would put Match away for a life sentence, as well as emptying his gun, most conveniently for the police. And in case Alec's lawyers, who would certainly be the most expensive and effective money could buy, tried to discredit police evidence, there was also Miss Calli Francis, bringing up the tail of the procession uninvited, and until the last moment undetected. Not that she wasted time consciously recording what she had witnessed, once her eyes fell upon Willie, lying against the wall spread-eagled under his treasure chest like an obstinate non-pleader sentenced to *peine forte et dure*. She uttered a loud, outraged, possessive yell, and dived to her knees beside him.

Crummie Best and Slitter McGoy, bounding joyously to retrieve a fortune, ran full tilt into the arms of Wells, Pearce and Jones, backed up by two or three uniformed men who had entered on their heels. Slitter never even had time to ditch his current knife. That alone would provide a holding charge on him until they could get Alf's evidence, which hopefully would be more rewarding. Sievwright, at any rate, knew when he was cornered, listened to the charge and caution without comment, and made no fuss. He was one more prize in a profitable night's work. Preacher Tweddle, too, took fate calmly, and had enough self-possession to ditch his gun before they got to him. And as for Match. . . .

Alec emerged rather slowly from the red mist of hate to the chill of realisation. If the gun in his hand had not been empty he might have launched a massacre. Instead, he smoothed out the fury from his face to a dead stillness, white and heavy, and laid the empty revolver quite gently on top of the nearest glass case. He shut his mouth implacably, and made no reply when he was cautioned and charged with murder. His fight would begin later, through lawyers, but even they would have hard work to disentangle him from this. One concession he made to his own wishes and appetites. He turned suddenly and kicked Stan's body in the ribs with all his force before they were able to lay hands on him and drag him away.

'God, what a clean-up!' said Sergeant Wells, awed, staring round the wreckage of the Box Museum, and then turning his startled eyes downwards, as an imperious hand plucked him by the sleeve.

'Hey, you!' commanded Calli urgently. 'Help me get this thing off him. It's heavy.'

Willie lay with his head awkwardly propped by the wall, and the rest of him flat on his back, hands collapsed loosely at his sides as they had fallen from the handles of the green leather chest. Cope came hurriedly to take one handle, Wells took the other, and they swung the chest aside. Its front was pierced dead-centre by Alec's first round.

'And what a turn-up,' whispered Sergeant Wells regretfully, 'if we've got a clean sweep, and the star turn's dead!'

The body opened it eyes, and said muzzily but crossly: 'Dead, my foot!' Willie lay still a moment longer, glaring from one face to another to determine who had written him off so lightly. Then he remembered his treasure, and struggled up in short order to look round for it. 'You'd better take good care of that,' he said, and heaved deep breaths into him, and then winced and embraced his own stomach tenderly.

'I ought to have known,' said Calli, between complacency and resignation. 'You *can't* kill him!'

Cope, with all his captives secured, went on his knees almost reverently to examine the sacrifice, and could find no bullet-hole anywhere in Willie's clothing. Nor was he acting like a casualty. He continued to massage his ribs and belly as though they were sore, but that was all.

'Then where the hell *is* it? said Cope, with immense relief, once he was sure of his facts.

'Somewhere in that lot, I suppose,' said Willie, fondling his solar plexus ruefully. 'All I seem to have got is a terrible kick in the wind from that load, and it chucked me backwards and I bashed my head against the wall. I know how hard-packed paper weighs, now I'm finding out how solid it is. You try penetrating that density of treasury notes, plus two boxes, at forty feet! Even with that cannon he was carrying!'

'And you really don't have any holes in you at all?' demanded Calli, marvelling.

'Only inside,' said Willie, reminded, and quickening into renewed life immediately. 'I haven't eaten since lunchtime, and then it was only a sandwich. I'm starving!'

They remembered, when everything else was cleared up, to instruct Jessamine's police shadow, kicking his heels and awaiting orders at the *Highwayman*, to notify the widow, sitting cold, bored and annoyed at the wheel of her hired car in the car-park, that Stan would not be coming, tonight or ever. He was fundamentally a kindly young man, this constable, willing to believe the best of everyone, even that Jess had genuinely felt for the deplorable husband she had lost, though in fact her regrets were mainly for the money, and her fears chiefly for her own possible involvement as an accessory before and after any number of offences. But on the whole, no one was really anxious to push Jess, if she behaved herself from now on. She had a little girl to bring up, and so far no police record of her own. And some sense, if few scruples. Also, they knew where to find her when they did want her.

It was to be morning before somebody discovered Beattie, shivering helplessly by another car, which she could not drive and would have to pay for, poor kid, on the car-park by the bridge. But she was young, and shallower than a village pond. She'd be all right. She might even benefit from the shock, and recoil into respectability. Probably they could have made a nice little case against her, too, but who wants the crumbs?

As for Willie, at Central they fed him on a steak and kidney pie and chips, fetched from the canteen, and asked if he felt fit enough to make a statement at once, which astonished him, since after the steak and kidney pie he felt on top of the world. While his statement was being typed they insisted on the police doctor going over him to make sure there were no delayed injuries, but all he found was some chest bruises and a lump on the back of the head – no cracked ribs, no dents in a skull which Willie admitted was held to be pretty thick from birth, not like those eggshell affairs you read about in the freak assault cases.

'Not everybody,' said Willie, marvelling, 'gets knocked out by a quarter of a million quid. I say,' he added in sudden misgiving, 'I hope it really is in there, after all that?'

It was, as they hastened to convince him by producing the chest itself, opening it before his eyes with Stan's key, and hoisting out a well-made wooden box, made in suitcase style like some tool-kits, with a brass handle, and fitting the interior of the chest very snugly.

'Custom-built,' said Sergeant Wells, smoothing the

dovetailed joints with an appreciative finger. 'Possibly even made it himself, he'd been considering a go at the bank for some time, by the look of it.'

The inner case was fastened only with brass hooks, needing no key. He opened it on the table, and there they were, the close-packed, neatly bound bundles of notes, filling the space within as an egg fills the shell. A slight, oblique bulge, like a healed scar, crossed the surface, beginning above the hole where the bullet had entered, and showing how the pressure of its passage had distorted the wadded notes. Willie followed its course right to the back, and there, sure enough, was the hole of egress. He began to feel as though some highly suspect form of invulnerability had been conferred on him, and while it had certainly been useful, he wasn't sure he wanted to be any different from other people.

'You've got me feeling like that chap who catches bullets in his teeth for a cabaret act,' he said. 'If it isn't in there, and it isn't in me – and I don't *think* it is – then *where is it*?'

'It had just about dented the leather at the back of the chest,' said Sergeant Wells, 'and was hanging in the wood when it gave up. Half an inch of good, solid hide between you and a .38 Special. That's something to remember!'

'Or forget,' said Willie, not sure yet which. He gazed at the greyish surface formed by the edges of all those bundles of notes, and marvelled that it had all been for something so uninteresting, when it came down to it. He poked curiously at the money, to see if it gave him any more stimulus to touch it than to look at it, but he didn't notice any frisson. 'It's only a lot of paper, really,' he said.

'You tell that to the bank,' said Sergeant Wells, and brought him his statement to sign.

It was while he was doing that that the agitated female voices made themselves heard from the outer office, and then, just as Cope came in very contentedly from his own room, in came the desk-sergeant also, with a slightly dazed look in his eyes, but a furtive grin hovering.

'Excuse me, sir, but I've got two ladies here who want to report a missing person.'

'You deal with it,' said Cope. 'It's routine stuff.'

'Well, not quite. And I don't think it's going to take a lot of dealing with,' said the desk-sergeant with a deprecating cough. 'They want to report the disappearance of a young chap called William Banks.'

'Good God!' said Willie, stricken. 'I knew I should have telephoned home. Bring 'em in – that's the quickest way. Let 'em see for themselves I haven't disappeared far. But why on earth *two*?'

But they were already in, anxious and resolute on the desk-sergeant's heels, Mrs Dutton with her beads heaving and her fringe bristling like a terrier's hackles, and with her a slender, well-preserved lady with silver-blue hair, in a party-annual-meeting hat and a very elegant black grosgrain suit. Her eyes fell upon Willie, and she uttered his name in a cry that could be read as expressing joy, astonishment, annoyance and reproach all at once. Mainly, reproach. But with that she was a day or two too late. Calli watched, fascinated and critical, as Willie rose promptly, wincing a little because his bruises were beginning to stiffen, shook hands apologetically with Mrs Dutton, and heartily embraced his mother, all in one competent operation.

'Hullo, Mum! Sorry I've put you in a flap, but you ought to know I'm capable of taking care of myself, and I wouldn't neglect you unless I was up to the eyes. I'm very sorry to have complicated your life, too, Mrs Dutton – you *are* Mrs Dutton? We haven't managed to meet until now, of course! I'll explain everything quite satisfactorily later. The Chief Inspector here will tell you the emergency's over, I shan't be vanishing again.'

Chief Inspector Cope, whose problem for the past few days had been the elusive but ubiquitous presence of Willie rather than his absence, gravely indicated that Mr Banks had been of considerable service to the police in a very important case, now happily concluded. He had a long night's work ahead of him yet before he could hope to get home, he wanted them all out of there.

'But surely,' complained Mrs Banks fretfully, 'you could have let me know! And poor Mrs Dutton here, too . . .'

'That's just it,' said Willie briskly, 'I couldn't. Especially not Mrs Dutton. I tell you what, Mum, now you know everything's OK, why don't you occupy my room at Mrs Dutton's for tonight, and I'll come round and we'll go into everything in the morning. Well, not first thing, because I want to break it gently to poor old Tommy Penfold before he gets into his museum and finds the mess we've made of it, and a policeman in charge. I daresay he'll have been told officially, but I feel responsible. But I'll come as soon as I can. We'll have lunch together somewhere. We could pick up Calli, too . . .'

'Calli?' said Mrs Banks faintly, annoyance fraying the edges of her bewilderment, but helplessness not far behind annoyance. 'What *are* you talking about, Willie? And may I ask where *you* intend to spend the night?'

'Willie's living with me,' said Calli, smooth as cream, and with a smile that began in malice and ended in complacency, because she so patently had nothing whatever to fear. Not considering the way Willie picked up that ball!

'This *is* Calli, Mother! May I present Miss Calliope Francis, the muse of eloquence and heroic poetry. I don't want her to think I'm taking her for granted if I call her my fiancée, because I haven't had time to ask her yet. But I just want to make a declaration of intent. I mean to marry her as soon as she'll have me. Calli'll do what she likes, but I shan't change my mind, so we'd all better get used to it.'

Poor Mrs Banks's face lost all its integral colour, leaving her delicate make-up plainly revealed, and her nose turned pinched and blue with shock. Some remnants of reasoning remained, and prompted her to dig in her claws now, or she might never have another chance. In a thin, tight voice she said: 'Marry? On what, may I ask? Really, Willie, you *can't* be so irresponsible.!'

Sergeant Wells put in an unexpected oar, saying, deadpan: 'We rather expect there'll be a fairly substantial reward from the bank – for the recovery of their money. That will make a nice little nest-egg.' His offside eye winked shamelessly at Calli.

'And of course,' said Calli, 'we've already got a flat.' Not that she was committing herself totally, not yet, and not this easily, but she couldn't resist it.

'It takes more than a nest-egg,' said Willie's mother, fighting on the defensive, and well aware of it, 'to establish a home and a marriage on a sound basis. Some sense, for one thing! Why, you haven't even got a job!'

Willie picked up Calli's coat from the back of her chair, and helped her into it.

'I soon will have,' he said confidently. 'A good job, interesting, with good promotion prospects, early retirement, pension, the lot.' He mustered his bemused womenfolk towards the door, and surprisingly they all went where they were shepherded, without resistance. In the front office Willie looked round, and encountered Detective Chief Inspector Cope's speculative gaze fixed upon him, curiously divided between misgiving and approval. The penny had already dropped. He was busy weighing the perils of having Willie inside the police force against the terrors of colliding with his undoubted gifts outside it. But on the whole the verdict appeared to be cautiously favourable.

'I think I may even be good at it,' said Willie.

ELLIS PETERS

The author of the bestselling *Brother Cadfael* novels

MOURNING RAGA

AN INDIAN WHODUNNIT

**As a favour to his girlfriend Tossa's beautiful
but erratic filmstar mother, Dominic Felse agrees
to escort a teenage heiress back to her father in
India. But travelling with the spoilt, precocious
Anjli is no sinecure – and the task of delivering
her to her family proves even less easy.**

**Dominic and Tossa find themselves embroiled in
a mystery that swiftly and shockingly
becomes a murder investigation. For behind the
colourful, smiling mask of India that the
tourist sees is another country – remote,
mysterious – and often shatteringly brutal...**

*'Strongly plotted story of kidnapping and murder
in a well-observed Delhi. Exciting and humane.'*
H. R. F. Keating, The Times

FICTION/CRIME   0 7472 3121 4

A selection of bestsellers from Headline

MONSIEUR PAMPLEMOUSSE ON LOCATION	Michael Bond	£4.50	☐
THE CAT WHO WENT INTO THE CLOSET	Lilian Jackson Braun	£4.50	☐
MURDER WEARS A COWL	P C Doherty	£4.50	☐
CURTAINS FOR THE CARDINAL	Elizabeth Eyre	£4.99	☐
ROUGH RIDE	John Francome	£4.99	☐
MURDER AMONG US	Ann Granger	£4.99	☐
DEADLY ERRAND	Christine Green	£4.99	☐
IDOL BONES	D M Greenwood	£4.50	☐
THE END OF THE PIER	Martha Grimes	£4.50	☐
COPY KAT	Karen Kijewski	£4.99	☐
CLOSE UP ON DEATH	Maureen O'Brien	£5.99	☐
THE LATE LADY	Staynes & Storey	£4.50	☐
SWEET DEATH COME SOFTLY	Barbara Whitehead	£4.99	☐

All Headline books are available at your local bookshop or newsagent, or can be ordered direct from the publisher. Just tick the titles you want and fill in the form below. Prices and availability subject to change without notice.

Headline Book Publishing PLC, Cash Sales Department, Bookpoint, 39 Milton Park, Abingdon, OXON, OX14 4TD, UK. If you have a credit card you may order by telephone – 0235 831700.

Please enclose a cheque or postal order made payable to Bookpoint Ltd to the value of the cover price and allow the following for postage and packing:
UK & BFPO: £1.00 for the first book, 50p for the second book and 30p for each additional book ordered up to a maximum charge of £3.00.
OVERSEAS & EIRE: £2.00 for the first book, £1.00 for the second book and 50p for each additional book.

Name ....

Address ....

....

....

If you would prefer to pay by credit card, please complete:
Please debit my Visa/Access/Diner's Card/American Express (delete as applicable) card no:

Signature .... Expiry Date ....